GENE RODDENBERRY'S

DESTRUCTION of ILLUSIONS

GENE RODDENBERRY'S

Andromeda

NOVELS FROM TOR BOOKS

Destruction of Illusions

Keith R.A. DeCandido

Visit the *Andromeda* Web site

at www.andromedatv.com

DESTRUCTION OF ILLUSIONS

KEITH R.A. DeCANDIDO

A TOM DOHERTY ASSOCIATES BOOK

NEW YORK

TOR®

GENE RODDENBERRY'S ANDROMEDA™:
DESTRUCTION OF ILLUSIONS

Copyright © 2003 by Tribune Entertainment, Inc., and Fireworks Entertainment, Inc.

This book is printed on acid-free paper.

Edited by James Frenkel

A Tor Book
Published by Tom Doherty Associates, LLC
175 Fifth Avenue
New York, NY 10010

www.tor.com

TOR® is a registered trademark of Tom Doherty Associates, LLC.

Library of Congress Cataloging-in-Publication Data

DeCandido, Keith R. A.
    Destruction of illusions / Keith R. A. DeCandido.—1st ed.
        p. cm.—(Gene Roddenberry's Andromeda)
    "A Tom Doherty Associates book."
    ISBN 0-765-30483-X (acid-free paper)
    1. Space ships—Fiction. I. Title.

    PS3554.E1773 D47 2003
    813'.54—dc21

                                                    2002072871

First Edition: February 2003

Printed in the United States of America

0 9 8 7 6 5 4 3 2 1

FOR RHW

ACKNOWLEDGMENTS

Many people deserve copious thanks for help in making this first *Andromeda* novel a reality, primary among them being Tor Books editor James Frenkel. I've known Jim longer than anyone else in the SF field, and he was the one who came up to me at the World Science Fiction Convention in Philadelphia and said, "Hey Keith, how'd you like to write an *Andromeda* book?" (We've come a long way since you drove my parents home from that wedding, huh, Jim?)

The behind-the-scenes folks at *Andromeda* have been especially helpful. In particular I'd like to heap gratitude on current producer Ashley Edward Miller and former producer Ethlie Ann Vare for assistance above and beyond. (Special thanks to Ethlie for letting me steal a cut part of her script for "It Makes a Lovely Light.")

Special thanks must also go to actors Kevin Sorbo, Lexa Doig, Gordon Michael Woolvet, Brent Strait, Laura Bertram, James Marsters, Dave Ward, and most especially Keith Hamilton Cobb and Lisa Ryder for their excellent work in giving me voices to work with.

Andromeda has a solid presence on the Web, and two sites in particular were helpful. The first is the show's excellent official Web site at www.andromedatv.com, which is one of the best resources of its type, and from which I cribbed mercilessly. The second is the fan site at www.slipstreamweb.com, especially the bulletin boards and the episode reviews/summaries by Heather Jarman and Michelle Erica Green. I'd also be remiss if I didn't mention the thought-provoking reviews of the show by Jamahl Epsicokhan and David E. Sluss.

Many thanks go also to Christopher L. Bennett and the afore-mentioned Heather Jarman, who were magnificent beta readers, providing boatloads of help on things plot- , character- , history- , grammar- and science-related. Dave Galanter provided some much-needed research assistance. Fred Herman at Tor Books kept everything running smoothly. And GraceAnne Andreassi DeCandido was her usual overwhelmingly helpful editorial self.

Finally, the most thanks have to go to the love of my life, Terri Osborne, for keeping me on track, kickstarting me when I needed it, watching old episodes with me, and perhaps most of all for Byr Anasazi out of Victoria by Bear-barossa.

Illusions are certainly expensive amusements, but the destruction of illusions is even more expensive.

—FRIEDRICH NIETZSCHE, CY 6808

GENE RODDENBERRY'S

Andromeda™

DESTRUCTION OF ILLUSIONS

PROLOGUE •

The trick isn't to be a hero when a cat is stuck up a tree. The trick is to be a hero when the cat goes into the tree willingly, and will kill you if you try to get it out.

—EFRAIM KARFOL, "MUSINGS ON THE ART OF SOLDIERING," CY 9778

Everyone I know is dead.

The thought ran endlessly through the head of Captain Dylan Hunt, as if his mind needed to repeat the concept before it could finally accept it.

Part of him was convinced that he was going to wake up any minute to find the crew bustling about the decks of the *Andromeda Ascendant*. Corporal Cooper would give him a report on how the Lancer Corps was holding up, Lieutenant Refractions of Dawn would be sitting in the pilot's chair, providing her usual snide commentary, Lt. Commander Hassan would be standing at attention at fire control, and the other four thousand members of his team would be in tip-top shape and ready to serve him, just as they were only a few subjective hours ago.

But Dylan was too much of a rationalist to truly believe that. They were all dead.

Sara . . .

He focused on this stunning revelation because, of all the revelations he had gotten on this three-century-long day, it was the easiest to deal with. The *Andromeda Ascendant* had become trapped near the accretion disk of a black hole, the artifical gravity field combining with the time-dilation effects of the black hole to render the mighty vessel immobile like a fly stuck in amber—only the ship was stuck there in time as well as unable to move in space. In the outside world, three hundred years had elapsed while less than a second had gone by for Dylan and the High Guard vessel under his command. Salvation from this entrapment had finally come in the form of the *Eureka Maru*, a salvage ship with a crew intending to sell the warship—and, most importantly, its mighty arsenal—to the highest bidder.

His odd journey through time, at least, was something Dylan could understand. Though the *Andromeda* winding up in exactly that spot, too far from the event horizon of the black hole and yet also too far from normal space, was mathematically unlikely, it was not impossible. It could be explained.

Dylan found the other revelations of the day much harder to wrap his mind around. Gaheris Rhade, his best friend, confidant, and first officer, the Nietzschean who had served dutifully and faithfully by his side since their covert mission to Mobius, who had agreed to be the best man at Dylan's forthcoming-yet-never-to-happen wedding, had turned on him. The betrayal of the Nietzscheans in general, Dylan could accept—the genetically engineered offshoot of humanity had always been arrogant and an attempted coup was not out of character—but Rhade's actions hurt Dylan personally. The man had murdered Refractions of Dawn in cold blood, and would have done the same to Dylan, had the captain not killed him instead.

Most incomprehensible of all to Dylan, however, was the long-term result of that Nietzschean betrayal: the Systems Commonwealth, the government that had ruled several galaxies for ten thousand years, had somehow fallen.

The whole idea was patently absurd. The Commonwealth had kept stability in the Known Worlds since humans were still getting the hang of agriculture as a sensible alternative to hunting and gathering. The idea that a mere three hundred years could go by with such a catastrophe happening—and Dylan missing it—was ridiculous.

He refused to accept it. Science explained his being out of his own time. Nature explained Rhade's betrayal. But *nothing* could explain why the Commonwealth had fallen. And he would not stand for it.

Dylan sat in his quarters, reviewing the computer records that Andromeda—the warship's artificial intelligence—had downloaded from the *Eureka Maru*. Gerentex, the Nightsider who had hired the *Maru* for the salvage of the *Andromeda Ascendant*, had been dispatched, with the aid both of the *Maru* crew—who had needed little motivation to turn on their double-crossing employer—and of Tyr Anasazi, the Nietzschean mercenary Gerentex had hired.

Those records told a story that Dylan found appalling. The

order and stability of the Commonwealth seemed to be nonexistant in this post-Commonwealth universe. A Free Trade Alliance had formed ostensibly to create a semi-stable economic structure, but in reality did little more than make it easier for the wealthy to exploit. Many of the different parts of the Commonwealth, such as the Than Hegemony, had become their own concern. The Nietzscheans had fractured into squabbling Prides. The Vedrans had disappeared, Tarn-Vedra itself cut off completely from the Slipstream.

Not only is everyone I know dead, but my homeworld is lost to me as well.

"Are you sure this is a good idea, Dylan?" a familiar voice asked. Dylan looked up to see a holographic representation of the ship's AI standing on the other side of his desk. "Rommie," as Dylan had nicknamed her when he first came aboard, was the only link he had left to the past. At times, he almost thought she was the only real thing left—ironic, given that she only took the form of insubstantial light or a flatscreen image.

Though in truth his answer to her question was no, Dylan said, "What's the alternative, Rommie? You've read these records—if even half of it is true, the Known Worlds are in total chaos."

"I don't mean trying to restore the Commonwealth. I mean using these—people to do it."

Dylan smiled. Whoever programmed Rommie had given her a typical military disdain for civilians—a disdain Dylan himself had never felt, and had hoped to someday ease the AI out of.

"We need a crew, Rommie. You, me, and a bunch of maintenance droids are not going to be able to staff a warship." He let out a long breath. "Even if all of them agree, we'll still be operating with a skeleton crew."

"Perhaps. But we can't trust them."

"Of course not." Dylan got up and started pacing his quarters. "Trust has to be earned. By the same token, they can't trust me, either."

Rommie looked incredulous. "Why shouldn't they trust you?"

"I appreciate the loyalty, but look at me. I'm a relic. Everything I know is three centuries out of date. Conversely, I've also got the most powerful ship any of them have seen." He snorted. "If anything, that proves that we have to do this. If technology has actually regressed in the last three hundred years, then the universe is in worse shape than we thought."

"They're not High Guard, Dylan. They haven't taken the oath, they don't know what it means."

Dylan sighed. "No, they're not. But they do know the territory. They know how things work. We can use that." He walked back over to his desk. "We need them, Rommie."

"All right, say that's true—do you think they'll agree? Do you really think that Captain Valentine will cede her authority to you? That a Magog and a Nietzschean will be able to work together—and work under a human?"

"Honestly?" Dylan couldn't help but laugh. "I have no idea. I'm still struggling with the image of a peaceful Magog." Of all the things Dylan had seen in his short time in the future, it was Rev Bem—the Magog who subscribed to a new pan-spiritual faith known simply as "the Way"—that had driven home to Dylan the utter strangeness of this new world. "But I've been reading up on what they've been up to for the past few years. Trust me, what I'm offering is a much better alternative to what they've been doing. . . ."

ONE • TAKILOV DRIFT, 302 AFC

> "We can do this one of two ways. There's the hard way,
> which involves hours of discussion, tons of negotia-
> tion, half a dozen bribes, and no guarantee of success."
>
> "What's the easy way?"
>
> "Liberally placed high explosives."
>
> —MAJE AND KLIMNOS, *ON THE RUN,* EPISODE 97:
> "GO WEST, OLD MAN," 287 AFC

It was a quiet day at Takilov Drift Impound Lot.

Teena Harwall preferred quiet days.

She and her partner, a Than named Song of the Ocean, had opened the Impound Lot seven years earlier when the previous company that provided impounding services to Drift Security had met with an unfortunate accident involving a landrover laced with explosives that had somehow been missed by Security's scans. Harwall and Ocean had bid for the rights to pick up the contract. Though their competition consisted of three multi-system companies, the pair of them, with much lower overhead than their huge corporate competition were able to lowball the offer and win the contract.

They had operated in the red for the first four years, but that had been part of the business plan. They had come into money after a successful series of grifts on San-Ska-Re, then left while they were flush and before the Than Hegemony's assorted law-enforcement branches caught wind of them. They had just enough to bribe six members of the Drift Security Contracts Appropriations Committee and plant the explosives in that land-rover. Once they got the contract, they were eligible for a loan to actually set up shop. When they paid that off—which they did two years ahead of their projections—it was all profit.

Harwall had relieved Ocean an hour earlier while the other one went to sleep. Although they had support staff, of course, they always made sure that one of them was present at the lot at all times—each taking a fifteen-hour shift per thirty-hour day. After all, this was Takilov Drift. You never knew which of your employees was plotting your downfall.

After all, if Harwall or Ocean were one of those workers, it was what they would be doing.

Calling up the manifest, Harwall saw that only three items had been added during Ocean's shift.

One was a planet-hopper that Sergeant Hong had brought in, supposedly belonging to a flash dealer who'd been arrested on half-a-dozen counts of possession, distribution of an illegal substance, loitering, and adultery. Harwall smiled in amusement at the last charge, and suspected that Hong's wife was cheating on him. Again. *And this time, it's either with a flash dealer,* she thought, *or with somebody Hong could easily set up as a flash dealer. Why he just doesn't divorce that woman is beyond me.*

The second was a taxi that had been left abandoned for two weeks in a casino parking bay, and the third, a cargo ship that had been put up as bail for a suspected grifter. According to the file he was attempting the old Neidermeyer con—by himself. Harwall shook her head in disbelief. Any idiot knew that Neidermeyer was a two-person job.

The official paperwork wasn't nearly as important to Harwall as the numerical designation that Ocean had entered. The cargo ship had a *1* next to it, which meant that it had come along with a top-level bribe, which was Security's way of telling them, *Don't sell this one, we really need it.* That meant that the case against the failed grifter wasn't especially strong, or Security needed the ship as a negotiating bargain chip. Or maybe they already had their own buyer for it.

The planet-hopper had a *2,* indicating a mid-level bribe: *Don't go out of your way to sell it, but if a good offer comes along, knock yourself out, just make sure I get a cut.* As it happened, Harwall knew a Perseid who was after a planet-hopper. She put in a call to him. If she recalled the conversation right, ten percent of the price he was willing to pay for the planet-hopper would be more than Hong's bribe, so the poor cuckolded bastard would come out ahead in the whole deal. This made Harwall happy—she had always liked Hong.

The taxi had a *3,* which meant no bribe at all. Ocean had already set the wheels in motion to sell that one for parts.

She called up the full scan data for the cargo ship. It didn't look like much on the outside, but whoever ran the engine room had done a fine job. The ship had almost none of its original parts, but every change was an upgrade. *Pity this was a number-one bribe—we could get a bundle for this one.*

The 'com beeped. Harwall slapped at the button. "Yeah?" A Than face appeared on the viewscreen. This was Ocean's deadbeat cousin—or podmate or egg-brother or whatever it was Than called their relations; Harwall had never been able to figure it out—whom they had hired last year out of pity. Or, rather, out of Ocean's pity and only after she had spent two days pleading with Harwall to take her in.

"Hey chief, there's a Nightsider on the line for you. Says he's interested in the luxury yacht."

Harwall winced. "What luxury yacht?"

"Y'know, the one in Bay Nine. I figure—"

"What did you tell him?" Harwall asked angrily.

"I told him we had a yacht, but he'd have to talk to the chief."

Harwall put her head in her hands. *I swear, Ocean, I'm going to kill her. I'm going to kill her until she is very, very dead.* "That yacht isn't for sale."

"It isn't?"

"No." They had gotten three separate number-one bribes on that one. It belonged to a businessman who had literally been caught with his pants down. It was a political hot potato of massive proportions. Accusations, payoffs, and lawsuits were flying back and forth, but if anything happened to that yacht while it was in Security custody, Harwall and Ocean would be shut down faster than a Slip skimmer pilot on flash. "Tell the Nightsider—" She hesitated. "Never mind, put him through."

The insectoid face of the Than was replaced with the rodentian features of a Nightsider. Harwall put on her public face and smiled sweetly. "Greetings. This is Teena Harwall, I'm the proprietor of this establishment. How may I be of service?"

"I wish to purchase a yacht."

Harwall pursed her lips and frowned. "I'm sorry?"

"Are you deaf, human? I said I wish to purchase a yacht."

"Yes, sir. I heard you the first time." She added a touch of confused outrage to her tone. "What I'm afraid I'm unclear on is why you've come to us. We're an impound lot, sir—simply a holding facility. For us to sell items in our care would be highly illegal, not to mention unethical." Tossing in a dollop of aghastness, she went on: "I'm frankly appalled that you would think us capable of such a vile act. We are a public service, sir. I'm sure you've heard stories about the poor quality of service and the dubious behavior found here on Takilov Drift, but I can assure you that those rumors did *not* get their start here. Nor are they based on any foundation of—"

"Madam, you're trying my patience. Please don't pretend that you are anything but a scam artist like everyone else on this damn drift. Now do you have a yacht for sale or don't you?"

"Sir, if you're going to make such *public* accusations, I'm going to have to cut you off."

The Nightsider got the hint. She didn't want to discuss such things on an open channel. *"Perhaps we can arrange a meeting, so you can convince me of your ethical purity in person?"* He smiled, a facial expression that had no business on a Nightsider, and it made Harwall's skin crawl.

She was about to dismiss him out of hand—there was simply no way that yacht was going anywhere—but just because he said he wanted a yacht didn't mean he wouldn't settle for something else. *Maybe he can outbid the Perseid for the planet-hopper.* "If you insist, sir, I can give you an appointment at thirteen this afternoon."

"Excellent. I look forward to seeing further examples of your law-abiding operation. Farewell."

The screen faded to black. Harwall sighed. *Potential for profit there, certainly, but not without possible costs.* She opened a com channel to Ocean's cousin and spent the next twenty minutes informing her, at great length and at a very loud volume, to *never* speak to anyone who didn't actually work there ever again.

It was just when she got to the part about letting someone else answer any calls that came in when the explosion rocked the lot.

Several more explosions followed, accompanied by the insistent wail of an automated alert klaxon. Harwall grabbed her desk to steady herself, only to find she couldn't get her footing. She tried to get her feet settled under her, but they wouldn't gain purchase. That, combined with a sudden queasiness could only mean one thing: *The AG field's been knocked out. Great—just great.* Zero gravity always made Harwall nauseous.

Swallowing down the digested remains of her breakfast, she held tightly onto the side of her desk with one hand, and called up the visuals from the security cameras on her screen with the other. Over half the cameras were out, but enough were working for her to see that robots were taking care of the fires and the staff was evacuating. An uncharitable part of Harwall hoped that Ocean's cousin was caught in one of the explosions, but she saw her, as well as the nine others, heading for the exits.

The Impound Lot was located on the outer portion of the drift, with a portal to space on the north wall. It was through there that the assorted vehicles were brought in, then put in their respective bays. Thankfully, none of the explosions were in that area, but were instead on interior bulkheads, or walls between bays. No danger of exposure to the vacuum of space, and no apparent loss of cargo that way.

Still plenty of damage to cargo, though, she thought angrily. Even if everything was accounted for, that didn't mean it was unscathed. Most of the damage was concentrated in Bays 1–4. Fear clenching her spine—right around where she kept her money pouch—she checked Bay 9, and was relieved to see the area near the luxury yacht had also remained untouched. The first obvious suspect of any kind of attack on the lot would have been someone wanting to complicate that particular situation even more than it already was. But that didn't seem to be the case here.

The AG field restored itself, sending Harwall stumbling to the floor in a heap. This time, she was unable to keep her breakfast down, and she spent several seconds on all fours, vomiting on the carpet.

Her first thought when her stomach was done heaving was, *It's going to cost a fortune to clean up this mess. Should've thrown up on the metal floor.*

Common sense reasserted itself. *After what just happened, cleaning the carpet is going to be the least of our expenses.*

The klaxon, which had been blaring a loud honking noise every second, had, with the restoration of the AG field, cut back to a not-so-loud beeping noise every two seconds, which meant that the crisis was being dealt with, but people should be on alert and avoid any part of the drift that might be compromised. Technically, that meant that Harwall should leave the lot immediately, but she wasn't going anywhere until she knew the precise nature and extent of the damage to her property. *This is Ocean's and my livelihood, dammit!*

She tried not to think about the fact that the previous holder of the Security impound lot contract had had its term ended by an explosion.

The direct line to Security beeped urgently, the sound clashing with the alert klaxon. Harwall quickly tapped the red button as much to stave off the impending headache as anything. The face of Lieutenant Jrinto appeared on her screen. Harwall resisted a new urge to throw up. Jrinto was a half-breed—human mother, Nietzschean father—who spent far more time than Harwall was comfortable with flirting with her. His flirting might have been more successful had he been a full-blooded Nietzschean, and therefore had the mole on his cheek, the blackheads on his nose, and the greasy hair bred out of him. *"Teena, what the hell just happened?"*

"I wish I knew. Somebody's trying to blow up the lot."

"Is—"

"Bay Nine is secure."

A look of relief spread over his unfortunate face. *"What's the rest of the damage?"*

"I'm still trying to figure it out." She started comparing the current scan to the manifest. There were some incomplete matches, which she chalked up to damage from the explosions. "So far, everything's—" Her face fell. "Oh, crap."

"What is it?"

Harwall muttered a series of Than curses that Ocean had taught her.

The cargo ship was gone.

She turned on external cameras, but they just gave her gray nothingness. Since they were on the space side of the bulkhead and nowhere near the explosions, they had obviously been taken out independently. She also noted that the arresting officer whose name was attached to the manifest entry for the cargo ship was Jrinto himself.

"We've got a breakout," she told the lieutenant. "Manifest #63904B."

"*That little tinkerer I busted last night? His friends didn't have enough cash, so they put the ship up for bail.*"

Harwall resisted the urge to point out to Jrinto that she knew that already. "I'd say his friends are making a getaway."

"*Damn, I should've expected something like this. But I didn't think they'd be bright enough. I mean, c'mon, who tries to pull off the Niedermeyer con as a single?*" He shook his head, causing a lock of greasy hair to fall over his eyes. "*I want a full damage list within half an hour, Teena. We need to account for this.*"

Right, Harwall thought, *so we know who to pay off to keep the lot running.* "You'll have it."

"*Meanwhile, I'm getting that ship back. That's* my *collar, dammit, they aren't getting away that easily.*"

The screen went blank. Harwall continued her scan, to make sure no one else was taking advantage of this confusion to make off with any merchandise.

This, she thought with a deep sigh, *is why I prefer quiet days.*

Having changed into his specially modified spacesuit, Malthazar Jrinto climbed into his Banshee and started the countdown sequence. Around him in the Drift Security Port, four officers did likewise, all wearing more standard-issue spacesuits, since they didn't have to have the sleeves adjusted for Nietzschean forearm spikes. His spikes were smaller than that of the average male Nietzschean—the price for his half-breed status—but luckily, most tailors were used to accounting for them in their designs.

That con artist's cargo ship already had a several-minute head start on them, so Jrinto and his people needed to move quickly. *Luckily, the ship hasn't been built that can outfly one of these babies, much less five of them.* Invented by a particularly clever Chichin (or, at least, that's what the Chichin who sold them to Drift Security claimed), Banshees were small, compact one-person craft that were as small as possible and still able to accommodate a Slipstream drive. They were faster and more maneuverable than anything else out there, and had been worth three times what they paid for them, given the hundreds of occasions on which they'd proven useful. Their success rate in chasing down suspects had increased a thousand-fold since buying these babies.

Certainly no way some clapped-out old wreck will stand a chance, Jrinto thought with glee. They'd bring these bastards in and return them to Teena and that Than partner of hers. *And then maybe—maybe—Teena will finally agree to go out with me.*

Jrinto didn't understand it. He had Nietzschean blood—the spikes on his forearms were a testament to that—so he should have been a superior specimen in the eyes of any woman. His mother had never talked about Jrinto's father. Given that his mother had grown up on Avilan, it was as likely as not that she didn't know who the father was among the dozens of Drago-Kazov men who had raped her when they took the planet.

The computer indicated that the checklist was done. His status board showed that the same held true for the other four. "Let's move," he said into the intercom. "Base, this is Jrinto. Have the sensor drones found anything yet?"

"*Aye, Lieutenant,*" said whoever was on duty at Base Command. "*Transmitting coordinates. They're about two LMs out.*"

Jrinto grinned. At full speed, they'd make up the two light-minutes in no time at all. He adjusted his spacesuit's cooling unit to maximum—Banshee engines tended to burn hot, and the cockpit was only half a meter from the engine housing.

"All units, set course, maximum speed. Let's bring them in."

"Make it fast, Lieutenant," Base said. *"They'll be able to Slipstream in twenty minutes."*

"Fast is what we do." Jrinto settled his hands into the pilot's grips and moved out. The force of the acceleration pushed him back into his heavily cushioned chair—basically an oversized pillow—as the five Banshees screamed out of the hatch.

Based on the sensor drones' report of the cargo ship's location, Jrinto and the other four would arrive at the appropriate spot on the ship's projected course in ten minutes. *And won't they be in for a shock,* he thought happily. That little twerp had been nothing but a pain in Jrinto's backside since his arrest. It wouldn't have been so bad if he had just gone quietly. Most grifters knew how the game was played—if you get caught, you pay the price. This guy, though, seemed to think he was entitled to special treatment. *As if being able to talk a mile-a-minute actually works on Security. Did he think I'd let him go just to shut him up? He wasn't that annoying.*

Though he was pretty close.

When nine minutes had elapsed, his console beeped, and Jrinto immediately pulled on the grips. At the speed they were going, they'd need to dump velocity at a great rate to slow down enough to come alongside the cargo ship. The already oppressive heat got worse as the ship's engines had to almost literally work against themselves to slow the ship down. Instinctively, Jrinto checked to make sure his suit's cooling unit was on maximum—and was disappointed to see that it was, and he was *still* sweating like a pig.

Wishing he could wipe his forehead, but unable to do so through his helmet, he checked the Banshee's viewscreen, to find—

—nothing.

"Where the hell's the ship?"

"*I don't see it anywhere.*"

"*Me, either.*"

The other two Banshees had similar reports.

"Base, this is Jrinto, what happened to the ship?"

There was a two-second lag before Base answered. "*Damn, they must've seen you coming and gone evasive. Hang on, I'll relaunch the drones.*"

Jrinto gritted his teeth. "Why the hell were the drones recalled?"

Two seconds. "*That, ah—that's SOP, sir. Those things are expensive, we don't like to leave them out any longer than necessary.*"

The biggest problem with the cramped confines of the Banshee cockpit, Jrinto decided, was that there wasn't room to throw a proper tantrum. The best he could do was shift slightly in his seat, and feel his face turn even redder. "If I lose this ship because of the damn *budget*, I swear I'm going to find the nearest—"

"*Got 'em! Sending fresh coordinates.*"

The coordinates came in two seconds later—right near a Slip point.

The drones' images also finally arrived, showing the ship heading for a Slip point—the area proximate to the Drift that was also far enough from the nearest star's or planet's gravity well to safely go into Slipstream. The coordinates were a hundred light-seconds away, which meant the image he was seeing was almost two minutes old.

Gripping the pilot controls, Jrinto slammed the engines forward, propelling the Banshee toward the Slip point at top speed and propelling Jrinto deep into the cushion.

You're not getting away from me, oh, no. I need you back so I can look heroic in front of Teena. If I get the ship back then maybe she can stay in business—hell, maybe that's the way to get her to go out with me. I'll be the big hero who kept her from losing her livelihood. Yeah, that's it. Perfect. Besides, it's my collar. . . .

"All units, prepare for Slipstream."

"*Uh, can we do that?*" one of the units asked.

Snidely, Jrinto asked, "Did you uninstall your Slipstream Drive when I wasn't looking, Officer?"

"*No, sir, it's just—well, if they go to Slip, that's kinda out of our jurisdiction, isn't it?*"

Technically, the officer was correct, but Jrinto was in no mood for legal niceties. Such things were mutable on Takilov in any case. "We're in hot pursuit—our jurisdiction extends to wherever that ship goes until that pursuit is ended." He had no idea if that was legally true, but enough greasing of palms could probably make it so.

Sure enough, the cargo ship entered Slipstream just as the Banshees approached. "Go in after them!" Jrinto said as he activated his Slip engines and gave chase.

The jerking of the Banshee's acceleration felt natural—the expected effect of inertia. On the other hand, the shifting of reality Jrinto experienced when entering Slipstream was the most unnatural thing he could imagine. It felt as if someone pulled his stomach out through his belly button.

Once someone had tried to explain what the Slipstream actually was to Jrinto, and it just gave him a headache. Supposedly, it was some kind of other dimension that intertwined with the real world, whatever that meant. All Jrinto cared about was that the place *worked*—when he went in, his engines harnessed the energy of the strings that made up the 'stream, and he came out the other side where he wanted to be, most of the time. Without the Slipstream, there would be little practical interstellar travel and no practical intergalactic travel.

The only part of the process Jrinto didn't like was the actual piloting. It was akin to someone taking his already-removed stomach and tap-dancing on it.

Jrinto and the other four doggedly followed the cargo ship as it went through the 'stream. It was a rough ride—Banshees were tough to handle in the 'stream generally, being so small and fragile, but the fact that they had a point of reference in the cargo ship made things easier.

Or, rather, it would have if that ship's pilot wasn't zipping around the 'stream like a crazy person.

They finally transited back to normal space—about three seconds behind the cargo ship, and not a second too soon, as far as Jrinto was concerned. He felt his stomach at last being put back in place, via his right ear.

Three seconds can be an eternity.

Most of the time in space, things took a very long time because space was just so *big*. While the discovery of the Slipstream made the distances between solar systems, between sectors, between galaxies all but irrelevant, the actual distances between things in normal space was still of a scale that made three seconds a paltry amount of time. After all, even with the Slipstream, messages and transit times were sometimes measured in months and years rather than seconds and minutes.

As a result, Jrinto didn't think of the three-second lag time between the cargo ship exiting Slipstream and the five Banshees doing likewise to be all that significant.

One second after he transited into normal space, he was reminded that it doesn't take very long to drop a missile or three right behind you as you exit Slipstream.

As Jrinto watched two of the Banshees he came with get dotted with explosions, he realized what the cargo ship had done. They had primed the missiles to be dropped out of their cargo bay, then gone into Slipstream. As soon as they came out, knowing that Jrinto and his people were only three seconds behind, they dropped the missiles—effectively mining the 'stream exit point— and got out of range.

The two Banshees that were hit were still in one piece. Jrinto's status board indicated that the vital signs of both officers were not optimum, but they were still alive. Their engines, however, had to be shut down.

All right, that does it. Now I'm pissed. "Remaining units, acquire target and pursue."

"Sir, what about Anzen and Limnos?"

"We'll come back for them them," Jrinto said. "And now we can add assault on an officer to the charges. But we can only do that if we catch them."

"Yessir."

"Got 'em!" the other officer said. *"They're just a few LS away."*

The coordinates came up on Jrinto's board. Gritting his teeth, blinking away the sweat that was now pouring into his eyes, he clutched the pilot grips and fired up the engines.

Jrinto's ship's computer had also found a nearby sun and examined its spectro reading—it appeared to be Mudwat's Star, the home of Caldonia, an independent world, and one with which Takilov Drift had many dealings. For one thing, they exported a fruit that fermented into the best wine Jrinto had ever had. His dream date with Teena Harwall had included several bottles of the stuff, in fact. *Perfect. I can take them here with no problems, and the Caldonians will at worst look the other way, and at best testify that they fired deadly weapons in their space.*

A beeping sound indicated that the engines were starting to overheat. Jrinto ignored it. "Arm missiles." Any chances of this ending peacefully were now gone. Jrinto was determined to get these guys no matter what.

They were at four light-seconds and closing. Optimum firing range for the Banshees was two LS. "Prepare to fire."

"They're firing up their Slipstream drive!" one of the officers cried out.

Jrinto blinked. "Are they nuts?"

The cargo ship then opened a Slip portal and was gone.

His mind working faster than he was accustomed to making it work, Jrinto said, "Remaining units stay here, prep to escort—" *what the hell are their names?* "—Anzen and Limnos back to Takilov. I'm going after them."

"Sir, I don't think—"

The rest of the officer's sentence was lost as Jrinto activated his own Slipstream Drive. He ignored the computer's protestations that activating the Slip engines so soon was ill-advised and went against the specifications of the Banshee vessels.

This time, Jrinto's stomach was wrested from his body through his nose with a very sharp, very rusty metal object. He'd never felt so sick in his life. The Banshee slammed against the stray strings of the 'stream as he desperately clutched to the string that the cargo ship was on, barely keeping up.

Some people had what was called the Slipstream touch. Jrinto had never really had it, though he'd always had adequate enough skills to pilot the 'stream without incident. Well, without major incident, in any case.

Whoever it was piloting that cargo ship didn't just have the Slipstream touch, but the Slipstream taste, smell, sight, and hearing as well. By the time they transited back into normal space, Jrinto was mentally exhausted, his Banshee beeping more alarms than he had known the thing was equipped with, and he was physically incapable of summoning the strength to fire the missiles he'd armed.

This time, he caught up to the cargo ship. In the back of his head, he noticed that they were near a red dwarf star. There wasn't one near Takilov that he was aware of, so they must have Slipped rather far. Once he was close enough for real-time communication, he activated ship-to-ship. "This—this is Takilov Drift—Drift Security. You will heave to and—and prepare to be boarded."

"*Sorry, Officer,*" a pleasant female voice said, "*but we've got to see a man about a dog.*"

"It's 'Lieutenant,' actually," Jrinto said. His anger at her misstatement of his rank gave him strength. "You're in violation of several laws of Takilov Drift, and the longer you stay out of my custody, the higher the number of those laws will be. I have missiles armed and ready, and I will use them if you don't stand down."

"*So you want me to heave to and stand down, huh? Well, sorry, Lieutenant, but I'd rather just Slip away.*"

The computer told Jrinto that the cargo ship was preparing to go into Slipstream *again*. The same computer also told him that he was about six seconds from overheating his engines. If he even tried to put the Slip engine back online again, the safeties would kick in and shut the whole ship down.

She's insane. That has to be it. Only a madwoman would go into three straight Slips like that. Especially to go this far.

Jrinto watched as the cargo ship went into Slipstream.

Rationalizations immediately started filling his sweat-drenched head. *I hate dealing with crazy people. They're always a problem in lockup. And they almost never plea-bargain properly because they're too busy following instructions from the invisible one-inch-tall Vedran resting on their shoulders transmitting data directly into their neckports.*

He started the cooldown procedure on the engines. He'd need to wait at least another hour before he'd be able to Slip back to Caldonia to retrieve the others.

I can tell them they were destroyed. They refused to surrender and I was forced to fire missiles on them. To make a good show of it, Jrinto fired the missiles and detonated them at roughly the same spot where the cargo ship had been. *No survivors.* The captain would be pissed, of course, since he had lined up a good buyer for the cargo ship, but that was life in the drift for you. The worst that would happen would be that the cost of repairs on the Banshees—not to mention replacing the missiles— would come out of his salary, but he had enough savings to cover it.

Besides, these people *had* done considerable damage to the Impound Lot. They *had* to be treated as armed and dangerous.

Confident in his ability to sell the story, Jrinto sat back, waited for his engines to cool down, and once again envisioned his dream date with Teena Harwall.

Aboard the erstwhile object of Jrinto's pursuit, the pilot took the ship out of Slipstream into space near Olivares Trust. As soon as they settled into normal space, the pilot leaned back and exhaled. Engaging the autopilot and pushing the seat back to its standby position—a move accompanied by a loud squeaking noise—she turned around and looked at her engineer, who at least had the good graces to look abashed.

"Next time, Harper," Captain Beka Valentine of the *Eureka Maru* said, "you can post your own damn bail."

TWO • THE *EUREKA MARU,* OLIVARES TRUST, 302 AFC

Welcome to Olivares Trust. If you can't fix it here, it can't be fixed.

—SIGN IN EVERY LANDING PORT ON OLIVARES TRUST

Beka maneuvered the *Eureka Maru* toward one of the drift's docking ports. At this speed, they'd be there in twenty minutes, and in range for instant communication in ten. She could've gone faster, but after playing cat-and-mouse-in-the-Slipstream with Takilov's Banshees, she wanted to be as gentle with her ship as she could. The *Maru* had once again come through in a pinch, and Beka believed in rewarding her with gentle treatment where possible. Especially since gentle treatment wasn't often the norm.

She loved drifts. They combined the best elements of ships and planets—though, to Beka's mind, there were far more like the former than the latter. They had a regulated atmosphere and gravity, they had structure and stability, and they controlled their weather. Floating in space under their own steam near Slip points, drifts served as ports of call, repair stations, rest-and-recreation facilities, shopping centers, and interstellar post offices. In fact, their stopover at Takilov Drift—a snake pit Beka would happily have avoided, all things being equal—had been made solely in order to pick up a cargo-load full of mail. Beka had always thought the universe would be a much better place if it was just drifts and ships and they did away with planets altogether.

Well, okay, we'd need somewhere to grow food and things like that, she thought grudgingly, *but you can automate most of that. It's not like anyone should have to, y'know, set foot on a planet or anything.*

"Boss?"

It was the third time Seamus Harper had said that word, and Beka, for the third time, replied with a terse, "Shut up, Harper." For good measure, she added, "You're still at the top of my list of People I Want to Beat Until They Bleed."

From one of the aft control stations, Fred Vexpag chuckled. "Hell, I thought ol' Bobby had the top spot on *that* list."

Beka spared a glance behind her at Vexpag, from whom she did not appreciate the mention of her now-very-much-former lover Bobby Jensen. "And you're next after Harper. I told you I wanted a *small* diversion, not a re-creation of the Battle of Witchhead."

Vexpag shrugged and spit out the toothpick that had been residing in the right-hand corner of his mouth. "Needed cover to steal the ship back. Explosions gave us cover. We got the ship. Don't see the problem, really." He pulled a fresh toothpick out of his pocket and stuck it in the left-hand corner of his mouth.

"The *problem* is that explosives are expensive. Our repair list was already long before I had to make three Slips in a row. Speaking of which . . ." She glanced over at Harper. "Get to the engine room. That'll serve two really useful functions."

Still looking abashed, Harper said, "What's that, Boss?"

"One, I need a damage report. Two, I need you out of my sight."

Harper grunted an acknowledgment, and Beka heard the heavy sound of his work boots on the deck. Then they stopped, and he said, "Can I just say something here?"

"Can I stop you?" Beka muttered. Keeping Harper quiet was always a temporary prospect at best.

"I had no way of knowin' that guy was a narc. I mean, c'mon, usually I can smell a cop a mile off, but this guy practically had 'hardened criminal' tattooed on his forehead!"

Beka blew out a breath. "It's Takilov Drift, Harper. The cops are the most hardened criminals there."

"Well, yeah, I know that *now*, but my point is, I thought for *sure* that—"

Beka pressed a button on her handgrips. The computer intoned, *"Autopilot engaged."* Then she turned around to face her engineer.

"Harper?"

"Yeah, Boss?"

"Damage report."

"Right, Boss."

He turned and left.

Beka sighed. Harper was a good kid. Her current animus against him notwithstanding, he was probably the most valuable member of her crew. Not bad for a short, dirty, pale, hyperactive, sickly human she and Bobby rescued from the wastes of Earth years ago. But he'd made huge improvements to all of the *Maru*'s systems, in ways that Beka didn't think were possible with the equipment at hand. Hell, she wasn't sure it was possible with top-of-the-line height-of-the-Commonwealth equipment. She sometimes wondered what Harper could accomplish on an old High Guard ship or a Nietzschean fighter.

At the mental image of the very unmilitary Harper in one of those archaic High Guard uniforms, Beka couldn't help but smile. Even more absurd was Harper—who didn't even have the standard enhancements most humans got done to their DNA, much less the genetic overhaul of a Nietzschean—on a fighter belonging to the Drago-Kazov or the Sabra Prides.

As soon as Harper was gone, Vexpag picked up an old conversational thread. "Look, you didn't say we were on a budget or nothin', you just said to create a diversion."

"Odd, isn't it, how your diversions tend to involve high explosives?" That was the Reverend Behemiel Far-Traveller—or Rev Bem, as Harper had taken to calling him after mangling the pronunciation of "Behemiel" for the ninth time—who spoke in his usual dry tone.

Beka added, "Really expensive high explosives."

Vexpag glanced over at Rev and grinned. "Don't remember you complainin' all that much back on Havnil when I saved your hairy hide." He turned back to Beka. "'Sides, they deserved it. Wouldn't let me on board to get my spare box'a toothpicks."

Rev bared his teeth. "Certainly an offense worthy of explosive decompression."

Looking back to Rev, Vexpag said, "Hey, I know what I'm doin'. Nobody got hurt, and I kept the big booms away from the outer hull. I ain't no murderer."

"Enough, you two!" Beka said, unable to help but smile. "Look, I'm not really that mad at you, Fred, but—I just wish you'd chosen a diversion less—costly."

"Like I said, you didn't say we were on a budget."

"I shouldn't have to by now." Beka slid the pilot's chair into standby mode, which caused it to make another squeak. She climbed out of the pilot's well to the aft of the flight deck. "We're *always* on a budget. We've always *been* on a budget. And at the rate we're going, we're always going to *be* on a budget."

"Fine." Vexpag tossed his toothpick onto the deck. "I'm gonna shower. 'Scuse me."

He turned on his heel and walked out.

As his footfalls faded, Beka turned to Rev, who looked at her with irritatingly placid blue eyes. "I know that look, Rev."

On any other Magog, the smile Rev hit her with would have been the prelude to a fine dining experience on Beka's spleen, but the Wayist had been with Beka for six years now, and she knew better. At first glance, of course, there was no mistaking him for anything but a Magog: the leathery skin, the wild mane of fur that covered him from head to toe, the razor-like claws, the menacing teeth, the flattened nose, the tapered ears, and the sharp horns that protruded from his forehead, cheeks, and chin.

And yet, a second glance showed that this could not possibly be the Magog that still provoked nightmares in children—and adults—throughout the Known Worlds. Where most Magog hunched over, using all four limbs to propel themselves like fighting-mad gorillas, Rev stood upright with perfect posture and didn't so much walk as glide. Magog eyes were usually bloodshot and wild, but Rev's were blue and gentle. He had eschewed the traditional Magog garb of the skins of slain prey in favor of a cloak in the muted orange color of the Way, with the additional adornment of the Wayist symbol that he wore on a thick necklace, and which sat prominently in the middle of his chest. Being in his presence, it was impossible to be scared of him.

Mostly. Every once in a while he would growl or snarl, and suddenly you remembered just what species he was—and what they were capable of. Magog had literally swarmed throughout the Commonwealth, and later through the remains of the Commonwealth-Nietzschean civil war that left both nations destroyed. Of all the horrors that a horrible universe could throw at a person, Magog were in many ways the worst because the method to their madness was both simple and brutal: they kill you or use you as food.

"What look would that be?" Rev replied to Beka's statement with a question asked as sweetly as his grinding voice would allow him to sound.

Running her hand through her red hair in a futile attempt to untangle it—the environmentals were off again, and the flight deck was much too hot—Beka said, "The you're-being-too-hard-on-them look. The Divine may be forgiving, Rev, but the Divine doesn't have a billion creditors to keep at bay."

"True. However, while I cannot, of course, condone Harper's actions—"

"The Divine forfend," Beka said with a small smile.

"—I can appreciate the motive behind them. The very creditors whose existence you lament are precisely why Harper felt the need to attempt his grift."

Beka refused to be placated. "Yeah, and about that, did he have to try Niedermeyer—solo? I mean, c'mon, what kind of idiot does a classic two-person con by himself?"

"So are you angry that he made the attempt—or that he got caught?"

Biting back a reply, Beka instead closed her eyes, counted to ten in Vedran, and then blew out a long breath. "I'm just mad, okay? The latest round of repairs were already going to go through the entire petty-cash reserve. Now I'm probably going to need to dip into my own funds—again—which means that much less I can pay my Dad's creditors—again. I'm barely keeping up with the damn interest." She rested against the railing over the pilot's well. "I'm tired of the circle, Rev. Take on a job to help pay off the debt. Job goes wrong, or Harper pisses somebody off, or Vexpag blows up something he shouldn't have blown up, or I look at somebody cross-eyed, or someone decides he won't work with a Magog, or everything goes right but the *Maru* gets banged up, and we're back to square one."

"How can you be back to square one if you're going in a circle?" Rev asked.

Almost involuntarily, Beka let out a bark of laughter.

Before she could explain her explanation, the computer intoned, *"Incoming transmission from Olivares Trust."*

Hopping back down into the pilot's well, Beka said, "Answer it, will you, Rev?"

As she settled back into the chair, loudly shifted it forward into the operating position, thinking, *I've got to get that squeak fixed*, and disengaged the autopilot, Beka heard Rev say, "This is the *Eureka Maru* requesting permission to dock."

"That depends," said a familiar voice.

"On?" Rev prompted when the conditions were not forthcoming.

"On where you want to dock."

Beka chuckled, finally placing the voice. "Manteen, do you really think I'd come back to this dump for any reason *other* than to dock at Vasily's?"

"It is you, Beka," Manteen said with a chuckle. *"Glad to see you've still got the* Maru. *I was sorry to hear about your dad. He was a good man. How's Sid doing?"*

"Wouldn't know," Beka said quickly. She hadn't heard from "Uncle" Sid since before her father died. "So you gonna let us dock at Vasily's, or what?"

"That depends."

"On?"

"You gonna finally say yes to that dinner offer I made you?"

Beka smiled. "Is the offer still for Cavanaugh's?"

Manteen snorted. *"Please. If I could afford Cavanaugh's, I wouldn't be working a portmaster's job on the ass-end of the Milky Way."*

"Cavanaugh's or nothing, Manteen, sorry."

"Ah, hell. Permission to dock granted anyhow. I always had a soft spot for people named Valentine. In fact, that's probably the only reason your brother's still breathing right now."

"Rafe was here?" This surprised Beka. Olivares was far too respectable a place for her older brother to be seen. A pit like Takilov was more his speed.

"About six months back. He did his usual job of making friends and influencing people."

"I'll bet." Rafe was one of the more gifted grifters around. *Hell,* Beka thought, *he probably* could *pull off Niedermeyer by himself if he had to.* She hadn't seen him since before Dad died, either.

"Anyhow, you're cleared for Vasily's port. You're in Bay Twenty-two."

"My lucky number. Thanks, Manteen."

"No problem. And hey, even if you won't go to dinner with me, how about a drink? Say, Girzin's at fifteen?"

"Maybe next time, Manteen. Right now, I just need to get my ship up to snuff and head out. Thanks, though, I appreciate it. *Maru* out."

She closed the connection.

"I was unaware that we were on a timetable at Olivares Trust," Rev said after a moment. "In fact, I was assuming—"

"I know, I know, I just—" Beka sighed. "Manteen'll want to talk about old times."

"My impression of humans has always been that they enjoy speaking of the past."

Beka maneuvered the ship toward a port that had Vasily's stylized logo painted over it. "That kinda depends on whose past."

"An excellent point. You, for example, very rarely speak of your past."

Glancing back at the Magog, she said, "Rev? You know that, if I ever need to talk to somebody about anything, you're the first person I'd go to, right?"

"I am flattered that you hold me in such high regard."

"When I'm ready to talk about this, you'll be the first to know."

Rev nodded his head in understanding. "Very well."

It wasn't that Beka didn't want to share a drink with Manteen. He wasn't a bad guy—though he was, in fact, three times Beka's age, and they both knew that his flirting was utterly harmless.

But Manteen knew Beka from when she was a teenager, when her father and Rafe and Uncle Sid were all on the *Maru* together. The conversation they'd just had indicated that he'd be full of questions about Dad's death and Rafe and Sid. The fact that Ignatius Valentine's oldest child and best friend were absent from his funeral was a wound that Beka had no interest in reopening.

It was the work of only a few minutes and some maneuvers that Beka could do in her sleep—indeed, *had* done in her sleep on more than one occasion—to land the *Maru* in Bay 22 of Vasily's port.

Once they were settled down, Beka hit the intercom. "Talk to me, Harper." She could have gotten the report from Harper in person, but that would have necessitated setting foot in the engine room. That was Harper's domain, and Beka had learned it was best to leave him to it. Besides, there was only so long she could stand there breathing through her mouth.

"Well, Boss," and Beka noticed that Harper's abashed tone was all but gone, *"we got us a classic case of the good, the bad, and the ugly—and by that, I don't mean me, a Nietzschean, and Rev Bem. No offense, Rev."*

"None taken," Rev said indulgently. "My people were not bred for aesthetics."

"Ain't that the truth. In any case, the good is that the Slip drive is just peachy, even after pinballing here from Takilov."

Beka let out a sigh of relief. That had been the biggest risk in doing so many Slips so quickly. She hadn't worried about her own ability to focus in the Slipstream—she could have gone on for hours more without slowing down—but the *Maru*'s battered old drive had its limits. *One of these days, I really need to upgrade the thing to something built in this decade. Maybe by next decade . . .*

"The bad is that there's a crack in the fuel tank, and it's not on a seam this time. We try welding and it'll shatter. It's gotta be replaced."

"Dammit," Beka muttered. "And the ugly?"

"The A/P valve's totally shot."

Wincing, Beka said, "Are you sure? Don't you know what those things cost?"

"Yeah, anywhere between prohibitively expensive and Oh-God-shoot-me-now. That's why when the valve first failed six months ago, I managed a jury-rig to keep us going so we wouldn't have to sell Vexpag's limbs to pay for 'em."

Beka blinked. "Harper, you can't jury-rig an A/P valve." The anti-proton valves were very particular parts that had to be aligned on the molecular level by nanobots, and had to be tailored to each individual ship. That was why they were so expensive.

"Maybe you can't, but it's nothing that a little genius couldn't figure out how to accomplish."

Smiling, Beka said, "That's my little genius."

"Unfortunately, even my godlike powers only extend so far. All I did was stave off the inevitable. Besides, we're at Vasily's right? At least we know we'll get good parts here."

"True." Six months ago, when the valve had first gone, they were in even worse financial straits and deep in the heart of the Andromeda galaxy. They would not have been able to get to Olivares Trust, and even if they could have, replacing the valve would have been beyond their means. "Good work, Harper. Draw up a list that I can give to Vasily."

"Will do, Boss."

Vasily wasn't available when they docked, so Beka left Harper behind with the repair list and gave everyone else liberty on the drift.

Harper, of course, whined about this as Rev, Vexpag, and Beka gathered at the airlock. "How come *I* get stuck playing guard dog to the *Maru*?"

Beka glowered at him. "Harper, cast your mind back a mere twenty-four hours. I realize your short-term memory isn't the best in the world, but surely you remember me putting *my ship* up for bail because of what happened the last time I gave you liberty on a drift."

"Aw, c'mon, Boss, I've learned my lesson. I'm a new man."

"*That's* a relief," Vexpag muttered. "Maybe the new you won't leave s'damn many Sparky Cola cans lyin' around."

Harper snorted. "This from the guy who leaves a trail of toothpicks wherever he goes."

Before the argument could continue, Beka stepped between them. "Harper, this isn't a debate. That's why it says 'captain' in front of my name. Got that?"

Not giving Harper a chance to reply, Beka turned around and headed toward the exit. Behind her, she heard Harper say to Rev at a volume he probably didn't think Beka could hear, "Hey, Rev—how long am I gonna be in her doghouse?"

"If I were you," Rev said sagely, "I would consider the efficacy of taking up bone-gnawing as a hobby."

Beka couldn't help but grin as she exited the *Maru*.

The remaining three members of the crew went their separate ways. Vexpag headed for the commerce section. "Gotta get somethin' for my lady." In the three years Vexpag had served on the *Maru*, Beka had never seen, met, nor been able to get the name of Vexpag's "lady," but he got her some kind of gift at every port of call and shipped it to her in secret.

It was one of many things about Fred Vexpag that Beka did not know—a list far longer than the reverse. A tall, lanky human with short legs for his height—he was basically all torso—he had a talent for weaponry. A few jobs that got unexpectedly violent had convinced Beka to seek out someone who could be violent right back. That was Fred Vexpag in spades. The man had a way with ordnance and a capacity for mayhem that belied his laid-back appearance. He kept his thick long brown hair tied back in a ponytail, with the bangs hanging over his eyes, making him look like a very tall sheepdog.

Beka never liked dogs. She wasn't entirely sure she liked Vexpag, either, but she couldn't deny that he'd been valuable. The incident on Havnil that he mentioned to Rev was a prime example. If not for his timely intervention with some very big booms, Rev would have died, and so probably would have the rest of them before long.

Speaking of Rev, he had gone off to the drift's local monastery—what Harper once called a "Wayist-station"—to check in with his fellow monks and see what was doing in the wonderful world of the Way. That left Beka on her own.

After the day I've had, that may be a good thing, she thought. Being forced to steal back her own ship because her engineer had gotten them all into trouble combined with a yet another rash of expensive repairs to put her in a dark mood.

Beka didn't drink, nor partake of any illicit substances, but she felt the need to sit alone in a bar. Maybe meet some stranger and have a lengthy chat about absolutely nothing. Maybe do more than chat.

Or maybe even just sit and stare at a wall for half a day.

She avoided Girzin's, since she might bump into Manteen there. Checking the directory, she found a place not far from Vasily's called the Slip Point. The name of the establishment caught her eye—given the name and the location, it was likely a place that catered to pilots. This appealed.

On the way, several people sidled near her and tried to entice her to spend money: flash and other narcotics, stocks and bonds, entertainment of a wide variety of types ranging from harmless to stupid to out-and-out deadly, sporting events, and much more. She ignored them with the ease of long practice. Beka had survived this long by knowing who to disregard, and people who peddled their wares in the brightly lit corridors of drifts were near the top of that particular list.

Also lining the corridors were a different set of people, most of them sitting in the corners, up against the walls, and under the windows and next to the doors of the establishments that emptied onto the corridor. They were trying to seek shadows in a place that had none. Space on a drift was far too limited to waste on such luxuries as nooks, crannies, or places without artificial light. So they were stuck in the open, just like everyone and everything else.

Whereas the peddlers dressed to impress, these people put on whatever they could scrounge—or beg. What Beka found ironic was that these beggars probably came to Olivares with plenty of cash, and made the mistake of actually listening to one of the peddlers. *The full circle of drift life in one place*, she thought with a bitter smile.

She noticed one person in particular—a woman dressed in half a coat, three-quarters of a pair of pants, and two shirts. Her face was streaked with dirt that covered several open sores, and most of her teeth were missing. She huddled in the space between a gaming emporium that promised "thrills, spills, and excitement" and a fast-food stand. How she could stand to sit that close to the aroma of food and drink that she obviously couldn't afford to obtain was beyond Beka. She supposed that it was possible that the owner would give her leftovers, or she counted on customers taking pity on her by virtue of that very proximity.

There but for the grace of the Maru *go I,* Beka thought. When her father died, her inheritance consisted of a broken family, a pile of debts that stretched from San-Ska-Re to Infinity Atoll, and the *Eureka Maru.* The third was the only remembrance of the first, and the best way to deal with the second.

It was the only home she had ever known. And it was more of a home than that woman had.

She reached into her pocket, took out a few coins, and gently placed them on the torn blanket the woman slept on.

The gesture was fruitless, pointless, and frivolous. Beka had never been one for noble causes. In fact, she generally avoided them like the plague. Her disdain for such things had been one of the many factors that led to her break-up with Bobby Jensen.

But in some bizarre way, giving this stranger some of her hard-earned coins improved Beka's mood. *Maybe because it's a not-so-nice reminder that things could be worse.*

Entering the Slip Point, Beka found herself surrounded by her people.

It wasn't anything she could pinpoint. Well, no, that wasn't entirely true: if you looked closely enough, you could see the calluses on the insides of their fingers from constant use of the grips. But even without that, all pilots had a certain bearing that was really only identifiable to other pilots. Part of it was attitude, the confidence combined with a mild dose of insanity that you needed to successfully navigate the Slipstream. Part of it was just the way like drew to like, so to speak.

Beka was among her own.

The bar was about half full. It reeked of sweat, alcohol, and the fumes of assorted illicit substances. Beka found the odor off-putting—she preferred the more regulated atmosphere of the *Maru*—but the place didn't smell qualitatively worse than Harper's engine room. Besides, at least it wasn't something really awful like dirt or animals or some other mudfoot olfactory disaster.

She found an empty stool at the bar and ordered a fruit punch.

"You call that a drink?" said a voice next to her.

Turning to her left, she saw an Umbrite holding a glass with an amber liquid inside it. He was wearing a simple black jumpsuit, with a corporate logo Beka didn't recognize on the chest. Beka also noticed he wore a thin gold chain around each of his facial pincers, a bit of body decoration she'd never seen on an Umbrite before.

More to the point, though, he wasn't a pilot. All the other people at the bar sat with the same posture one used in Slipstream: back rounded, arms spread, legs straight and half a meter apart. The Umbrite, though, was slumped over and had his legs crossed.

"Yeah," she said in answer to the question, "I do."

"Wanna know what I call it?"

"Not particularly."

The bartender brought her the fruit punch, and Beka handed him a credit chit.

Hurry back, she thought at the bartender as he went to verify the chit. She didn't want to be stuck next to the Umbrite any longer than necessary.

"I call it the sign of a smart pilot."

Beka blinked.

"I've been sitting here for days waiting for the right person to come in. I'm willing to bet another one of these," he held up his own drink, "that you're in here for repairs you can't afford and in need of work, right?"

Smiling, Beka said, "What do I get if you're wrong?"

"Doesn't matter. I'm not wrong."

The bartender came back with the chit and a nod. Beka let out an involuntary sigh of relief. She knew intellectually that her credit was good, but that didn't stop her heart from beating a little faster every time she handed over the chit, half-expecting it to come up empty.

Of course, I lived that nightmare half the times I went somewhere with Dad . . .

The Umbrite offered a callus-free hand. "My name is Goran. I work for Divrot Salvage and Recovery."

"Never heard of you," Beka said, not returning the handshake. She took a sip of the punch, which was too acidic.

"We're new. Well, kind of new. There are a bunch of wrecks a couple of systems over on Tychen."

That got Beka's attention. Tychen had been the site of a rather brutal war during the early days of the Commonwealth, but the radiation levels were obscenely high. Beka had heard through the grapevine that the levels had gotten low enough to make salvaging a possibility instead of a pipe dream. "Let me guess," she said. "Divrot was formed by some entrepreneur who thought that the opening of Tychen would translate to easy money."

"A cynical but accurate assessment of my employer's motives, yes."

So Goran here isn't the boss. Or he's pretending he isn't. "Tell your employer that no money is easy."

"Neither is securing a pilot." Umbrites generally didn't smile, but Goran did look a bit more amused than he had a second ago. "We had a ship all lined up to run salvage for us, but she turned out to be—unreliable in Slipstream."

Beka shuddered. In Slipstream, *unreliable* translated to anything from "dead" to "permanently lost in the 'stream." She wasn't sure which fate was worse.

"So what makes you think I'd be more reliable?"

"The fact that you came into a seedy bar near a repair depot looking haggard—you humans really need to figure out some way to mask how tired you are, it's written *all* over your faces—"

"I'll take it up with the designer," Beka said dryly.

Again, the amused look. "In any case, you come in here in a situation in which ninety-nine people out of a hundred would order something alcoholic. But you ordered fruit punch. That, to me, bespeaks reliability. And good judgment. Both qualities one wants in a pilot. On top of that," he looked down at her fingers, "those are some of the hardest calluses I've ever seen, which means you're experienced. Add to that your presence at the bar closest to Vasily's, and that indicates that you've not only got a steep repair bill, but you know enough to go to the best."

Beka quickly revised her estimate of Goran upward. He was observant, talked a good game, and was a possible source of income.

Of course, that didn't mean she was going to do anything silly like *trust* him.

"Tell you what," she said. "Why don't we find us a table in good light close to the exit, and you can give me your sales pitch." She emphasized the good light. The Umbrite homeworld of Zhu-Zhu Hwai consisted of a huge network of underground warrens—Umbrites were as well-adapted to low-light conditions as Nightsiders, and that gave him every advantage in the dimly lit bar. Beka wanted him to know that she knew that.

"Very well," Goran said, and he climbed off his stool.

While she didn't get her hopes up—she never got her hopes up, because it almost always led to disappointment—she did feel better about coming to the Slip Point. At best, the *Maru* might come out of this with another job.

At worst, she thought, *I get to spend some time with a clever Umbrite. I've met worse in bars. . . .*

THREE • MALANI'S HAVEN, 302 AFC

There is an old saying that people get the governments they deserve. This is only occasionally true. It is, however, universally true that governments get the people they deserve.

—KING BISIME OF MALANI'S HAVEN, 257 AFC

Thirty years ago, Bisime, the supreme ruler of Malani's Haven, told his son Prince Nwari that a good king was bold in everything he did—even his mistakes. The important thing was to make all your moves in the open and to show confidence in your decisions. If you're sure of yourself, your subjects are more likely to believe in you.

As he walked through the tunnel beneath the surface of Malani's Haven now, surrounded by mercenaries hired for the express purpose of getting him and his queen off-planet before the Liberators captured and killed them as the final blow of their successful coup d'état against the monarchy, King Nwari wondered what his long-dead father would think of him now.

Probably not much, Nwari thought.

Father, of course, made everything look easy. Worse, he made it *sound* easy. Ruling a planet was effortless for him. It was all well and good for King Bisime to say that his son should be confident in his decisions, because he himself usually only took a fraction of a second to mull over them. Once it was made, that was it. And, more often than not, it was the right decision.

Nwari, though, faced every thought, every question, every dilemma with a terrible sense of dread and fear of failure. He agonized, sometimes for days at a time, and then when he *did* make the decision, he fretted afterward about whether or not it was the right one.

It wasn't that he wanted to raise taxes, but the money for the desperately needed restoration of the crumbling spaceport had to come from *somewhere*. It wasn't that he wanted to increase the number of flybys by Enforcement, but he had to respond to the rise in crime in the cities.

It wasn't that he wanted to be king, but he was the son of the old king.

He knew what Father would say. "You think I wanted to be king? Bah! I wanted to be a farmer. But sons of kings don't get to be farmers, they get to rule the world. And someday, so will you."

Maybe, but not for long . . .

Looking back on it, the biggest mistake had been cutting the military budget. Malani's Haven had been successfully fending off the local Nietzschean Pride since before Bisime's time, but the Ursa Pride hadn't come anywhere near Malani's Haven for two decades, and Nwari simply couldn't justify military readiness for a campaign that didn't exist, and wasn't likely to exist—not when there were so many other things that needed the money.

Unfortunately, the higher-ups in the military dealt with the cuts by slashing the salaries of the rank-and-file. That made said rank-and-file an easy target for Liberator propaganda, and when the rebels made their move, they had the support of three-quarters of the soldiers. Nwari and Hamsha found themselves backed by the aristocracy and the upper ranks of the military, who were helpless against the sheer numbers of the people and lower ranks.

General Orkani had arranged to hire mercenaries to get the king and queen away to exile on Terra Verde before the palace was taken. Within the day, a group led by a tall, powerful looking Nietzschean arrived.

Nwari had always thought of his father—who stood almost half a head taller than Nwari and was broad-shouldered and full of girth besides—as the biggest person he'd ever known. That was before he met this Nietzschean—who, Nwari learned after he rather pretentiously introduced himself, was named Tyr Anasazi, out of Victoria by Barbarossa, of the Kodiak Pride. (Nietzscheans loved their genealogy so much, they made it part of their full names.) He was taller than Bisime, with shoulders at least as wide. However, he had none of the previous king's girth. If there was a micron of fat on him, it wasn't readily evident. There were thousand-year-old redwoods on Malani's Haven whose trunks were smaller than Anasazi's arms. Where the six forearm spikes usually made the average Nietzschean look more fearsome, on this one they seemed redundant. Anasazi's physique was framed by a mane of braided brown hair that extended to his lower back. The hair combined with intense brown eyes to complete the image of a predatory animal about to strike.

The moment Anasazi had entered the throne room—which had been carefully designed and refined by palace decorators over the centuries to make the two raised thrones in the back of the room the first place the eye fell—he suddenly became the focus of attention. People seemed unconsciously to shift position to allow him to be at the center. Just by his very presence, he became the sun around which all else revolved.

Nwari had been at once scared to death to be in the same room—indeed, the same universe—as Anasazi and also relieved that the mercenary was on *his* side.

It was Hamsha who had told them of the secret tunnel under the capital city of Amorin. Neither Nwari nor Orkani had heard of it, but Hamsha said she had discovered the tunnel by accident when she was a girl. She often played there when she wanted to get away from her governess. Nwari, who had been hearing tales of what a troublesome child Hamsha was from that selfsame governess all of his life, would have found this revelation a lot more amusing under different circumstances. When she came of age, then-Princess Hamsha did some research and found that King Yoblan—Nwari's great-great-great-grandfather—had had the tunnel constructed during a time of political unrest. It was an escape route from the palace to the spaceport.

Obviously, Nwari thought, *Yoblan didn't believe in doing everything publicly . . .*

From there, the plan for getting them away was simplicity itself. To the best of Hamsha's knowledge, no one but she and the palace archivist knew that the tunnel even existed. The Nietzschean had a ship waiting in a part of the spaceport that was in the process of being refurbished. Guarded by two of his people, the area was comparatively lax in security, and so the ideal place for a getaway vehicle, especially since the Liberators had very little air support. Once they achieved escape velocity, they'd be home free.

"The problem," Anasazi had said in his deep, resonant voice, "is that the Liberators probably are smart enough to know that that part of the spaceport is where you will try to get away."

"If they're thinking that at all," Orkani had replied. "They probably expect Nwari to hold his ground and withstand the attack, not run away."

Nwari had bristled at that, even though the characterization was perfectly accurate. He *was* running away. Bisime no doubt would have faced whatever was coming to him as openly as he did everything else, and then would have died needlessly. Nwari preferred breathing to being right.

"Even so," Hamsha had said, "it is unlikely that they know about the tunnel."

"True," Anasazi had said.

So now five mercenaries, three aides, and the king and queen of Malani's Haven proceeded down a secret tunnel that was, at last, being used for the purpose for which it had been constructed. They left Orkani behind with a cadre of trusted soldiers—a number that was distressingly small—to defend the palace.

The Than mercenary was up front, probably because she had the best eyesight, by virtue of the bionic attachments to her compound eyes. She was followed by one of the two impossibly large human mercenaries, then Nwari and Hamsha, then the Nightsider mercenary, then the three aides, then the other human, with Anasazi bringing up the rear. All of Anasazi's people were armed with pistols of some kind, and many also wore edged weapons.

Anasazi's weapon was the largest by far—Nwari had seen one-person spacecraft that were smaller than the gun, which rested on the Nietzschean's shoulder via a leather strap.

The tunnel itself was carved out of the bedrock that Amorin was built on. No attempt had been made to smooth the walls or the floor, so both were uneven. Nwari started to develop a sore hip from the constant brisk tramping over such awkward terrain. He also noticed a slight limp in Hamsha's step as they continued, and one of his aides was breathing much heavier. The tunnel was only a meter wide, so they had to go single file.

Lighting for the tunnel was provided by old-fashioned Everlites: half-a-meter-diameter flat discs that were attached to the uneven wall surface every twenty meters or so. They provided more than ample light to see by—in fact, the tunnel was better lit than half the rooms in the palace. The company that manufactured them promised that they'd last for two hundred years, and it seemed that they were at least three-quarters accurate, given that these were still going a century-and-a-half after they were put in place. *If I live through this*, Nwari swore, *and am someday restored to power, Everlite will get every government lighting contract I can possibly give them.*

As they were about to round a corner, the Than held up an arm—if one could call it an arm on the insectoid Than. "Something up ahead."

"That's impossible," Mucri, one of the aides, said as they all stopped walking forward. "Nobody knows about this tunnel."

"Quiet," Anasazi said from the rear. "What do you see, Air?"

"Trip wire," she said.

Anasazi pushed his way to the front of the line. "You're right," he said.

Peering past the human in front of him, Nwari saw just the tunnel. "I don't see anything."

"You're not meant to, Your Highness," Anasazi said. He somehow managed to say those last two words with token respect and a sneer at the same time. "The trip wire's too thin for inferior eyes to make out."

"Why Tyr, that's the nicest thing you've ever said to me," the Than said.

Anasazi looked at the Than. "It would be foolish to disregard your superior eyesight, Air."

"And you're never foolish."

"Never." Anasazi spoke with a confidence that bordered on arrogant. "The question is, is it the prelude to an ambush, or simply an alarm?"

"Or a detonator," the Than added.

"A bomb?" Mucri said. "Nobody said anything about a bomb! We've got to go back!"

"We *can't* go back," Nwari said. Images of the palace in flames, of Orkani making a final, but ultimately futile, attempt to stop the Liberators filled his mind. The image sickened him. Orkani deserved better than that.

We all do.

"Don't be a fool," Anasazi said. "Conveniently, we're dealing with amateurs. The trip wire is low enough to step over." He knelt down next to the right-hand wall and held his weapon at a position that was approximately Nwari's mid-shin level. "The trip wire is here." He depressed the trigger, and a bolt of energy flew from the muzzle and hit the bedrock on the left-hand side. It left a smoky black indentation. "Make sure you lift your leg over that spot."

Hamsha looked at Mucri and the other two aides. "Them first."

"Your Highness, no," Mucri said. "Your noble personage is—"

"Less important right now," Hamsha said, giving Mucri a stern look. "You are innocents in this. You must go first."

Mucri gave Hamsha a frightened look back, and Nwari knew that Hamsha wasn't fooling anyone. The aides were going first because they were expendable, and would therefore more likely be the first ones hit if something went wrong.

As each aide lifted their legs and climbed over something they could not see, Nwari came to a realization.

He was going to die.

When the Liberators first started agitating, he figured that they were just a bunch of rabble who would never be organized enough to constitute a proper threat.

When they became organized, he figured they would simply push for political change through proper channels and he would deal with it that way.

When they started staging protests, military strikes, and raids on government targets, he figured the military would deal with it.

When many members of the military pledged their support to the Liberators, he figured General Orkani could still handle it.

When Orkani suggested hiring Anasazi to get him and Hamsha off-planet, he figured that they would take him to their allies on Terra Verde and he could wait until the heat blew over.

Now, though, he knew that this hope, like all his others, was to be dashed. He was going to die, not as Bisime did—in his bed, surrounded by loved ones and admirers—nor as his grandfather Kantu did—in victorious combat against the Ursa Pride—but while running away through an unknown tunnel under Amorin, at the hands of a bunch of rebels who had succeeded in overthrowing him.

Hamsha insisted the other mercenaries precede her and Nwari, and save for Anasazi, they all did.

"I will go last," Anasazi said. He spoke matter-of-factly, yet Nwari knew that it was not a suggestion, but a statement of fact, and nothing either king or queen could say would alter that fact.

Nwari stared at the corridor ahead of him for several seconds.

He did not doubt the existence of the trip wire, of course, but he simply could not see it. Squinting his eyes, he tried once again to capture it in his sight. For a second, he was able to make out—something. But then, a moment later, it was gone again.

Paranoia gripped him suddenly. *Did Anasazi make it up? Is it all a trick to—*

Then common sense returned. What, exactly, would such a trick accomplish? If Anasazi had wanted to betray him, or deliver him into the arms of the Liberators, he'd hardly work to maneuver him *around* a trap. And what point would making up a trip wire serve, except to make them even more nervous than they already were?

You're overanalyzing, he admonished himself, *again. That's what got you into this mess—thinking too much. So stop it, and get a move on!*

He lifted his left leg over the spot indicated by Anasazi's weapons fire and his own half-seen vision of the wire, then brought it down as far ahead as he could manage without straining a muscle. His hip, already sore from moving through this wretched tunnel, howled in protest, but he ignored the pain that now shot through his entire pelvic region. As soon as his left foot found purchase, he lifted his right leg up as high as he could and brought it forward, mumbling a quick prayer to deities that he had never, until this precise moment, believed in.

Fearing his heart would escape his rib cage, it was beating so fast, he turned to see Hamsha do the same thing he did, only leading with her right leg. As soon as she made it to the other side of the trip wire, she all but collapsed into Nwari's arms. The king embraced his queen, never more grateful to feel the warmth of her body against his.

Anasazi jumped over the trip wire, landed, and strode forward in one elegant motion. "The group hug can wait until later. Let's move."

They got back into the same formation and started walking once again.

Nwari's heartbeat didn't slow down.

His surviving the trip wire did nothing to alleviate his fear that he was going to die today.

Just as they went around a sharp bend, Anasazi cried out, "Everyone, *down!*"

Around him, the mercenaries all smoothly moved down to the ground—the Than actually looked more natural down on all fours. Mucri, Hamsha, and the others clambered down to the ground more awkwardly.

Nwari did not move.

He couldn't make his muscles work.

Looking up at him with those pitiless brown eyes, Anasazi said, "Your Highness, get on the floor or I will shoot your legs out from under you."

That did it. Nwari got down on the ground, keeping his arms between his chest and the filthy tunnel floor.

Finding his voice, Nwari asked, "What's going on?"

"Someone's coming behind us." Anasazi crab-walked over to the side then peered back around the corner. "Footfalls—sounds like thirty troops."

"I don't hear anything," Nwari said, then realized it was foolish. Nietzscheans had superior hearing too, after all.

"I suspect that General Orkani's ability to hold off the Liberators and keep them from finding these tunnels was overrated. We need to—"

Anasazi's words were cut off by a massive explosion.

Nwari put his hands to his ears, which did nothing to alleviate the bone-jarring noise of the explosion. He felt the ground shake, and closed his eyes.

A deep voice that wasn't Anasazi's said, "The trip wire?"

"Yes." That was Anasazi. "It seems that it was a bomb—and the Liberators aren't the ones who planted it."

That was enough to get Nwari to open his eyes. "What?"

Lying next to him, Hamsha said, "You mean that bomb was left over from some previous—"

The queen was interrupted by a violent quake that shook the tunnel.

Nwari looked up, and saw some cracks in the bedrock. "This isn't good."

"No, it isn't." Anasazi got up. "I hear more footfalls—fewer, but they're there. Some of the Liberators survived. They'll be after you. Glasten, Brexos, Air, get the others to the spaceport."

"What'll you be doing?" Nwari asked as he got up.

Hefting his impossibly large weapon, Anasazi said, "Finishing what the bomb started." He nodded to the Nightsider, who held up two much smaller pistols.

The Than said, "C'mon, let's go."

Now they ran—except when they stumbled thanks to another quake. Nwari now felt a searing pain in his lungs and aches in his knees to go with the soreness in his hip. He'd spent his life sitting—with his tutors, with his father, in meetings, on the throne. The most physical activity he ever engaged in was when he swam in the royal pool, and he hadn't had time to do that for months. He was in no shape for this. His heart, already pounding from nerves, now added the stress of keeping him alive through this exertion to its labors.

"I don't like this," the Than said. "I don't think this tunnel is much longer for this world." She turned around to look at Hamsha as they ran. "How much further to the spaceport?"

Between heavy breaths, Hamsha replied, "Another hundred meters at least."

Another quake. Mucri fell to the ground. One of the other aides helped him up, even as one of the human mercenaries kicked him. "Move!"

Nwari didn't know how long they ran through the tunnel before they reached the ladder that would take them up to the trapdoor that led to the back room of the security office of the spaceport. Time had lost all meaning. All he knew was that it took forever to get there, and he was obscenely grateful to see it when they finally did arrive.

The Than, Air—presumably a shortening of whatever five-syllable phrase made up this particular Than's designation—said, "I'll go first." She looked at the two humans. "Keep an eye out for Tyr and Gerenmar—or for the Liberators."

One of them snickered. "You think those jerks're gonna get past Tyr?"

Nwari couldn't read Air's expression, but he definitely heard a tinge of humor in her voice. "First time for everything."

Then she nimbly climbed up the ladder.

The two humans stood with their weapons ready. One positioned himself so he could shoot at anything that came down toward them, the other stood at the foot of the ladder. Nwari had no idea which one was Glasten and which was Brexos—indeed, even if he had been told, he doubted he would be able to tell them apart. They were of approximately the same height, same build, with the same close-cropped black hair, and the same lack of a discernible neck. They even both had deep voices.

Air made no noise as she skittered up the ladder. However, Nwari did hear a popping sound, similar to the noise a jar made when opened. *Probably releasing the seal on the trapdoor.* If the information Hamsha had found in the archives was accurate, that door hadn't been touched in a hundred and fifty years, but it also could be opened with a simple pull of a lever.

Two seconds later, Nwari heard blaster fire. But the king couldn't tell whether it was from down the corridor or above in the spaceport.

Both mercenaries tensed. The one at the ladder looked up and yelled, "Air!" Only then was Nwari able to pinpoint the source of the noise: the spaceport. The Than had found opposition up top.

By the time the blaster fire stopped, the human mercenary was already halfway up the ladder. Nwari exchanged a frightened glance with Hamsha. "An ambush?"

Hamsha gave a frightened shrug.

"We're going to die," Mucri said miserably.

"Be *quiet*, Mucri!" Nwari said angrily. "These people have been hired to keep us alive, and they will do just that."

"Yes, Your Highness." However, Mucri didn't sound like he was very encouraged.

"Son of a *bitch*!" That was the human, who was now all the way up the ladder.

The other human now stood at the foot of the ladder, pointing his weapon up toward the trapdoor. "Brexos, what is it?"

Brexos yelled down. "There were ten of these bastards waiting for her when she came up."

"What happened?"

"She got 'em—but they got her too."

Glasten snorted. "Fine by me—means we split the money six ways 'stead of seven."

Nwari shuddered.

He also tried to remember the prayer for the commendation of the soul to the afterlife. Unfortunately, it had been decades since he'd last had any kind of religious training—once, the king of Malani's Haven also served as the spiritual guide to the people as well, but that function had fallen into disuse in direct proportion to the declining number of the devout among the population—so he could not recall the words. He wasn't even sure if Thans had souls. But Air died protecting the king and queen of Malani's Haven, and, even if that sacrifice meant nothing to her own comrades, it meant a great deal to him.

At the sound of approaching footsteps from down the tunnel, Glasten once again raised his weapon. Panic started to well in Nwari until he realized that the steps were even and at a regular pace. If it was the Liberators, they wouldn't be so straightforward. Which meant it had to be—

"Tyr!" Glasten said as the Nietzschean came into view, the Nightsider alongside him. Nwari noticed that the Nightsider looked a bit worse for the wear—he had lost the leather cap he'd been wearing, and there were scuff marks and rents on his jacket and pants—but Anasazi didn't have a braid of hair out of place. The only change was the red stain on the tips of each of his three left arm spikes.

"What happened?" Nwari asked.

"Nothing especially surprising." Anasazi looked at Glasten. "Where are Air and Brexos?"

"Topside," Glasten said. "Air went up and got into an ambush. She took care of it, but—she didn't make it."

Anasazi's eyes went wide. "That *is* surprising."

Another quake shook the tunnel. Nwari almost fell over—one of his aides did, and everyone stumbled.

Except, he noticed, for Anasazi, who not only didn't lose his footing, but barely seemed even to acknowledge the tremor's existence.

"We need to get a move on." The Nietzschean sent Glasten and the Nightsider up the ladder, then the king and queen and their aides, and finally he came up himself.

When Nwari reached the midpoint of the ladder, he started to notice the stench.

By the time he reached the top, it was overwhelming.

King Nwari had seen plenty of dead bodies in his time, but they were always at funerals or in hospitals or other less chaotic situations. The only time he had seen a newly dead body was that of Bisime, when the royal physician declared him dead, the old king having died in his sleep.

Until now.

The security office into which the trapdoor led was a fairly ordinary looking room, with three desks, several wall screens that showed a variety of vistas, some rather dull wall hangings, and the royal crest painted onto the floor.

That last was somewhat obscured by the eleven corpses on the floor.

Nwari tried not to breathe through his nose, but found that nothing could keep out the stench of blood mingled with burned flesh and clothing. Red blood pooled underfoot, occasionally mixed in with the turquoise blood of the Than who was both responsible for and the final victim of the carnage in the room.

All at once, the words to the Prayer for the Commendation of the Dead came back to him.

Brexos was shaking his head. "She took down all ten of 'em. Didn't even have time to cry out or anything—was all over before we even knew what was happening."

Looking down at her body, Anasazi said, "The only anomaly in that is that she died as well. I thought she was better than that."

"What was her name?" Nwari asked.

Anasazi stared at him. "What does it matter to you?"

"I wish to say a prayer for her, and it requires her full name."

"Your Highness, we really don't have time for this."

Hamsha put a hand on his shoulder. "It's a grand gesture, my love, but he's right, we can't—"

Shaking off the hand, Nwari said, "I am still the king of Malani's Haven! I may have been a bad king, I may not be even a quarter of the man my father or his father were, and I may be in the middle of the most cowardly act ever performed by a monarch on this world." He pointed at Air's corpse. "But this person died in the service of the crown, and I will see to it that she receives at least the minimum funerary rites that I can provide. If I can do *nothing else* right, I will do that at least! Now tell me, Nietzschean, *what was her name?*"

For several seconds, Anasazi stared at Nwari with those unreadable brown eyes of his. What was going through his genetically engineered brain? Nwari wondered. Was he looking on the king with new respect? Or was he—as was far more likely—thinking what a fool he had for a client?

Nwari found he didn't care one way or the other, as long as his question was answered.

"Her name was Element of Air," he finally said in an unusually soft voice.

"Thank you."

Nwari knelt down next to Element of Air's body, again ignoring the shooting pains through his upper legs and hips. "O creators of all things, hear my plea. You made our form from the stuff of stars and our souls from the stuff of yourselves. Element of Air's form is no more. Please take her soul back into yourselves, and treat it with reverence and respect, for it is a soul worthy of your glory."

When he was done, he stood, wincing, but holding back a grunt of pain. He put his hand over his heart. "Blessings."

Hamsha, Mucri, and the other aides did likewise and intoned, "Blessings."

"Are you finished?" Anasazi asked impatiently.

Nwari looked up—and noticed that he now stood in the center of the room. Anasazi and his mercenaries stood by the door, off to the side. It was a small victory, but Nwari decided to bask in it.

He also noticed that the Nietzschean no longer intimidated him.

"Yes, I'm finished."

"Then, if you please, Your Highness, let's get out of here."

They moved through the corridors of the spaceport—which had been ordered shut down two days earlier for security reasons once the coup started, and so were quite empty—with Anasazi now in the lead, leaving Brexos to bring up the rear. Nwari was relieved to be moving on the ergonomically designed manufactured floors, though it did nothing to improve the pain to his hips, which had finally started to adjust to the bedrock.

The smooth construction and walls lined with advertisements and paintings soon gave way to half-finished walls, half-ripped-up floors, and barricades indicating the ongoing refurbishment. Nwari felt a twinge. *Ironic*, he thought. *The very spaceport project that I raised taxes in order to complete is now providing cover for the escape necessitated by the coup that started in part because I raised taxes.*

Two humans, a man as dark-skinned as Nwari himself and a woman whose joints made a slight whirring sound when she moved, indicating that she was a cyborg, stood at one airlock.

As soon as they were in sight, Anasazi asked angrily, "What have you two been doing, exactly?"

The two exchanged a glance. The woman said, "Standing guard on the ship. It's been quiet."

"We were ambushed in the security office by a team of ten. Air didn't make it. When I tell you to stand guard, it means to be *alert*."

Anasazi did not give the two mercenaries a chance to explain their lapse—not that Nwari could see how they could possibly have known anything about an ambush that was almost a hundred meters away—but instead strode past them into the airlock.

The vessel they had waiting was a cramped passenger ship, the flight deck for which was a large space full of chairs. Four comfortable ones were placed at a large multi-consoled station against the front bulkhead. Ten very uncomfortable-looking metal chairs were in the rear, with a Slip pilot's chair in the middle. The flight deck had one trapdoor in the back, one airlock, and no other way in or out. Nwari had the feeling that this and the engine housing made up the sum total of the ship's interior. As far as he knew, the journey to Terra Verde was one of several days' duration, and he was not encouraged by the lack of any kind of private quarters on this ship.

He expressed this concern to Anasazi, who said, "And if we were going to Terra Verde, that would be a valid concern. However, we're going to Haukon Tau."

Once again, fear of betrayal gripped Nwari. "What happened to Terra Verde?"

"To the best of my knowledge, not a thing. I have a contact on Haukon—he'll be providing the transport to Terra Verde from there."

Fear loosened its grip. "Ah." Haukon Tau was also only one Slip jump away—a few hours' journey at most.

"Assuming you don't have any more irritating questions, Your Highness, I'd ask you to please take your seats before the Liberators wonder why their assault team in the security office hasn't checked in yet."

Nwari nodded, relieved. As Anasazi went to sit in the one of the fore seats—the third human, the dark-skinned one who had stood guard, took the pilot's chair—the king moved to one of the chairs in the rear. It was even more uncomfortable than it looked.

Hamsha took the seat next to his, and put her hand on his

shoulder. "That was a wonderful thing you did for that Than, my love."

Before Nwari could reply to that, Anasazi turned and looked back at them. Again, Nwari found he could not read the Nietzschean's eyes. "For the record, Your Highness, if you had ruled Malani's Haven with the same passion and resolve with which you commended Element of Air's soul to the afterlife, you might not be running away with your tail between your legs right now."

Anasazi then turned around and ran through the preflight checklist. He did not acknowledge the existence of any of his passengers from Malani's Haven for the duration of the flight to Haukon Tau.

Nwari, however, spent the entire duration of the flight thinking about Anasazi's last words to him.

FOUR • OLIVARES TRUST, 302 AFC

That which is impossible is only impossible until it is accomplished, at which point it becomes possible, if not necessarily probable.

—WAYFINDER FIRST ORDER HASTURI,
A.K.A. "THE MAD PERSEID," 217 AFC

Beka Valentine made two decisions: the first was that she was going to be a blonde. She was tired of the red hair.

The second was that she was going to take the job with Divrot.

The first decision was implemented with a simple shake of her head, activating the nanobots that her father had designed to make her hair whatever color or style she desired. She briefly contemplated making it curly as well, then decided to stick with straight for the time being.

The second had taken a couple of days, but could be implemented as soon as Vasily was done working on the *Maru*.

At their initial meeting, Beka had spent two hours talking to Goran about the nature of the job, ending with her finishing her second fruit punch (which Goran had paid for) and promising to talk it over with her crew and get back to him.

The crew's reactions all boiled down to, "We're with you whatever you decide," a predictable loyalty that reminded Beka why she had picked the crew she did. So she had another meeting with Goran, this time in his office at Divrot—a neat and tidy place decorated with soft-colored paintings, a plush carpet, comfortable chairs, and with no clutter to speak of—where she explained what she brought to the table, and they worked out a verbal agreement. Goran promised to have a written agreement sent to the *Maru* by the next day.

Now for the fun part, she thought as she headed back to Vasily's. He had done the preliminary work on the ship and had a bill for it, along with an estimate for the more detailed work that needed to be done—like the A/P valve.

Vasily's office was the diametric opposite of Goran's: a cramped room that was piled high and deep with machine parts. If there was a pattern to the piling, she couldn't see it. A hydrospanner from an ancient Castalian cargo ship sat next to an armrest from a Than royal yacht, both balanced on top of an ultramodern panel of Slip drive casing. The floor space—what there was of it—was taken up almost entirely by these random ship droppings. Beka had to step over one of the piles to get to the guest chair—only to find that it too had a pile.

"Just put stuff on floor," Vasily said from his chair on the other side of the desk—which, naturally, had its own collection of piles.

Vasily himself was fiddling with a piece of copper wire, which he then tossed onto a radiator grille from a landrover.

The mechanic himself was a short, squat human who gave the impression of being made up entirely of perfect spheres: head, torso, even his arms and legs were circular. Wispy white hair peeked out from a gray cap that was covered in stains of many colors. Similar stains mottled his face and his gray one-piece jumpsuit. He stared at Beka with eyes that had long since been replaced by bionic implants that gave him almost microscopic vision, and probably contributed to his general lack of personal hygiene, since those eyes allowed him to see the details of the bark and miss the forest altogether.

After unceremoniously dumping the guest chair's pile on top of a collection of a dozen different brands of fuel tubing, Beka sat down. "So what's the good word?"

Vasily shrugged as he liberated a list from the morass on the desk. "Is some good, is some bad. Like life, you know?"

"Tell me about it," Beka muttered.

"I've done most of simple fixes. Big fixes take longer."

"A/P valve?"

Vasily nodded, a gesture which on him encompassed his entire torso. "That and fuel tank. Have to wait for delivery."

Beka winced. Deliveries of this sort could take months. "How long a wait?"

Another shrug. "Just one or two days. I got old wreck for parts yesterday. Take boys a while to break down, but fuel tank just the thing for *Maru*."

Blowing a sigh of relief through her lips, Beka said, "Anything else?"

"Not beyond what young Seamus gave me. Only extra thing is, I fix squeak in pilot's chair. No charge for that."

Smiling, Beka said, "Thank you. That's been driving me batty."

"I only fix because it drive *me* batty when I test equipment." Vasily returned the smile, showing yellowed teeth. "He's a good boy, young Seamus. You should keep him."

"Only way I wouldn't is if you steal him away from me."

Putting a pudgy hand over his heart, Vasily said, "Would I do that to favorite customer?"

"I don't know, why don't you ask her?"

They both chuckled, then Vasily handed her the list.

At the sight of the bill amount, Beka paled. The number was considerably higher than she was expecting—right at the limit of credit she had available. Trying to keep her voice calm, she said, "That's a lot of money."

Another shrug. "You want cheap, go somewhere else. You want good, come to Vasily."

Now Beka was even more grateful that she'd taken the Divrot job. Then she noticed something that distressed her even further.

"This doesn't include the estimate for the A/P valve or the fuel tank." She had a harder time keeping her voice calm this time.

"No. That is bill for services rendered. Valve and fuel tank not rendered yet." Vasily gave another yellow-toothed smile.

Her lips widening in a gesture that was halfway between a smile a scream of panic, Beka asked, "I don't suppose you can put this on my tab?"

Vasily's smile vanished. "You mean Iggy's tab, yes?"

Slowly, Beka nodded.

Leaning forward, Vasily said, "Beka, you know I cannot do this thing. You're good girl and good customer, but Iggy—he not either one."

Beka refrained from pointing out that her father couldn't have been a good girl. "Vasily, I—I can't afford this."

The mechanic leaned back. "That is problem."

"At least not yet," she added quickly. Visions of the *Maru* being impounded danced in her head. It was one thing to steal the *Maru* back from a garbage heap like Takilov, but having to do so from Vasily's meant burning a bridge she knew she'd have to cross again some day. "I just took a job with Divrot, doing salvage on Tychen. I'm going to have a contract from them within the day. If you want, you can garnish the money from them directly, but I need you to extend the credit and fix the ship so I can *take* the job."

Vasily picked the copper wire back up and started fiddling with it.

"Talk to Goran at Divrot—he's the one who hired me."

That got Vasily's attention. "Goran? Umbrite, wears chains on pincers?"

Hoping this was a good sign, Beka said, "That's him."

"Okay. Talk to him, then talk to you. We work this out."

Relief washed over Beka. "Thank you, Vasily."

"This mean you don't pay more of Iggy's debt, yes?"

"I'm trying," Beka said. "I promise, this'll just slow it down a bit."

"Is okay," he said holding up a hand and smiling again. "You've done more to pay off Iggy's debt than Iggy. Like I said, you good girl."

Standing up—and almost knocking a circuit board off the desk—Beka said, "You're not so bad yourself."

"Ah, Beka?"

She frowned. "What?"

"Still need payment for that." He pointed to the bill she was holding.

Beka started to protest, then decided she'd better quit while she was behind. Reaching into her pocket, she handed over the credit chit with the usual sense of dread. *I didn't need to eat this month anyhow. . . .*

While he waited for the authorization of the transaction, Vasily said, "By the way, you good blonde. I say keep it."

Since the remaining repairs had to wait until the verification of Beka's contract with Divrot—and wouldn't happen for a day or two in any case—she retired to the *Maru*. As much as she liked drifts, the *Maru* was still home, where she was born and raised. She entered the airlock with the hopes of a long hot shower and an even longer nap.

It wasn't until she had removed her shirt and started to take off her pants that she remembered that the water system was probably offline. And even if it wasn't—or she could turn it back on— the water heating system was also offline, and was going to stay that way until the fuel tank was replaced.

"Dammit!" she said, and pounded the bulkhead of her cabin. Cold showers had their place in life—she remembered several dozen after she and Bobby broke up—but this wasn't one of them. *I guess I'll have to find a place on the drift . . .*

"Boss, you here?"

Beka closed her eyes. *Harper. Just what I needed.* "Be right out!" She grabbed what she thought was a fresh shirt, got a whiff of it, winced, put it back, grabbed another shirt, almost gagged, then just put the old shirt back on.

Looks like I'll need to use the drift's laundry too.

She walked out onto the flight deck to see Harper carrying a blue ball.

After a second, she realized that Harper was, in fact, standing next to a very short Perseid who was standing with his head lowered. With his arms in front of him, it looked like he was trying desperately to disappear down into the grillework of the deck.

Upon Beka's entrance, he looked up for a second before going back to studying the deck. He either had small features or pursed his lips and squinted so much that it just seemed that way, but he had everything you'd expect from a Perseid: blue skin, hairless, extended chin. The initial impression he created was that of painful shyness.

This, of course, was in direct contrast to Harper. "Heya Boss! Wantcha to meet a new buddy of mine who's got this *great* idea. And any buddy of mine is a buddy of yours, right?"

"Maybe." She put out a hand, deciding to at least give this guy the benefit of the doubt. "Captain Beka Valentine." Beka didn't often flaunt her captaincy, especially since it was more an indication of ownership than any kind of rank designation, but she wanted to emphasize who, precisely, was in charge, especially since Harper had been known to forget once or twice. "And you are—?"

The Perseid seemed surprised that someone was talking to him. He again looked up briefly, returned the handshake just long enough to make contact, then put his hands back down and again lowered his head. The deck was apparently *much* more interesting for him to look at. Beka tried not to take it personally. "Oh, I'm nobody that interesting. Uh, my name's Nabrot." Beka noted that his handshake was clammy.

"I met him at this great café on the south side called the Mainline," Harper continued. "Great booze, great entertainment, loud music—trust me, you'd hate it. Anyway, Nabrot and I started talking, sharing our mutual appreciation of the quality of the entertainment—"

Beka chuckled. "Blonde, brunette, or redhead?"

"Exactly. Anyhow, after we left the café—"

"Well, actually," Nabrot said in a small voice, "they threw us out."

"Hey, who's telling this story? Anyhow, we went to another place and started talking—it turns out that we have a few interests in common."

"Besides the type of entertainment that comes in cafés?" Beka asked.

"And Sparky Cola."

"Actually," Nabrot mumbled toward the deck, "I don't much like Sparky Cola."

"See, my pal Nabrot here," and here Harper put an arm around Nabrot's shoulder, a gesture that made the Perseid look even more uncomfortable, "also shares our love for flipping great wodges of cash and grand larceny."

Beka didn't like the way this was going. "Harper, I'd like to stay on the right side of the law as long as we're here, okay? After Takilov—"

"It won't be here, Boss, that's the beauty of it. It'll be on Beros Prime."

It took Beka a moment to place the planet. "That's the homeworld of the Ursa Pride. What could—" Then she realized what Harper had to be talking about. "Oh, no."

"Oh, yes. It can be *ours*, Beka. All ours. Think about it!"

"Forget it, Harper." She turned and headed back toward her cabin.

"C-captain?" Nabrot said. "It's true. We can do it. If you follow my plan, you can steal the Sword of Terpsichore."

Keep going, Beka told herself. *Just walk away*. But her feet stopped moving.

"I've spent three years coming up with it, and it's foolproof!" Nabrot now sounded almost animated. "The only thing I don't have are the resources to pull it off, but Seamus here says you've got everything I need!"

She turned around. "Forget it. The Sword of Terpsichore is the holiest of holy relics for the Ursa Pride. It's got more security than the mint on Tarn-Vedra—*after* the planet was cut off from Slipstream. We'd be better off trying to steal the Crab Nebula."

Harper held his hands up. "Look, Beka, I was skeptical too, but Nabrot showed me his plan. I think we can pull it off."

"What part of 'forget it' did you miss? Even if we could do it, the ship's being fixed, we're gonna need to work for Divrot for a month just to pay off the repairs. And it doesn't matter, because it can't be done. The Sword of Terpsichore is—"

"The most secure artifact in the Known Worlds, can't be stolen, never happen in a billion years, yadda yadda yadda—I know, Boss, I've heard the same stories you have."

Beka shook her head. "They're not *stories*, Harper, they're facts."

"Aw, c'mon, Beka, how many times've I told you, you're never gonna get anywhere in life if you keep clouding the issue with facts? Look, what's the big deal about just taking a gander at the plan? It's in the *Maru* computer."

Right next to the Divrot contract, probably, she thought, the irony of that possibility not lost on her. "Harper, I really don't think we should—"

"Why not just *look* at it? What's the worst thing that could happen?"

Regarding him with a you've-*got*-to-be-kidding-me look, Beka said, "You'll use this as a precedent for forcing me to listen to more of your cockamamy schemes?"

"And this is a bad thing, how?" Harper smiled. "C'mon, Boss, just *look* at it. I *guarantee* you won't regret it."

"Little late for that," she muttered. "Fine, I'll *look* at it, but no promises. And no matter what, we're not doing anything until I pay for these repairs. We can't afford to piss Vasily off."

"Yeah, we wouldn't want to do that. He might breathe on me."

"Harper . . ."

"Hey, c'mon, Beka, have you smelled his breath? You could wipe out an entire Nietzschean regiment just by having him exhale."

Beka rolled her eyes. "Glass houses, Harper."

Panic filled Harper's eyes. "What do you mean? Is something wrong with my breath?" He put an open palm in front of his mouth and exhaled. Then he turned to Nabrot. "Maybe *that's* why that girl wouldn't talk to me."

In a barely audible voice, Nabrot said, "I think she just wanted to be left alone."

Or maybe she just wanted to be bothered by someone else, Beka said, but didn't say aloud, though it was tempting right now to kick Harper while he was down.

"Whatever," Harper said, already over his anxiety on the subject. "C'mon, Nab, I'll show you the some of the hot spots."

"I thought that's what we were doing *last* night," Nabrot said, now with a somewhat whiny tenor.

Putting an arm around the Perseid's shoulder and leading him out of the *Maru*, Harper said, "Nah, these spots are even *hotter*. We're talkin' Supernova."

"I don't like supernovae."

"No, no; Superno-*vuh*, not no-*vay*. That's the name of the place, the Supernova. Trust me, you'll love it."

Beka shook her head. *Somehow, I find it hard to believe that that little nebbish has come up with a master plan to steal the Sword of Terpsichore.*

"Hey, Boss!"

Turning to look at Harper, who was gazing at her over his shoulder and smiling, she said, "Yeah?"

"I like the new 'do, You make a good blonde."

"She's right, actually, Captain," Nabrot said to the deck, "you're a very pretty blonde."

The compliments might have meant more to Beka if the two of them weren't trying so hard to get her to read that idiotic plan. Dredging up as much sincerity as she could, she said, "Thank you both."

She watched the pair depart, then she continued back to her cabin. *What a pair*, she thought. Somehow she didn't picture the little Perseid as a master thief. And even if he was, Terpsichore was one of the Holy Grails of valuable objects, and second on Beka's list only to the demi-mythical Engine of Creation (the existence of which, Beka freely admitted, was a pipe dream that she never fully expected to see realized). Ursa Pride was one of the quieter Nietzschean clans. They had mostly avoided the internecine conflicts that had ravaged the assorted Prides since the fall of the Commonwealth, choosing to maintain order over their small-but-stable demesne in the Andromeda galaxy.

The Sword itself was the one used by Ogun Bonaparte to slaughter his brother Olorun and lead the Ursa Pride to glory. Beka had no idea as to the truth of the story, but it didn't matter that much. The point was, *they* thought it was the most important relic of their history. They charged a bundle for visitors to view it at the museum that housed it, and its security had taken on mythic proportions in the thieves' community.

And even if by some miracle that little guy came up with a foolproof plan, then what? Its fame gave it even better security than the weight sensors, nanobots, laser sights, unbreakable glass, and who-knew-what-all-else that protected the sword. After all, even if one did steal it, then what? Who could you possibly sell it to? The instant it was stolen, everyone would *know* it was stolen. The Ursa muckity-mucks could hardly replace it with an exact duplicate—the cost to create such a thing was prohibitive to say the least, especially since it still has the dried blood of the late Olorun Bonaparte on it, splattered in a very complex and distinct pattern. Beka actually knew a forger who would love to take a stab—so to speak—at creating a fake, but, again, it would be so expensive as to render any monetary gain from the theft redundant. *If* you could find a buyer. Which Beka doubted could be found.

She entered her cabin and punched up recent downloads. The two on top of the list were from Harper and from Goran. *Good,* she thought, *the contract*. After that were bits of mail they had picked up at Takilov that she hadn't gotten around to looking at yet. She wasn't going to get around to it now, either. The most important thing at the moment was the Divrot contract.

Harper and his friend's silly fantasies could wait.

FIVE · HAUKON TAU DRIFT, 302 AFC

The problem with a work of true genius such as this is that the people who appreciate it most are the ones who already knew what the genius was trying to convey, and the people who most need to know what is being conveyed are the ones who don't appreciate it at all.

—HAMMOND MARKINSON, REVIEW OF
"THE COLLECTED SAYINGS OF DRAGO MUSEVENI"
IN *THE COMMONWEALTH LITERARY
SUPPLEMENT*, VOL. 782, #14, CY 9669

Tyr climbed.

"The support is rotting through—it'll collapse within the week, if not sooner."

He sat in the desert, the sun beating down severely, burning his sixteen-year-old body. Eventually, he knew, a sand rat would appear. If he caught one—no, when he caught one—that was another day's worth of food. Two days, if it was an adult rat and if he rationed it properly.

Tyr climbed.

"I said no lip, boy!"

*The blood tasted metallic in his mouth after the overseer hit him.
Oddly, he felt the impact of his arm with the floor more than the actual
blow to his jaw, even though the former did almost no damage, and the
latter resulted in a cut.*

Tyr climbed.

"Double his work shifts!"

*It had taken an hour just to shift the rock off his leg, which had some-
how managed not to break, after the tunnel collapsed. The pain was
sheer agony, slicing through his entire body like a knife, but he put it
aside. There was no light, no sound save for his own breathing and
heartbeat; the only taste was the salty tang of his own sweat and blood.
This time it didn't taste metallic, it tasted like fire. He used that fire
to stoke the flames of his own desire to survive—to escape—to exact
vengeance.*

Tyr climbed.

"Oh, and cut his rations in half."

*The sun blinded him when he first hit the surface after his two
hundred-meter journey through the collapsed mine. He didn't care—he
shouted his victory to the heavens until his throat went dry.*

Tyr climbed.

"What's happening? Why is the ground shaking?"

*The sand rat's blood felt more nourishing than the seep water, but he
knew that it would do much less to stave off dehydration.*

Tyr climbed.

"Why do you think, fool?"

*When he came to after the tunnel collapse, he was surrounded by
corpses: the other slaves, the guards. But he survived. Again. Just as he
had lived through the massacre of the Kodiak by the Drago-Kazov, now
he had lived through this.*

Tyr climbed.

"You're not working hard enough, Anasazi—pick it up, or I'll be using those things on your forearms to pick my teeth!"

He clawed his way through dirt and rocks and mud and filth and diamonds. Great wealth and insignificant lives had been lost, but he lived, and he would not succumb.

Tyr climbed.

"So who's this child, then?"

Often he wondered why they needed slaves. Automated mines were considerably more efficient. The only thing he could imagine was that it was cheaper to buy people than it was to buy and set up the equipment so far underground. That and a healthy dose of sadism, a desire to hold power over others. Of course, true power came from strength and guile, not through a business transaction, a lesson he hoped to some day teach the overseer. . . .

Tyr climbed.

"He's named Tyr Anasazi. Nietzschean we bought 'im from said he's the last survivor of one of their clans."

The seep water tasted like death. He had seen insects with more meat on their bones than what he picked off the largest sand rat he could find. Yet a sand rat was better than the taste of dirt and mud that accompanied him on his slow ascent from the collapsed mine. More importantly, eating them would keep him alive. That was all that mattered.

Tyr climbed.

"There's diamonds in those caves, boy, and I intend to make sure that you dig out every single one of them."

The most glorious sight he had ever seen was the shocked expression on the overseer's face as he choked the life out of him.

Tyr climbed.

For two hundred meters, he climbed.

Against all odds, the sixteen-year-old Tyr Anasazi, out of Victoria by Barbarossa, last of the Kodiak Pride, survived the collapse of the diamond mine, survived living in the desert on Zocatl for a season, and survived his journey to the new headquarters of the slavers so he could kill the overseer with his bare hands.

Tyr climbed.

Tyr awoke to the sound of beeping.

He was in the apartment he maintained on Haukon Tau Drift. Small, functional, barely furnished, it provided him with a place to sleep whenever he came here, which was fairly often, as it was his main point of contact for mercenary work.

The transition from sleeping and fitfully dreaming of his experiences as a slave to wide awake and fully alert was nearly instantaneous. Tyr did not bolt awake and scream after an unpleasant dream—he was made of sterner stuff. Indeed, if he was affected by once again dreaming of his nightmarish experiences on Zocatl as a teenager, he showed no sign of it.

Tyr sat up from his cot and did the same thing he did every time he awakened: visually and aurally checked every aspect of the one-room dwelling to make sure nothing threatened him.

The beeping was the apartment's computer. "What is it?" he asked once he was satisfied that the apartment was secure.

"Incoming message," the mechanical voice intoned.

"Play it."

"Tyr, it's me," said the distinctive voice of Ferahr al-Akbar. *"Two things—your clients're all on their way to Terra Verde. Don't worry, they can't be traced back to you or to me."*

Nodding, Tyr got up from the cot and went to the sink. Part of the deal with getting the royal pair and their tiresome entourage to safety was that Tyr and his people would not be able to say precisely how they got to Terra Verde. It was an added layer of security that General Orkani had suggested, and of which Tyr approved.

A pity such a sensible mind was no doubt sacrificed to get those two idiots to safety. Tyr supposed it was possible that the general survived the attack on the palace. Whether he did or not, Tyr had no sympathy for the king and queen in whose service the worthy Orkani had no doubt sacrificed himself. If Nwari and Hamsha were so incompetent as to be overthrown by rabble, they deserved their fates. Not that he had any confidence in the efficacy of the Liberators' long-term goals of a democratic government to replace the monarchy. Power was held by the strong. To simply grant it to a collection of idiots only served to weaken that power and therefore weaken the government. Tyr confidently predicted that the new government wouldn't last a year before it descended into anarchy. *If Orkani survived the coup, perhaps he would be able to seize control.* Military dictatorships could be well run in the hands of the right military.

Ferahr's recorded message continued. *"That Nietzschean ship you wanted to meet up with came outta Slip. Got a message from some field marshal named Alaric Augustus saying he'll get together with you at midday in my office."*

Again, Tyr nodded. This was good. With Element of Air's death, the fee for the Malani's Haven endeavor was higher than expected, split as it was six ways instead of seven—and as leader, Tyr's share was the largest. In the years since freeing himself from captivity on

Zocatl, he had been working toward a single goal. While Ursa Pride may not have been the most ideal of the Nietzschean clans for Tyr's purpose, they were certainly a worthwhile place to start.

Tyr spent the morning putting himself through a wide variety of workouts, all of Nietzschean design, combining the best elements of human and Than martial arts forms and Vedran meditation techniques. The exercises were many and varied, and accounted for different environments. If necessary, he could do the physical forms in an area no more than a meter squared. Sometimes he had the luxury of doing them in an open space with appropriate accoutrements—a staff, perhaps, or knives, depending on his mood. There was also a two-person form, but Tyr had not practiced it in some time. He had attempted it with each of his fellow mercenaries, but the only one who had shown any aptitude was Brexos, and he grew bored with it quickly. He occasionally sparred with Varastaya, but the cyborg had no technique, simply relying on brute strength and her enhanced agility. These abilities were sufficient to serve her in most situations, but Tyr's attempts to get her to improve them thus far had been met with disinterest.

The loss was hers. While Tyr trusted the work done by his parents to secure the best genes for their son, he had never made the mistake far too many of his fellow Nietzscheans did in thinking that he was perfect. To Tyr, the genetic engineering was the beginning, not the end, of the process. There was always room for improvement. Most of the Nietzscheans Tyr encountered had believed themselves to be the best possible specimen upon birth and saw no reason to go any further. Plato had once spoken of the ideal form, with the reality being but shadows made by firelight on a cavewall. Tyr knew that, while Nietzscheans were closer to that Platonic ideal than most, it was the height of stupidity to assume that they had achieved perfection.

So he pushed himself harder and harder, working to hone his mind, his body, his very self.

After three hours of physical workout, sweat glistening off his bare chest and down his forehead, Tyr then stripped, showered, instructed his nanobot shaver to trim his beard, and spent the remaining two hours before his meeting with Field Marshal Augustus reading a copy of *The Artha-Shastra* by Chandragupta Maurya—the ancient Indian emperor better known as Chanakya. This was a new edition that had been published in the original Sanskrit. Tyr had always preferred to read works—especially important ones like this—untranslated. Tyr was ever mindful of the Italian proverb: *traduttore, traditore*. "The translator is a traitor" was the appropriately imprecise translation. Nuances were lost when converting from one tongue to the other, which prompted another proverb: the devil is in the details.

Tyr of course did not believe in the devil, having assumed him to have died alongside God.

Idly, he wondered if the situation on Malani's Haven still would have deteriorated so disastrously if Nwari or Hamsha had been familiar with Chanakya's work. *Probably not*, he quickly concluded.

When midday arrived, he walked through the corridors of Haukon Tau, taking in every detail of his surroundings and ignoring them once they proved not to be a threat. He passed the usual collection of shops, eateries, temporary dwellings, meeting places, and other establishments that competed for both the attention of the people on and the limited space in the drift. Tyr gave them no thought beyond what they might do for him or to him—which, today at least, was nothing.

Ferahr maintained an office in a large windowless space at the center of the drift. The open area in the middle of the room was surrounded by shelves full of a variety of items—the type of items changed daily, depending on what bit of business Ferahr was conducting. Tyr neither knew nor cared about the nature of that business. All he knew was that Ferahr had proven himself reliable.

Tyr had never been foolish enough to assume that non-Nietzscheans were automatically useless any more than he assumed that all Nietzscheans were automatically superior. The universe never made things that easy. While he wouldn't go so far as to say he trusted Ferahr—Tyr trusted no one and nothing but Tyr—the fat human was probably the only person in the Known Worlds who Tyr might consider calling a friend.

Upon arrival at the office, Tyr found Ferahr sitting at his desk, eating a vile concoction that had been provided by one of the local food-poisoning establishments not-very-cleverly disguised as a restaurant. Of Field Marshal Augustus, there was no sign.

"It's midday. Where is he?"

Through a mouthful of soup, Ferahr said, "'Hello, Ferahr. How're you doing? Good to see you. Oh, and hey, thanks for helpin' me out with those folks you wanted to get to Terra Verde.'"

"You were paid, were you not?"

Ferahr finally swallowed the soup. "Yeah."

Tyr smiled. "Then what possible reason do I have to thank you?"

"Right, why start now?" Shaking his head, Ferahr put the soup aside. "Anyhow, that field marshal guy said he'd be here at midday. S'not my fault he's late. And hey, you think maybe you could reschedule?"

Raising his eyebrows, Tyr asked, "Why would I wish to do that?"

Ferahr squirmed in his chair, never a pretty sight. "Well, not so much reschedule as relocate. It just seems t'me that you could have your little confab somewhere, y'know—safer."

"Do you think I won't be safe here?"

"I meant safer for *me*." Ferahr scratched his stubbly chin. "Look, Tyr, I'm just a regular businessman—"

"There are many adjectives I would use to describe you, Ferahr. 'Regular' is not one of them." As Tyr spoke, he heard the sound of three sets of footsteps approaching the office from down the hall. *Ferahr's concerns are about to become moot.*

"Fine, whatever, but I really can't afford t'get in the middle'a whatever you got goin' with your Nietzschean pal."

"I would not characterize myself as a 'pal' in these circumstances," said a rich voice from the doorway as the footsteps arrived.

Tyr turned to see a Nietzschean shorter than Tyr, but with broad shoulders and a soldier's bearing. This, he assumed, was Field Marshal Alaric Augustus. He had large, almost perfectly round hazel eyes, and a softer face than Tyr would have expected from someone of Augustus's reputation. Nothing was soft about his clothing, though. The field marshal was covered neck to toe in armor, all white, and covered in a variety of insignia, one of which Tyr recognized as the crest of the Ursa Pride. It made him a perfect target, to Tyr's mind, though perhaps it was simply a dress armor that he wore to meetings. His jet-black hair was trimmed into a bowl cut, which, combined with the white ensemble, gave him an ancient Roman look—unsurprising, given his name, though his features were about as Roman as Tyr's.

Behind him were two soldiers, also Nietzschean, dressed in

similar armor, though theirs had no decoration save the Ursa Pride crest over the heart. The field marshal kept his weapon holstered, but these two had pistols out in a standby position.

"I have to admit," the field marshal continued, "that I was confused by the sender of the message. It was identified as 'Tyr Anasazi of the Kodiak Pride.' I was unaware of the existence of the Kodiak Pride."

Tyr wondered if he was being willfully obtuse, or if perhaps the field marshal's reputation was overrated. "Do you mock me, sir?"

Augustus gave a small smile. "Forgive me, I should have been more specific: I was unaware of the *present* existence of the Kodiak. I was under the impression that any discussion of that Pride would, of necessity, be in the past tense."

"The Kodiak Pride has not truly fallen until its last son lies dead. My own existence is testimony to the fact that that day has not yet come."

Augustus nodded. "So you survived the destruction of your Pride. That bespeaks either excellent survival skills, phenomenal luck, or treachery on your part."

Tyr leaned, arms folded, against the edge of Ferahr's desk. He did not want to sit in the guest chair, for that would put the still-standing Augustus on a physically higher plane than Tyr, but he wanted to show that he was relaxed in the field marshal's presence and not concerned—or, more accurately, not so concerned that he needed to be overt about it. Tyr noted that Ferahr was sweating even more profusely than usual and had shifted position so that Tyr was directly between him and Augustus. "I am not here to discuss the past, sir, but the future."

"Ah, but the past affects the future." Augustus walked over to one of the shelves and started inspecting one of the objects on it. "I am named for two figures from Roman history: Augustus, the first great emperor of Rome, and Alaric, the Goth general who sacked Rome. The play begins, the play ends, the play continues. I had thought the performance of the Kodiak Pride to be ended." He now looked at Tyr. "I take it you wish it to continue?"

Unfolding his arms, Tyr simply said, "Yes."

"And where does Ursa Pride fit into your story?"

"The Kodiak Pride fell when I was a boy. After my parents were killed, I was sold into slavery on Zocatl. I made my escape from a collapsed diamond mine and became free. I have spent the years since improving myself. I believe that I would make a good ally to your Pride and a good father to your children."

"After spending years as a mercenary?" Augustus spoke with a disdainful undertone.

"My record speaks for itself," Tyr said, trying to restrain his rising anger.

Augustus nodded. "Oh, it most certainly does, yes." He started to pace around the office.

Behind Tyr, Ferahr continued to shift the position of his chair, always endeavoring to keep Tyr in the line of any possible fire.

"I had heard stories about a very high-priced mercenary team led by a man named Tyr Anasazi. By the name, I took him to be a Nietzschean, and assumed him to be both a man without a Pride and a man without pride." Augustus had now worked his way around to the area next to Ferahr's desk, causing the desk's owner to practically cower.

Tyr did not move. "I am only the first of those, I assure you."

"Really? You take money from imbeciles and tramp about with

kludges. These are not the actions of someone I would want functioning in my jurisdiction, much less one I would want in my Pride. The Kodiak were genetic inferiors, who—"

Tyr stood upright and faced Augustus directly. "There is nothing 'inferior' about the Kodiak, Field Marshal. We were betrayed by the Drago-Kazov, and—"

"Is that supposed to mitigate your failure? If you were so incompetent as to allow yourselves to be betrayed so completely, you deserved your fate."

That brought Tyr up short.

"You are the last remnant of a failed Pride. If you truly wished to improve the bloodlines of the Nietzschean race, you would take that knife in your boot and plunge it into your own heart. I would shoot you myself, but I have no desire to waste ammunition on one such as you. The Kodiak's play *has* ended, Tyr Anasazi; you were simply never informed of its close. My recommendation would be for you to take your curtain call and remove yourself from the stage."

With that, Field Marshal Alaric Augustus turned his back on Tyr and moved toward the exit of Ferahr's office.

Ferahr swallowed audibly and said, "Well, that didn't go *too* badly. . . ."

SIX • THE *EUREKA MARU,* TYCHEN, 302 AFC

Restorians are people who fly around in ships in order to stop people from flying around in ships. Of course, by that logic, they should blow themselves up, which would certainly make the rest of us happy.

— KANT KORBLAN, STAND-UP ROUTINE, 300 AFC

Beka had avoided reading Nabrot's plan for the theft of the Sword of Terpsichore for a good three weeks.

First there was the matter of negotiating the contract with Divrot, which took her and Rev a full day. The two of them had gotten the contract terms from outright robbery to something closer to Beka and Goran's original oral agreement. She arranged for the payments to go directly to Vasily's until the remaining repair work was paid off. As an added bonus, Divrot agreed to pay for ten percent of Vasily's repairs, viewing it, according to Goran, as an investment.

Then Vasily had to install both the new fuel tank and the new A/P valve—the latter after crafting the part.

After all that was done, Rev and Beka spent a good two hours convincing one of the entertainers at the Supernova not to file harassment charges against Harper. Beka liked to think her own charm and talent made the difference, but she suspected that the girl was simply worried that Rev would eat her alive if she didn't drop the charges. Harper even paid her the amount that he might have been fined had he been found guilty—something he did only because Beka convinced him that *she* would eat him alive if he didn't.

Then, at last, they were able to start working salvage.

After two weeks, they had developed a routine.

Beka was soon reminded of why she hated routines. They were boring. They flew the *Maru* to Tychen, and found a spot no one had gotten to yet. They landed, put on their environmental suits, dug up stuff, put it in the cargo hold, and fended off anyone who tried to get in their way. The latter was the only part that was really interesting, but it only happened once. Tychen was still brand new, and full of unclaimed territory, so there was plenty of room for the scavengers to descend without getting in each others' way.

"What I don't get," Harper said at one point while they were flying back to Tychen, "is why we're wasting our time playing errand boys—and girls," he added with a look at Beka. "And Magogs," with a look at Rev. "And other," with a look at Vexpag, who spit a toothpick at him. "Why not just eliminate the middle Divrot and sell this crap ourselves?"

"Think of Divrot as our fence, Harper," Beka said from the pilot's seat. "They've already got clients lined up to buy this 'crap.'"

Rev added, "If we did decide to go into business for ourselves, we would waste valuable time seeking our own buyers and negotiating with them over price. That time is better spent finding more items to salvage."

"'Sides," Vexpag said, "our cut's better'n we'd get from any fence *I* ever dealt with."

"How much better?" Harper asked.

Beka smiled. "Twenty-five percent."

Harper's eyes widened to the size of two airlocks. "Exsqueeze me? They're giving us *that* much?"

"To be fair," Rev said, "the original contract called for fifteen percent, but Beka and I were able to talk them up via an incentive bonus."

"Whaddaya mean?"

"In these early days of salvage on Tychen, speed is of critical import. They knew the size of our cargo holds, so Beka and I convinced them that, if we provided a full hold's worth of material within one week, we would be entitled to a higher bonus."

Laughing, Harper slapped the Magog on the back. "Wayist to go, my buddy my pal. You know all those nasty things I said to you when we first met? I take most of them back."

Rev smiled. "That, of course, makes it all worthwhile."

Beka chuckled to herself. That was why she always made sure to talk out deals with Rev Bem present. Such discussions were much easier when you had someone on your side who either intimidated the opposing party or made them feel guilty about cheating you. In the Magog monk, Beka had both in one furry package, and she felt only a little guilty about using him that way.

Besides, Rev was also sharp, sensible, and canny, and an able negotiator. He often caught dodges, cheats, and loopholes that Beka missed.

An alarm beeped, but even before it did so, Beka realized that they were entering their final approach to Tychen. She only set the alarm as a backup in case she was in the bathroom or something when it happened. "We're approaching Tychen. Let's see if those fancy-shmancy sensor drones Divrot gave us are worth what they paid for them."

"Launching drones," Rev said.

As Beka eased the *Maru* into an orbit around Tychen that put them as far from any of the other half-a-dozen salvage ships in orbit as possible, Rev sent the drones that Divrot had provided. They would skim the surface, looking for a variety of energy signatures, mineral patterns, crust formations, or anything else that might prove to be indicative of something Divrot could sell for large sums of money—a quarter of which would go to the *Maru* crew.

Beka then moved to the standby position—and she had yet to grow tired of the lack of squeaking accompanying said maneuver; she once again gave thanks to Vasily's skills—and blew out a long breath. *Yet another salvage run.* This was the fourth run they'd made. The flat fee for this one would finally pay off Vasily's repair bill, which meant the bonus would go directly into their pockets, as would any subsequent income.

Sadly, it wasn't enough to get her excited about this latest run. Salvaging could be profitable, and it was certainly something they were good at, but it could also be tedious, frustrating, and bore no guarantee of profit. They were paid when they brought in a haul—if they brought in nothing, they got paid nothing, and their bonus was contingent on the quality of the merchandise.

And so, finally, while they awaited the information from the sensor drones, Beka gave in and decided to take a gander at Nabrot's plan to steal the Sword of Terpsichore. She downloaded it to a reader, sat down in her quarters with a bottle of water, and started perusing it.

Her first thought upon reading it through the first time was, *It's flawless. It'll work.*

Realizing that such a thought was patently absurd, that the little Perseid Harper had dragged onto the *Maru* couldn't possibly have come up with such a brilliant scheme, she read it again.

Her first thought upon reading it through the second time was, *It really is flawless. It really will work.*

Deciding this was the first sign of senility—or a true commentary on how boring salvage runs on Tychen were turning out to be—she read it one more time.

Her thoughts upon the third reading did not change significantly from the first two.

She consoled herself with the fact that the brilliance of the plan did nothing to alleviate her biggest concern about the plan for attempting to steal the sword: a buyer. Somehow, she doubted that Divrot would be able to toss it in with one of the lots from Tychen. . . .

Rev's voice interrupted her fourth reading of the plan. *"Beka, you should come up front right away."*

"The drones are back?"

"Yes. And they tell quite the story."

"I like a good story," she said, gulping down the rest of her water and putting the reader aside. *No sense in getting worked up over something that's impossible in any case.*

She reentered the flight deck. "So tell me the story, Rev."

"The drones have flagged two particular locations as potential salvage spots." He bared his teeth. "A story with a happy ending."

"Let's hope so. What've we got?" Beka asked as she walked over to the console on the wall.

Rev punched up a sensor display. It showed an area that looked to Beka like a cityscape. "Oh yipee, another lost city."

"More of a village than a city," Rev said. "It has a plethora of archaeological curiosities for which Divrot's university clients on Ugroth will no doubt pay handsomely."

"I dunno, Rev," Vexpag said. "Even them Perseids are gonna get mighty tired'a pottery shards after a while. This is the sorta thing that gets old real fast. And old is cheap in this business."

Beka peered at the display. "Yeah, but I think we'll make up for it in volume."

"In addition," Rev said, "most of the salvagers have been ignoring places such as this for more lucrative fare, so we probably won't be overburdened with competition."

"I assume the drones were programmed to ignore anything that had a claim on it?" Beka asked.

"Of course."

"Well, it's safe, that's for sure," Vexpag said. "But the one I wanna take dancin' is the other one."

"That entails a certain amount of risk," Rev said.

Vexpag grinned, his omnipresent toothpick flicking upward. "The good stuff always is risky, Rev, you oughtta know that."

"Want to fill me in?" Beka asked.

With obvious reluctance, Rev punched up another display. This showed a pyramid-like structure that Beka recognized from other locations on Tychen as a burial ground.

"Oh yipee, another empty tomb." Then she noticed something

on the display. "Waitasec, it's not empty. Why isn't it empty?" The tombs were the first places raided when the radiation levels died down. *Hell*, she thought, *half of them were raided before the rad levels were safe.*

She was able to answer her own question when she noticed one of the readings the sensor drone gave. For some reason, the radiation was still at lethal levels.

"This isn't an option. The drones should've just gone over it."

Rev said, "They were not programmed to ignore radiation—no doubt expecting that such things would no longer be a factor."

"Okay, fine, we head for the—"

"Now hang on a sec," Vexpag said, tossing his toothpick to the deck and walking over to the console. "Let's not dump this one too fast. Look here." He pointed to one reading. "See that geo reading from *under* the tomb?"

"Yeah," Beka said. "It's green—that means it's undefined."

"I *know* that," Vexpag said irritably, "so I ran it through the *Maru* and this is what I got." He punched up another display, which used the older graphics interface of the cargo ship, and didn't color-coordinate the readings, instead providing text accompaniment. Next to the reading in question it said DIAMOND 72% MATCH.

Beka shot Vexpag a look. "Diamonds?"

"Yup. And they're in a chamber that's completely uncontaminated."

"How'd the drones miss that?" Beka asked Rev.

"As far as anyone has been able to determine, there are no diamonds on Tychen," the monk said, "and none of the salvagers to date have found any, so the drones were not programmed with a means of recognizing them."

"Can't find what you can't find," Vexpag said. "Tychen was

space-farin' 'fore they bombed themselves all to hell. My guess is somebody found some diamonds somewhere, took 'em home, and was buried with 'em."

More and more Beka was liking the sound of this. Then she saw the look on Rev's face. "What is it, Rev?"

"The radiation. For whatever reason, the levels within that tomb have not fallen to tolerable levels. Even I would not survive for more than an hour. And the structure is built on unstable ground. There are tunnels below the surface that lead to where the readings are, but surface access to them is impossible. Based on the geological readings the drones took, there were quakes there within the last century that cut off any passageway down to the tunnels. The only way to them is through the tomb—which, obviously, is impractical."

A voice came from the aft corridor that led to the flight deck. "It's only impractical if you're not blessed with the greatest mechanical genius who ever accessed a dataport."

Upon Harper's arrival on deck, Vexpag actually smiled. "It worked?"

Handing Vexpag a reader, Harper grinned. "Like there was ever any doubt."

"What worked?" Beka asked. The prospect of salvaging diamonds was one that appealed greatly, but any time these two actually got enthused about something, Beka worried just on general principles.

"Fred here thought that we might be able to blow our way through the tunnels."

"Naturally," Rev said.

"Y'know," Vexpag said, placing another toothpick in his

mouth, "you folks really don't properly appreciate the value of a good explosion."

"Good explosions are fine. It's the bad ones that I worry about," Beka said. "Go on, Harper."

"Problem is that any big booms will just result in another quake, probably destroying the tunnels, possibly destroying the tomb, which would let all that radiation leak out, and we'd be looking at another ten-thousand-year sunburn for half the continent, which is not the sort of thing that keeps our contractors happy."

Beka snorted. "Not to mention our fellow salvagers. Contaminating the competition is bad for business."

"Bingo. So, looking for a more subtle solution, our intrepid demolition expert turned to *moi*."

Fixing Vexpag with a stare, Beka said, "You went to Harper for subtle?"

Rev smiled. "He said *more* subtle—it's all a question of degree."

Harper continued. "What I figured is that, instead of one big boom, hit it with a couple of little booms that would destabilize the ground enough to collapse a small part of the surrounding rock, giving us a nice little tunnel *under* all the big bad radiation and right to the diamonds."

While Harper had been talking, Vexpag had looked over the information on Harper's reader, then hooked it into the main display on the console next to Rev. "Nice one, twerp. Take a look, boys'n'girls."

The screen showed a computer generated aerial image of the pyramid, as well as the ground around it, which showed to the naked eye as totally barren, no doubt the aftereffects of those quakes Rev mentioned. Silently, Beka marveled at whoever constructed the tombs—they were obviously built to last.

A dozen purple dots showed up, spaced at uneven points around the pyramid—most were on the north side, but a few were on the south side, with three each east and west. They exploded in a particular sequence—Beka noted that the explosions themselves were small ones, the yield listed on the display very low by the standards of what she had come to expect from Fred Vexpag.

The display showed a minor quake, and what looked like a sinkhole opening in the ground. It rotated to show a side view, both above- and below-ground. The sinkhole extended downward to a lengthy passage that intersected with another passage that led to where the diamond reading was.

"Those new LT4s that Makdav put out last year oughtta do the trick," Vexpag said. "They been usin' 'em for asteroid mining. Great for precision bombing."

Beka inhaled through her nose and blew the breath out her mouth. "So let me see if I've got this straight. If we blow twelve of these LT4s around that pyramid, it *should* drop a sinkhole down to the passageways, which *should* lead to what we *think* are diamonds."

Vexpag fixed the captain with as penetrating a look as he could with his eyes half-hidden behind his brown bangs. "Bek, those *are* diamonds down there. I'm sure of it."

"As I recall, you were sure that that ship we were digging out of that asteroid near Mitalbo was a High Guard Slip fighter. *You* remember, the one that was—"

"Yeah yeah, a Nightsider moon shuttle, fine, so I ain't always right. But I'm right about this."

Beka stared at the display again, then punched up the geo readings the *Maru* had taken from the drones' information.

DIAMOND 72% MATCH.

She'd taken bigger chances on readings that were much less sure things—like that river that registered a fifty-two percent chance of having gold. And a twenty-five percent commission on what were probably refined diamonds that had been sitting out of circulation for several millennia. . . .

As always when her greed got hold of her common sense, she turned to Rev. "What do you think?"

The Magog paused before speaking in a grave tone. "I think the risks are great. If Harper's calculations are off, we risk contaminating the planet anew." Before Harper could comment on that, Rev smiled. "However, I have rarely known Harper's calculations to be off. And the rewards if we succeed are great as well."

That clinched it. Beka didn't trust Harper or Vexpag as far as she could throw the *Maru*, and she trusted herself even less. But it was a rare thing to have them working together on something, and Rev was never one to shy away from a dissenting opinion.

"All right, we'll do it."

Harper pumped his fist. "Yes."

"Let's get to it, then," Vexpag said.

"No, not yet." Beka called up the original display of the lost city. "We're gonna raid this little metropolis first."

"Why bother?" Harper asked. "We've got steak here, why settle for oatmeal?"

"Two reasons." Beka held up one finger. "One, we have to go back to Olivares to get your little bombs, and I really don't like the idea of going back there empty-handed. It's not a lot, but what's down there is basically free money, and we can't afford to pass it up—especially if what the drones picked up falls into the wrong twenty-eight percent and we create a sinkhole that nets us some zinc ore or something." A second finger went up. "Two, the orbital track has eyes and ears. If one of our friendly competitors notices that we came, we launched sensor drones, and we turned around and left without picking anything up, one of our distinguished competition might find that suspicious and investigate, and find our maybe-diamonds."

Vexpag nodded. "Good point, well made."

Smiling sweetly, Beka said, "I'm glad you approve." She moved down to the pilot's chair. "Prepare for atmospheric entry. We're gonna get us some pottery shards."

It took two days to gather up the assorted items lying about the "lost city of Dullsville," as Harper called it. Afterward, they headed back to Olivares Trust with a full cargo hold.

On the way back, Beka looked over the Terpsichore plan again.

No, she thought, *it's pointless. We'll get those diamonds and we'll have a ton of money and we won't need to do something as crazy as this.*

It was perfect for them, though. The plan required a brilliant pilot, a crack shot, and a computer expert—they had one of each in Beka, Vexpag, and Harper. She started imagining the prep work they'd need to do in advance, the equipment they'd need to secure, getting visas to visit Beros Prime. . . .

No, stop it, she admonished herself. *As great a heist as this would be, all it'll do is get us wanted the minute we try to sell it. And if we don't try to sell it, what's the point?* Beka considered herself a good thief, but only as a means to an end: money. She wasn't one of those tiresomely romantic rogues—usually only found in fiction, though she'd met one or two in real life in her time—who only stole for the challenge of pulling off a difficult robbery. That was a luxury that most actual thieves couldn't afford—literally. One stole because, at the end, one ended up with more money than one had if one didn't steal.

So no buyer, no heist, period, end of sentence.

Yet she found herself reading over the plan several more times on the way back to Olivares.

They arrived, and pulled into their spot in Divrot's docking bay. Once the *Maru* settled into that spot, the ceiling lowered to the top of the cargo hold. That ceiling was also the floor of a loading bay, complete with several access hatches. Divrot's staff would unload the *Maru*'s cargo through those hatches and bring them to the Sorting Center, where the objects were appraised and catalogued.

Shoving her chair back into standby, she turned to the crew. "Rev, get topside and keep an eye on the unloading." Beka had found that Rev was as good for watching over sticky-fingered loading-bay staff as he was for helping with contract negotiations, for much the same reasons. "Fred, talk to Goran at Divrot about getting those LT4s."

"I got my own sources, Bek, I don't need to—"

"It's not a question of need, it's a question of payment. If we're gonna use these explosives for Divrot business while under contract to Divrot, I want Divrot to shell out for them."

Vexpag nodded. "Fair 'nough." He and Rev both departed through the airlock.

"Harper, I want to have a chat with your Perseid friend."

Eyes widening, Harper said, "You read the plan?"

"I read it, and I think it makes a dandy exercise, but it's lacking in certain—practical aspects."

The engineer frowned. "Like what?"

"Like, oh, say, a buyer?"

"He's got one."

Beka started to say something, then stopped. "What?"

"He's got one," Harper repeated. "Cah-*mon*, Boss, you really think I'd try to sell you on a heist this big if there wasn't a buyer lined up? What do you take me for? Don't answer that," he added quickly.

"Do you know who this buyer is?"

"Who else? Another Nietzschean from some other Pride."

Shaking her head, Beka thought, *Now it all makes sense.* If anyone would want to get their hands on the holy relic of a Nietzschean Pride it was someone from a rival clan. *Fits in with the overall Nietzschean tendency to play mine's-bigger-than-yours.*

"Did he say which Nietzschean?"

"Oh yeah—I made sure to ask, in case it was the Drago-Jerkoffs."

Beka nodded. The Drago-Kazov Pride currently ruled Harper's home planet of Earth. Beka had, in fact, liberated Harper from living under their regime. Had it been one of them, Harper would have sent Nabrot packing to find some other thief. "So who is it?"

"One of the big dogs of the Jaguar Pride—guy named Charlemagne Bolivar."

That almost caused Beka to lose her footing. "Archduke Bolivar?"

"You know him?"

"No, but I've heard of him." Bolivar was a charismatic figure, a prominent leader among the Jaguar. Suddenly, this plan was looking better and better. The greatest heist ever *and* doing a favor for the Jaguar Pride. Unlike Ursa, Jaguar hardly kept to themselves—

they were in a near-constant state of conflict with both the Sabra and Drago-Kazov Prides.

Good people to have owe you a favor . . .

Then she remembered a display that said there was a seventy-two percent chance of there being diamonds on Tychen, and she banished thoughts of stealing the Sword of Terpsichore. *Let's go for the easy score, Valentine,* she admonished herself. *Those are safer. And less likely to blow up in your face.*

Four days later, everything was blowing up in Beka's face. *So much for the easy score,* she thought as she deftly maneuvered the *Maru* away from the kinetic missiles the Rester ship had fired on them.

Up until then, everything had been going smoothly. Divrot hadn't been willing to pay for the LT4s, but they were willing to reimburse Beka for them, should they result in the successful retrieval of a cache of diamonds. They were able to use the bonus from the "Dullsville" haul to pay for the explosives, obtained from a source of Vexpag's.

Soon enough they were back at Tychen, setting the charges, which performed exactly as Harper predicted. ("Like there was ever a shadow of a doubt.") Rev and Harper had then crawled into the sinkhole and through the tunnels and brought back what Beka estimated to be about eight million thrones' worth of diamonds, as well as a bunch of other, lesser jewels. It had taken a few trips to get it all out through the sinkhole, but to Beka's mind it had been worth it.

Then a giant ship claiming to belong to the Restorians showed up and started firing at every ship in orbit around Tychen.

One had decided to use the *Eureka Maru* for target practice, and that sent Beka running. Beka had no idea if these were legitimate Resters or just loonies who used the Rester cause as an excuse to fire on a bunch of salvage ships. One was as likely as the other. Certainly, it was in character for the Resters—environmental extremists who felt that space travel was an abomination and that people should remain planet-bound—to take on a group of ship-based folks whom they would view as grave robbers. *But did they have to hit us right when we got our big haul?*

The Resters had been hiding on the far side of one of Tychen's moons, and they caught the *Maru* completely off guard. They had fired a salvo of missiles before Beka could even get into the pilot's chair, and she had barely been able to break orbit and dodge the missiles, which dutifully followed their programming and reacquired their target: the *Maru*.

Only after the missiles had either been taken care of by Vexpag's countermeasures or dodged by Beka's piloting skills did she realize that the Rester ship was following them.

"Fred, get these bastards off my tail."

"Don't wanna blow my wad in one shot," Vexpag said. "Can you get me closer?"

"Uh," Harper said, "closer? Can I put in my vote for farther away? Like, say, back at Olivares?"

"We are still thirty light-seconds from the nearest Slip point," Rev said with refreshing calm. "And the Restorians are firing another round."

"From this distance?" Vexpag asked. "What the hell for? They ain't gonna come anywhere near us—we got tons'a time to get outta the way."

"They're herding us," Beka said, disappointed in the obvious tactic. The Resters were using textbook strategy, forgetting that most textbooks disappeared with the Vedrans centuries ago. "Changing course toward the missiles."

"Countermeasures ready," Vexpag said.

Rev said, "There is another ship bearing on our former position—now changing course. Three light-seconds and closing."

Beka nodded. That's what that missile fire was herding them toward. *Sorry, kids, you're gonna have to do better than that.* "Fred?"

"Countermeasures away. If they get too close, I'll toss everything we got at 'em, but—" Vexpag was interrupted by several alarms going off.

Harper ran over to the console next to Rev's. "Aw, crap and a half. One of the missiles got through—nailed us right in the cargo hold. We've got a hole wider'n the one in Vexpag's head."

"Seal it!" Beka cried.

Harper shook his head. "It's too late, Boss. Cargo's lost."

"We can retrieve it, we—"

"Resters at one light-second," Rev said by way of pointing out that they couldn't retrieve anything right now. "Slip point in ten seconds."

Slamming a hand on his console, Vexpag said, "Bek, we can't just leave the diamonds!"

Beka spared Vexpag a glance as she flew the *Maru* as fast as it would go toward the Slip point, compensating for the sudden change in pressure, mass, and hull configuration brought on by the Rester missile. "Can you take out both those ships with what we've got in the weapons bay?"

From the hesitation in Vexpag's face, Beka knew the answer before he said it. "No. One, maybe—or if we still had the LT4s, but—" Again he slammed his hand. "Dammit!"

Rev reported, "We've reached the Slip point."

Without another word, Beka engaged the Slipstream drive.

When they transited back to normal space near Olivares Trust, Harper was flailing his arms around. "I can't freakin' believe it. All that work crawlin' around Tychen, risking life and limb, just to have it taken away by the stupid Resters." He shook his head. "We shoulda taken a shot at getting the diamonds back."

"In all likelihood," Rev said, "we would have died in the attempt. What is more important, Harper, your money or your life?"

No answer was immediately forthcoming, prompting Rev to prompt, "Well?"

"I'm thinkin' it over!"

"The Divine gave life to all things, and made them each unique," Rev said. "Money, however, is interchangeable and easy to come by, under the right circumstances. Other opportunities will present themselves—but only if you are alive to take them."

"If that's supposed to make me feel better, Rev, it failed kinda dismally."

Beka ignored the babbling of her crew as she set the *Maru* on course for Divrot's bay on the drift. Right now, she was pissed. It never failed—every single time she was on the verge of the big score, something came along and took it away from her. *Typical Valentine—if we didn't have bad luck, we'd have no luck at all.*

She immediately started rehearsing what she was going to say to Goran. Luckily, they were not the only ship attacked. This drift—hell, every drift from here to San-Ska-Re—was going to be full of news about the Resters' attack on Tychen, so it's not like they were going to be accused of trying to pull a fast one. *Besides,* she thought, *I'm hardly likely to blow a hole in my own ship. Which reminds me . . .*

"Harper, Fred, the minute we're docked, I want a full report on how bad the damage is to the hold and how much it'll cost to fix it."

"Right, Boss," Harper said, still sounding distressed.

Not that Beka blamed him. *At least we paid off Vasily. Now I'm back to the same old debts. . . .*

"We're receiving an urgent transmission from the drift's traffic control."

Rev's report surprised Beka. "Put it through."

"Beka," Manteen's voice said, *"I hate to break this to you, but you're gonna need to find another place to dock."*

"Uh, why?"

"Divrot's port's closed, on account of Divrot being closed. Permanently."

Harper muttered, "And the hits just keep on comin'."

"What do you mean 'closed,' Manteen?"

"Well, the official story is that they were discontinuing operations due to cash-flow difficulties."

Vexpag made a noise somewhere between a snort and a laugh. "Cash-flow difficulties. Right."

Manteen wouldn't have used the adjective "official" if he didn't have gossip on the subject, and Beka knew he couldn't resist sharing it, especially with her. "And the unofficial story?" she asked sweetly.

"Their main investor pulled out—of the company and of the drift. He took back his investment and left Olivares this morning. The ship he was on was headed to Halcyon. So any cargo you brought back from Tychen? You're gonna have to find someone else to deal with it."

"Oh, if only it were that simple." Briefly, she filled Manteen in on what happened at Tychen.

"Resters, huh? Damn. That's gonna ruin a lot of people's days."

"Oh, it already has, believe me," Beka said. "So where *can* we park?"

"Right now, nowhere. All the ports are full. But if you hang tight for another seven hours, I can clear a space for you."

"Seven *hours*?" Harper whined, but Beka overlaid him quickly, knowing that the number was only that small because Manteen was doing her a favor.

"Thanks, Manteen." She took a breath. "And maybe afterward, we can have that drink at Girzin's?"

"I won't be off-shift for another hour after that—I just came on—but I'd like that. But you're buying."

Despite the situation, Beka laughed. "Fine. See you then. *Maru* out."

"So we're stuck here for seven hours?" Harper asked.

Bringing the *Maru* to a relative stop alongside the drift, Beka put the chair in standby mode. "Stuck, but not idle. We need to do a full damage-control assessment. Rev, you and Fred get to go to the great outdoors, see how bad off the cargo hold is."

"Of course."

"Check."

"And Fred? *Check* your EVA suit's seals this time? Last time we almost lost you."

Tossing a toothpick to the deck, Vexpag muttered, "Yeah yeah," in a tone that, Beka knew, indicated that he wouldn't check his suit properly.

"Harper, you and I will do internal damage," she said as the other two went to the airlock to prep for going out onto the hull.

"But first, I want you to get in touch with your little Perseid friend."

That got Harper's attention. He'd been sulking since the Resters first showed up, but now he was at last showing signs of life. The light came back into his eyes, the spring to his step, and the nasal whine to his voice that indicated he was happy. "Oh yeah?"

"*Don't* get your hopes up," she said, holding up a hand. "For now, my main concern is fixing the *Maru*. But I think it's safe to say our contract for Tychen is over—even if Divrot was still in business, I'm in no mood to tackle Resters. So I want other options."

"Boss, I'm telling you, this is the chance of a lifetime. All we gotta do—"

"All *you* have to do is find Nabrot and tell him that before I even think about this, I want iron-clad proof that Bolivar will buy this thing if it's lifted."

Despite Beka's attempts to rein him in, Harper was in full happy mode. "You'll have it. Trust me, Boss, you *won't* be sorry." He went aft, humming a happy tune.

"Too late," she muttered, "I think I'm sorry already."

SEVEN • HAUKON TAU DRIFT, 302 AFC

> The best things in life cost money. The worst things
> in life cost more money.
>
> — ARIDAR LOTHMANHIR, CY 8822

After finishing the message to Terra Verde he was sending on
Tyr's behalf, Ferahr al-Akbar took an antacid. *Working with Tyr
didn't* used *to give me stomach pains*, he thought sourly.

Ferahr remembered a time when dealing with Tyr was easier. It
was when he first walked into Ferahr's office, almost ten years ago.

No, not "walked." Tyr doesn't "walk" anywhere. He strides.

Tyr strode in, all those years ago, and said, "You have a ship for
sale. I will purchase it."

That was it. No "Hello," no "You must be Ferahr," no "Greetings, I am Tyr Anasazi out of my mother by my father from some Pride or other, how do you do?" Just "I will purchase it."

Which, of course, Tyr did. When a Nietzschean the size of a moon strides into your office saying he'll purchase the ship you just got your hands on, you sell it to him.

Ferahr had fully expected never to see Tyr or the ship again, but then two months later he returned, explaining in similarly terse terms that he had no more use for the ship, and would Ferahr like to buy it back? Expecting it to be some kind of Nietzschean con, Ferahr said he'd think about it after inspecting the ship—only to find that the wear-and-tear on it was no more than you'd expect after two months, and the price Tyr was asking was reasonable.

Never having met a Nietzschean who was willing to be reasonable in a business transaction with a "kludge," Ferahr was impressed, and decided he'd be willing to do other deals with Tyr. He even told him as much.

Tyr smiled and said, "We'll see."

Over time, Tyr and Ferahr came to see how useful they could each be to each other. Tyr found Ferahr to be a reliable source of a variety of services, from weapons to ships to equipment to personnel. Ferahr found Tyr to be a perfectionist, so he always wanted the best—which usually translated to the most expensive, which in turn meant more money for Ferahr, who worked on a percentage. For example, Ferahr had been finding a progression of bigger and bigger hand-weapons for Tyr to carry. Of course, no matter how big the gun was, Tyr wanted one bigger. . . .

Ferahr was starting to worry, though. Tyr had gone from being a solo merc to a leader of a group—in fact, Ferahr had recruited two of Tyr's team, Glasten and Brexos, two human bruisers who had worn out their welcome on Enkindu. The jobs Tyr took on were higher and higher profile—and also higher and higher profit. Ferahr had the feeling that Tyr was building to something, a feeling confirmed by the meeting with that crazy Nietzschean field marshal.

Obviously, Tyr wanted to restore his family pride or family name or genetic purity or some other crazy Nietzschean thing. All this served to do was worry Ferahr. Akbar al-Haroun had said many things to his son Ferahr when he was a boy. Most of them involved requests for more alcohol, but every once in a while wise words escaped his whiskey-soaked mouth. One was: "Never do a deal with someone who thinks of you as a lower life form." Aside from Tyr, the übers were bad for business—they had absolutely no concept of compromise. As far as Ferahr was concerned, they could happily wipe each other out and leave the Known Worlds for sensible folk.

So why is Tyr getting involved with them?

As he gulped the antacid down with a glass of beer, his computer beeped. *"New message has arrived via courier from Malani's Haven."*

Ferahr punched up the full manifest of the message. It was coming from Minister Saamm, who claimed to be the leader of Malani's Haven. *Funny, I thought the leader was on Terra Verde. . . .*

Knowing that he'd regret it, Ferahr said, "Play it."

"This is Minister Saamm, leader of the free peoples of Malani's Haven with a message for Ferahr al-Akbar. I seek out Tyr Anasazi. I am told that you know how to reach him. I will be arriving at Haukon Tau tomorrow. I hope you can arrange a meeting."

The recording ended. Ferahr debated whether or not he should tell Tyr about it.

Yeah, right, he thought after half a second. *As soon as that minister guy shows up, Tyr'll find out that I held out on him and then you can count the minutes of the rest of my life on one hand.*

"Send a message to Tyr Anasazi," he instructed the computer, "that I need to talk to him."

Surprisingly, Tyr responded right away. His face appeared on the small screen on Ferahr's desk. *"What is it?"*

He passed on the message from Saamm, finishing with: "Said he'll be here tomorrow."

"Good. Set up a meeting in your office."

Ferahr rolled his eyes. "Aw, c'mon Tyr, since when am I your personal secretary?"

Tyr raised an eyebrow. *"Since when aren't you?"*

"Very funny. Look, I got things to do. I got a whole shipment of, uh—" He thought fast. "Framberry ale comin' in for that, uh, Nightsider." It wasn't even a lie—of course, the shipment was just being dropped off, and the Nightsider wasn't picking it up for another week, but Tyr didn't need to know that.

"We'll try not to disturb your delivery people. Set the meeting for midday."

Before Ferahr could say anything in response, Tyr cut off the communication.

Great, he thought with annoyance, *just great*.

"There has been rioting in the streets, a rampant rise in crime—half the factions in the aristocracy that supported us are now trying to undermine us. We're barely able to maintain order. We want to bring about reform, but we can't do that if the people are agitating for additional food, for services, for—well, everything. We've tried telling them to be patient, that everything will improve in time, but they're not listening."

The minister had been pacing back and forth along the same path that Alaric Augustus had trod weeks earlier as he spoke. But,

Ferahr noted, where the Nietzschean field marshal had the same stride that Tyr utilized, Saamm was just walking. Worse, he was fidgeting. The leader of Malani's Haven was a short man, with lighter skin than most of that world's inhabitants—but slightly darker than Tyr's—and he didn't seem to know what to do with his hands. He also kept looking at the walls and the floor, rarely making eye contact with Tyr, and never for very long. Ferahr pegged him as an easy mark the minute he walked into the office, accompanied by a pair of very unsoldierlike bodyguards bearing weapons that they didn't look comfortable holding.

"And what does any of this have to do with me?" Tyr asked the question from the exact same relaxed position he maintained for the meeting with Augustus: leaning against the desk, arms folded. This time, though, Ferahr didn't fear for his life and so didn't make an effort to hide behind the Nietzschean.

"I have come here to request your aid," Saamm said.

Tyr actually laughed at that. "Really?"

"We need someone to organize our armed forces to deal with the unrest. To pacify the people until we can implement our reforms. You successfully evacuated the king and queen from under our noses, and you come highly recommended from many sources. The Malani Free Army needs guidance. We believe you can provide that."

"Let me guess," Tyr said. "General Orkani and his people are all either dead or unwilling to aid you, leaving you with an army full of low-ranking soldiers, none of whom has the first clue how to lead."

Saamm sighed and stared at the wall. "Something like that. General Orkani is dead, yes, as are most of his aides. We actually captured Orkani alive, but he killed himself rather than face a trial."

That's nuts, Ferahr thought, and Tyr said, "Really?"

"Yes," Saamm said, turning his gaze back down to the floor. "Unfortunate. Without him or Nwari or Hamsha we didn't have anyone to put on trial."

"So what?" Ferahr asked. "You already took over the government. What more d'you want?"

"A performance," Tyr said. "A visual aid to provide for the public so they can see that the old regime is gone. With Nwari and Hamsha safely in exile and with Orkani dead in his cell by his own hand, you don't have that symbol."

Nodding, Saamm said, "Exactly." He looked at Tyr. "Will you help us?"

"My fee is one million thrones for one month's work. After that—we can negotiate."

"That's fine," Saamm said without even a moment's hesitation.

Ferahr tried not to laugh out loud.

Tyr blinked. "When the money has arrived in my account, I will commission a ship to take me and my team to Malani's Haven. Once there, we will take stock of the situation and take command of your 'free army.'"

"Excellent." Saamm let out a breath, visibly showing his relief. "We look forward to your arrival." He handed Tyr a flexi. "This has all the information you will need—accounts of the riots, reports from my deputies, and economic forecasts. Plus other things—I wasn't sure what you might need, so I gathered as much as possible." After Tyr took the flexi and put it aside unread, Saamm offered a hand. "Thank you. The people of Malani's Haven owe you—"

"One million thrones for the first month." Tyr did not accept the handshake.

"Yes. Yes, of course." Saamm lowered the hand. "I look forward to seeing you on Malani's Haven within the week."

"That depends entirely upon how fast you can transfer funds."

"Right." The minister put his hands behind his back, which was the first sensible thing he'd done with his hands the entire time he'd been in Ferahr's office. "Good-bye."

Without even looking at Ferahr—indeed, Saamm hadn't even acknowledged Ferahr's presence the entire time, looking only at Tyr or the floor or the walls—the minister turned on his heel and left, his bodyguards walking quickly behind him. All three looked relieved to be leaving.

As soon as the door closed behind them, Ferahr burst out with the laugh he'd been holding in for the last half an hour.

"Something amuses you?" Tyr asked.

"Him," Ferahr said, pointing at the door. "Love to sit down across from *him* at a card table. He didn't even *haggle*."

"He's desperate."

Ferahr leaned back in his chair. "He's an idiot. Has *anyone* actually paid you the full million before?"

Tyr did finally smile a little. "No."

"My point. I don't care how desperate you are, you don't go with the first price offered, you work your way down. Listen, I wanna apologize."

Frowning, Tyr asked, "For what?"

"Askin' you to have the meeting somewhere else. That was the funniest thing I saw in *months*. How the hell did that jerk ever manage to overthrow a government?"

"The people he overthrew were even bigger—" another smile "—jerks." Tyr picked the flexi up and gave it a quick glance. "I'll need the *Abraxas* back."

That was the same transport Tyr had used for his last trip to Malani's Haven. It had been returned to the long-term storage lot. "No problem. May cost more to use it a second time, though."

Tyr shot Ferahr a look. "Just handle it."

Putting up his hands, Ferahr said, "Okay fine. I just wanted to make sure you didn't bust a gut when I showed you the bill."

"Have I ever busted a gut before?"

"No, but you never talked to Nietzscheans in my office before, neither. I'm just hedgin' my bets."

Tyr folded the flexi and placed it in his boot. "Just get me what I need. Let me worry about Field Marshal Augustus."

"I just think—"

Holding up a finger, Tyr laughed. "Ferahr, of the dozens of things I have needed from you or will someday need from you, I can guarantee that your thoughts will never be numbered among them."

Why do I bother? "Fine. I'll get the *Abraxas*—what about weapons?"

"We're fully loaded. In fact, more than fully, with Air dead."

"You want I should get a replacement?" Ferahr hadn't asked this before, but this was the first job Tyr had taken since then. Besides, Tyr usually requested replacements or reinforcements himself—but again, his behavior hadn't been entirely consistent lately.

Tyr snorted. "Unnecessary. I doubt we'll even need all six of us, to be honest. You took care of my message to Terra Verde?"

"Went off right before I first heard from Minister Nervous."

"Good." He turned to leave and added, without turning around, "Let me know when the money from Malani's Haven clears the account."

As the Nietzschean left, Ferahr found himself remembering something else his father said: "Don't make friends, son. They'll just confuse you, annoy you, and cost you money. You'll get enough of that from family."

Given how much Akbar al-Haroun confused, annoyed, and cost his son, Ferahr understood the wisdom of that.

What's going on in that genetically enhanced brain of yours, Tyr? Ferahr wondered.

Then he decided he just couldn't bring himself to be bothered by it. Tyr could confide in him, the Vedrans could reappear tomorrow and announce that there would be peace in the galaxies forever, or Ferahr would just go on doing business and not understanding Tyr. The second two were far more likely than the first.

Sighing, he put a call in to the storage lot to see how much it would cost to "borrow" the *Abraxas* again, and put in a call to the portmaster asking where the hell the Framberry ale was.

EIGHT · BEROS PRIME, 302 AFC

The best laid plans of mice and men usually go about the way you expect when you involve a rodent in the planning process.

—JACKSON FIORELLO, "APHORISMS," CY 9876

Seamus Zelazny Harper was in his element.

Well, one of his elements, anyhow.

His avatar wandered the VR landscape of the museum computer. The sword was housed in a huge building in the capital city on Beros Prime, and the building's security system was run through this computer. Harper's body was still safely on the *Maru* flight deck, but he had managed to gain remote access via the dataport on his neck through a series of back doors that only a true super-genius could have navigated without getting caught.

Beka was actually in the museum itself, walking through a main hallway wearing a borrowed Anwar Couriers delivery suit. She walked slowly, but not so much as to cause comment. She was waiting for Harper's signal.

Harper would provide that signal as soon as he was done convincing the security cameras that Beka was going to keep walking to the storage room for a pickup.

"Okay, Boss," he said when that was finished with a simple rearranging of flashes of light in the 'scape. "Time for the detour."

Beka, of course, said nothing, but simply made a right turn. Talking out loud to the air might, after all, alert someone to the fact that she was *not* making a pickup—or rather, not just making the scheduled pickup for Anwar Couriers that the guy she had bribed was supposed to make.

At least, Harper assumed she made that right turn. As far as he could tell from inside the computer, she was going to the storage room—which was as it should have been.

The most critical part of Nabrot's plan was the implementation of the various encryption codes that would allow one to jack into the computer network that controlled the security around the Sword of Terpsichore. Nabrot had a collection of codes, but wasn't sure what went with what.

That was where Harper came in.

Like most computers designed by people with no imagination—like, say, Nietzscheans—the landscape looked like little more than walls of circuitry. If he was ever in a position to design such a thing, Harper would have given the 'scape some personality: streets, large signs to indicate different sections of the mainframe, some benches where your avatar could actually sit while working, music playing in the background, things like that.

But the museum security computer took a safer route. This simplified Harper's life, because it made it much easier for him to find the areas he needed to rewrite and/or disable. As long as he had the codes, and used the codes in the right spots, no one would be the wiser—the computer would think he was an authorized user, because only an authorized user would have the codes.

Of course, most authorized users aren't short, adorable kludges. . . .

Most people with dataports tended to create an idealized version of themselves as their avatar when they entered the 'scape of a particular system. Harper, of course, did likewise, which was why his avatar looked no different from his actual body. Why improve on perfection, after all?

Nabrot had assured them that the codes would still be up to date, that, in fact, the Ursans hadn't changed them in fifty years.

The actual plan Nabrot concocted was now several years old. He had created it out of a sense of boredom as much as anything while working in data-entry at the museum. His work was tedious and uninteresting, so he spent months trying to figure out how to solve the unsolveable: how to steal the legendary sword that was the museum's centerpiece. Harper understood Nabrot's desire. His own mind was constantly coming up with things when he was bored, which usually meant that the *Maru* was about to get an upgrade or Harper was going to get yelled at by Beka. Or both.

Then, totally by accident thanks to a system glitch, the young Perseid found himself in possession of the encryption codes for the museum's computer—quite possibly the most closely guarded secret on Beros Prime. Nabrot quickly committed the codes to his eidetic memory and then made sure that no trace of the codes' accidental presence on his terminal remained.

Nabrot's harmless diversion suddenly became a practical reality.

He spent the next month living in fear for his life. Nietzscheans tended to be very direct when it came to security breaches—Harper still had scars from such direct actions dating back to his time living under the Drago-Kazov on Earth—and the Perseid was sure that someone would find out what had happened and have him killed. Or worse, tortured and killed.

But nobody ever found out.

The problem, of course, was that Nabrot didn't have anything like the resources or the skills to pull the heist off.

Luckily, he found me, Harper thought as he shut down the security to the sword's room but made sure that the status boards of the various guards gave no indication of this.

Then he hit another security wall. They had come up more and more often, but Harper was always ready with a code. The codes were nine characters made up of letters from the old Earth Roman alphabet—something Harper hadn't seen on anything since leaving his homeworld behind, save Beka's old music discs— and if you assigned a numeric value to them (one for the first letter, *A*, two for the second letter, which was *B*, etc.), they each added up to a different prime number, which was the same prime number that had been assigned to a particular subsection of the programming.

Then, to Harper's abject shock, he realized that the sword security had a designation of 109. Harper had one code of SDI-UWPAGI, and one of EHENZCTSI—both added up to 109.

Crap crap crap crap.

Harper found himself with too many options. One was that the Ursans had two codes for the same sytem, and it didn't matter which one he used. *Somehow, I'm thinking that's not gonna work*, he thought. Another was that the code had been changed at some point, which meant that one of the two codes was out of date, and if he used the wrong one, the jig was up. A third was that one of the codes was a totally false one, meant to cause exactly the problem Harper was facing now.

Then he realized something about the second code: it was an anagram for Nietzsche.

Could it be that easy?

Most people wouldn't even know that the letters corresponded to a rarely used alphabet, and fewer still would know what those letters actually meant.

So is it a clue for the brilliant or a trap for the clever—or Nietzschean arrogance, using the name of the jackass they decided to base their lives on as the security code for their oh-so-precious relic?

Harper had another three-and-a-half seconds to make a decision before Beka tried to open the door.

When in doubt, go with Nietzschean arrogance. He entered the second code.

He immediately got access.

"Yes! Wile E. Harper, *suuuuuuuuuuper*-genius!" he crowed as he rearranged the security so that the door would open and close without comment, the nanobots would ignore Beka's disruption, and the weight sensors would not acknowledge her footfalls. "Attention Beka Valentine, you are now free and clear to enter the room. Feel free to steal any swords you happen to find along the way, and have a nice day."

Harper then turned his attention to the security system in the huge glass case that held the Sword of Terpsichore. It was designated 127, and this time there was only one code that fit:

ZXYTQAABK. After plugging it in, Harper went about turning off the eyebeams, dismantling the alarms in the hard plastic case, and projecting false images of an empty room into the cameras.

Then he found one more security system. One he hadn't been expecting.

The hologram projectors.

What the hell?

By now, Beka would be starting on getting the case open, so Harper took a moment to see what the projectors were supposed to be creating a hologram *of*.

As soon as he realized what it was, his avatar's jaw fell open. He suspected that his real jaw did likewise back on the *Maru*, and he hoped that Rev or Nabrot was kind enough to close his mouth to keep flies from going in.

He confirmed his suspicions with a quick mass analysis of the inside of the case, which turned up enough for a cushion, and nowhere near enough for a one-meter-long piece of refined metal.

"Uh, Boss?" he said to Beka. "We got us a problem. There's nothing there."

That got Beka to break radio silence, though she spoke in a whisper. *"What?"*

"The Sword of Terpsichore, the pride of the Pride? It's a hologram. A damn good one, considering how much the entire Known Worlds have been fooled into thinking the sword was actually, y'know, *here*—besides, I'm checking these projectors, and they're *hot*, but—"

"Harper?"

"Yeah, Boss?"

"I just opened the case."

"What do you see?"

"Well, first I saw the Sword of Terpsichore. Then my hand went through it."

Harper didn't often hope he was wrong, but this had been one of those times. *Of all the occasions to be my usual perfect self . . .* "You gotta get outta there."

"Ten steps ahead of you. Stick to the plan so I can get out of here before the sweep."

"Okay." They still had a long way to go to get out of this in one piece—even if they didn't have anything to show for it. . . .

Beka walked calmly through the museum, retracing the route to where she needed to pick up the supplies that the Anwar delivery person she was subbing for was scheduled to retrieve. She was running out of time.

I still can't believe the whole thing was a damn fake! She had opened the case, and saw it right there. She could see the intricate fractal-like pattern of dried blood on the blade, the shining smoothness of the refined metal, the elaborate markings on the hilt. Hell, the case even had a vague metallic smell. Two of her senses told her that if she reached out to it, she would feel it with a third—yet her hand went right through. And when she removed the hand, it did nothing to shatter the illusion. It still looked like there was an ancient sword resting on the cushion.

Shaking her head, she continued on her path to the storage room. They had worked out a strict timetable because the one security element that could not be overridden even with the magical codes Nabrot had given Harper was that every twenty-three minutes and twenty-one-point-six seconds, the entire computer system was swept through with a "cleaner" program. People who made the mistake of being jacked in during the sweep would be forcibly ejected, and quite possibly killed. Even if they survived, the computer would be able to track them.

Less than five minutes remained until the next sweep. Harper needed to be out of the system by then, which meant Beka had to be out of the building.

Beka walked by various exhibits of Nietzschean paintings and statuary and old weaponry, trying not to calculate their fence value. *Stay focused, Valentine.* She caught her reflection in the glass covering one of the knives and had to keep in a smile. *I look really goofy in this getup.* Besides the delivery company jumpsuit, she had instructed the hair nanobots to go hot pink and adopt a style that vaguely resembled a mohawk. She had also inserted white contact lenses to simulate flash addiction. Once the Ursans realized the sword was gone, they'd likely commence their search for a drug-addicted Anwar employee with hot pink hair. On the off-chance that the cops investigating had two brain cells to rub together (admittedly, this was more likely with Nietzschean cops than the lowlife bribe-takers Beka was used to), they might do a detailed enough check of the security logs to realize that the eyes were contact lenses and the hair mutable, but by that time the *Maru* would be well on its way to the Jaguar homeworld.

The box was right where it was supposed to be. A bored "kludge" was standing guard—probably a slave. He didn't even look up from the book he was reading when Beka entered, and barely did so when she handed him the work order to sign.

Speaking in the rapid-fire tone one would expect from a flasher, Beka said, "This job's gotta suck, huh? I mean standing guard over über crap, am I right, huh, am I, I mean, really, this is *so* crap-ass as to be downright embarrassing isn't it?"

The guard looked up for a second, then went back to his book. "Whatever."

Score one for the hired help. Beka wanted to make sure he got a good look at her. *"I swear, Officer, it was a flasher with pink hair!"*

Carrying the box, she walked out toward the exit and risked whispering to Harper. "Time check."

"One minute, thirty-one seconds. Get a move on, Boss."

"Yeah, yeah."

She reached the exit without incident. The worry now was how soon they'd notice Harper's messing up the system after he left. Given sufficient time, he could cover his tracks, but that time simply wasn't available, and it was too risky for him to jack back in after the sweep.

Exiting through the rear door, she nodded to the guards and said, "Seeya later guys, nice meetin' ya, and—"

"Just get outta here, kludge," one guard said.

Beka noticed the arm spikes. *A Nietzschean guard? Hate to think how weak his genes are to be stuck with this duty. . . .*

Smiling as goofy a smile as she could manage, she climbed into the Anwar Deliveries aircar, placing the box on the passenger seat.

"Gotta go, Boss. Seeya in orbit!"

With that, Beka assumed that Harper had beaten a hasty retreat from the museum security computer.

Now's the time to stay frosty, Valentine. Thunder crackled through the sky, startling her. *God, I hate weather.* She eased the aircar into takeoff mode, forcing herself not to rush it. Slowly, she guided the small vehicle into the air, remembering at the last second to compensate for the wind. *I really really hate weather.*

Once she got the aircar to Anwar, she'd drop off the box—that had been part of the deal; Beka would actually make the scheduled pickup, which suited her, as it kept their tracks better covered if it was under legitimate business—pick up Vexpag, and head into orbit to rendezvous with the *Maru*. The aircar would be left adrift for Anwar to pick up later.

Or not. She didn't really care one way or the other, as long as it got them to the *Maru*.

She kept waiting for a planet-wide alarm that never came as she eased the aircar into the lot behind Anwar's box-shaped headquarters. Just as she did so, it started to rain.

Weather just sucks.

A young man and Vexpag both came out to greet the aircar. The rain plastered Vexpag's shaggy hair to his head, making him look even more sheepdog-like than normal.

"Have a box," she said to the young man, then she turned to Vexpag. "I've got good news and bad news."

"Where's the sword?" he asked.

"That's the bad news."

The young man opened the box. "Nice work. Try not to break this thing before you dump it." He hefted it and took it inside without a backward glance.

Hey, his butt's covered, what does he care? To Vexpag, she said, "There is no Sword of Terpsichore. Or if there is, it isn't in that museum. That was the single best hologram I've ever seen in my life."

"Dammit." Vexpag climbed into the passenger seat, holding a long-range P22 rifle. He was dripping on the seat. "So now what?"

"Now what? We hightail it to orbit, that's what."

"But—"

"Yes, Fred, I know exactly how much money we spent and how

much credit we took on in anticipation of selling the sword to Archduke Bolivar and now we're screwed. Let's just—"

The computer on the aircar console beeped just as Beka started to bring it up into the rainy night.

"*Alarm. Alarm. All vehicles are ordered to ground themselves immediately or be rendered inoperable.*"

"Well, either someone else did something naughty," Beka said as she ignored the warning and continued their flight upward, "or they found out that we broke and entered their light show. Get the big gun ready, Plan B just kicked in."

"Fine." Vexpag stuck a fresh toothpick into his mouth and touched a button on the door. A small hole irised open, and he put the muzzle of the rifle into it.

Beka followed the course that Nabrot had specified, should the planet go onto any kind of alert status. Under those circumstances, a network of hovering electromagnetic pulse emitter buoys were launched into the atmosphere. They each sent out several eye-beams across the sky, forming a nigh-impassable network. Any interruption of a beam would cause the nearest emitter to fire an EMP, which would disable any craft and send it hurtling to the ground. However, Nabrot had found that a well-placed shot at one of the emitters would open a five-meter-wide hole in the eye-beam network for seven-and-a-half seconds before the other emitters changed position to compensate. If they cut it close enough, there was more than enough time for Beka to get the three-and-a-half meter-wide aircar through the hole. Of course, it would take a perfect shot and precision piloting worthy of a Nietzschean.

Fred Vexpag was the only non-Nietzschean to ever win the annual sharpshooting contest on Razor's Vantage in the event's fifty-year history. In fact, he'd done so three times. *And I can out-fly any one of those damn übers any day of the week and six times on Sunday.*

Again, Beka had to compensate for the wind, which had picked up in the last few minutes.

"You wanna lay off the buckin' and weavin'?" Vexpag asked.

"Talk to the weather," she muttered as she ordered the display to show the eye-beam network. "About that—you gonna be able to make the shot with all this rain?"

"Long's you keep the car steady, I can shoot the wings off a fly." He closed his left eye and peered into the rifle's scope with his right.

Gritting her teeth, Beka said, "That wasn't what I asked." She looked down at the display. The eye-beams had spread across the sky, showing up on the computer's image as a red lattice over the entire planet—or, for the purposes of the image in front of Beka, directly in front of her on all sides. They were going to hit it in twenty seconds, and if the aircar disturbed the lattice even slightly, they were finished. "We're on the approach. You have the target?"

"Not yet." A pause. "Okay, got it."

Ten seconds. "Get ready." *Five seconds.* "And—now!"

Vexpag pulled the trigger. A shot flew out into the rain. *And why couldn't they have had the buoys* above *the stupid clouds?* Beka thought angrily. *I really* hate *weather.*

The wind had grown fiercer. Beka's knuckles were turning white as she held the aircar's grips, struggling to keep it steady.

A three-point-six-meter hole opened in the red lattice. It did not grow any wider. Nabrot's calculations had been off—or maybe they'd improved the design of the buoys.

A one-decimeter margin of error. In the rain.

Beka grinned.

The color returned to her fingers as she calmly flew the aircar toward the hole.

If Beka Valentine thought about what she did when she piloted under these circumstances, she'd have crashed and burned years ago. So she didn't think at all. She just trusted her instincts and *flew*. What Rev had once called "Zen and the art of ship piloting."

The aircar moved smoothly and steadily toward the hole.

Less than four meters from the hole, an updraft slammed into the rear of the aircar, jarring it half a meter off course.

Without even thinking about it, Beka righted the aircar's course, just in time to reach the buoys.

The aircar slid through without disturbing a single beam, into the cumulus clouds that were providing Beros Prime's capital city with such a miserable amount of rainfall.

Once she was through the clouds and into the stratosphere—and, at last, above the rain—she spared Vexpag a glance. To her surprise, he was smiling.

"Nice flying," he said.

She chuckled. "Nice shooting."

"Nah, I think I was off by a couple millimeters. Damn rain."

"I'm a results-oriented kinda gal. You shot it, it blew up—that's good enough for me."

Vexpag laughed. "Always nice to get kudos from a pink-haired flasher."

Beka frowned, then remembered her disguise. She shook her head, returning her hair to the blond look she'd been favoring since Olivares. *The contacts can wait until later.*

As soon as the *Maru* read as being in real-time communication range, she opened a channel. "Rev, Harper, the nanosecond we're on board, get us the hell out of here. I don't want to be anywhere near Beros Prime ever again."

"Understood," Rev said.

"And then I want to have a talk with our Perseid passenger." Nabrot had come along, mainly because Beka insisted—she had more confidence in the plan if the plan's creator was handy to consult.

"My 'pal' is right here, Boss," Harper said, sounding none too pleased.

Beka started the final approach to the *Maru's* airlock. "Hiya, Nabrot. Care to explain this one?"

"L-look, I don't know what happened. I had no idea, really! I don't see how the sword couldn't have been there!"

"You used to work here, how the hell could you—?"

Rev interjected. *"I believe our young friend is telling the truth, Beka."*

That brought Beka up short. Still, if Rev vouched for him . . . "All right, say he is. That doesn't change the fact that I went along with this cockamamy scheme and spent what little money we had, plus a whole lot of money we didn't have. Right now, the only way we could even buy a meal is to sell Harper's dataport."

"Hey, waitasec, nobody touches my—"

"Harper."

"Yeah, Boss?"

"Shut up."

"Sorry, Boss."

"L-look, I can—I can make this up to you," Nabrot said quickly. *"If we go to—to Schopenhauer, I c-can talk to Powell, my—my Jaguar Pride contact. Trust me, he'll—he'll take care of us."*

Douglas Powell was the Nietzschean whose recorded message

to Nabrot assuring him of Archduke Bolivar's interest in buying the Sword of Terpsichore "should it come on the market" was what convinced Beka to take on the job in the end.

"*I'm not sure being 'taken care of' by a Nietzschean would be wise,*" Rev said.

"Me either," Vexpag said. "My vote's for spacin' the little blue twerp an' fendin' for ourselves."

Beka thought a moment as she tethered the car to the airlock. "No."

"No what?" Vexpag asked.

Popping the hatch, she said, "We're going to Schopenhauer." She climbed out of the chair and onto the *Maru.* As soon as Vexpag and his rifle came out after her, they both left the airlock. "*Maru,* engage autopilot. Break orbit when I cut the car loose and set course for Schopenhauer," she said as she closed the door and depressurized the airlock.

The *Maru*'s deep, male computer voice said, "*Acknowledged.*"

"You sure this is a good idea?" Vexpag asked.

"Bolivar wanted the sword. If it's a fake, I think we owe it to him to tell him that, don't you?"

Vexpag spit out his toothpick. "Not really, no."

"Well, we're doing it anyway. And let's hope that they'll think the effort counts."

Snorting, Vexpag said, "Effort without tangible results? We're talkin' 'bout *Nietzscheans,* Bek."

She nodded as they entered the flight deck. "Yeah, I know." Beka noted that Rev was at his station, with Harper leaning on the railing. Nabrot was nowhere to be found. *Probably hiding in the bunkroom.*

Rev looked over at them as they came in. "We will reach the

nearest Slip point in three minutes. And Fred is right—Nietz-scheans, especially Jaguar Pride, are not likely to feel sorry for us."

"Right now I'm just hoping for payment for information," Beka said as she got into the pilot's chair.

"I hate this plan, Boss," Harper added. "I'm with Rev and Vex-pag—I vote for stayin' away from people with spikes in their arms."

"I wasn't kidding about selling your dataport for food, Harper."

"Did I mention how much I love this plan?" Harper said with-out missing a beat.

"Approaching Slip point," Rev said.

Beka moved the seat forward. "Let's go to Schopenhauer."

"And may the Divine guide our path," Rev said.

"Amen," Vexpag added as they went into Slipstream.

There are always choices. It's just a matter of finding
the one that sucks the least.

> —CAPTAIN JANZEN GIANNINI,
> "ON SOLDIERING," CY 8999

"Who are these people again?"

Charlemagne Bolivar, who listed archduke of the Jaguar Pride
among his manifold titles, asked the question of his aide Douglas
Powell as he sat on a massive, soft cushion covered in silk sheets,
holding a chilled glass of strawberry wine in his right hand. A
slave had just put a plate of fruits and chocolates next to him, then
retreated to the antechamber of the Palace Suite. The suite took
up the entire top floor of the Regency Hotel on Schopenhauer,
and was permanently reserved for Bolivar. The walls were deco-

rated with several spacescapes by a local painter whose career Bolivar had sponsored. Indeed, all of her work was on display in the various museums on Schopenhauer except for those in Bolivar's own private collection. His personal favorite, *Slipstream Overdrive*, which depicted an intersection between the Slipstream and normal space, hung across from where he lay. The colors never failed to enthrall him.

Powell spoke to him via a screen from halfway around the world at a much less posh hotel near one of the spaceports. *"It's a battered old cargo ship—the* Eureka Maru. *Crew of four: three humans and one Magog."*

Bolivar blinked. "These damn speakers must be on the fritz again. It sounded like you said their crew had one Magog."

"That's because I did say that. He's a reformed Magog—a Wayist monk, in fact."

Sipping his wine thoughtfully, Bolivar said, "Those Wayists have got to stop lowering their admission standards. They'll be letting Sabra Pride in next. So why, precisely, am I supposed to care about these people?"

"They just returned from Beros Prime, where they, with the help of that young Perseid I was telling you about, successfully broke into the case containing the Sword of Terpsichore."

Bolivar almost choked on his chocolate-covered cherry. He managed to maintain his poise and dignity as he swallowed the confection, but it was a close call. He leaned forward. "They have the sword?" *After all these years, I'll finally . . .*

"I'm afraid not. The rumors are true, Charlemagne."

"Damn." Bolivar fell back into the cushion, almost spilling some of his wine. He set the glass down on the end table. "I was really looking forward to holding it, feeling the hilt in my hand, the weight of the blade against my wrist. Besides, it matches the rug." He turned back to Powell's image. "You haven't answered my question. Why are they here?"

"Apparently, they put up a significant outlay of cash in order to finance the endeavor, which they now can't pay off due to a rather unfortunate lack of merchandise."

"My heart bleeds for them." Bolivar popped a grape into his mouth. "Send them on their way, and—"

"I was thinking they might be useful. And they did take on the task expecting to be paid by us."

"Their mistaken impressions aren't my problem, Douglas."

"No, but Catherine is."

Another grape stopped halfway to Bolivar's mouth. He set it back down on the dish. He regarded his advisor's pleasantly round, dark face for several seconds. "Let me see if I understand you, Douglas. You're suggesting I entrust Catherine's welfare to three kludges and a Magog priest in a clapped-out old cargo ship?"

"No. I'm suggesting that you entrust Catherine's welfare to four people who pulled off a theft that everyone in the Known Worlds has assumed to be impossible. Or, rather, they would have done but for a technicality out of their control."

"Douglas, my dear old friend and companion, that is without a doubt in my mind the single most brilliant idea you've ever had."

That prompted a look of relief on Powell's face. *"Thank you, Charlemagne."*

"Don't mention it." A pause. "I mean that literally, by the way. If my other advisors found out I gave you a compliment, they'll all want one." Bolivar sat upright, the folds of his silk dressing gown flowing down airily toward the floor, his bare feet now on the plush carpet. "It's too risky to bring them to the homeworld. I'll take my ship back home and fetch Catherine and her two thugs."

"Sacco and Vanzetti are the best bodyguards I could find, Charlemagne. They're not just 'thugs.'"

"Spoken like someone who hasn't watched them eat. In any event, I'll be back in four days. Keep these kludges occupied." He thought a moment. "I'll record a message to tide them over with a proper offer. Who runs this motley crew—not the Magog, I hope?"

"No," Powell said quickly. *"One of the humans—a woman named Beka Valentine."*

"Really?" Bolivar got up and removed the dressing gown, letting it fall to the floor. "Don't suppose you've got an image of her?"

In a long-suffering tone, Powell said, *"She's a kludge, Charlemagne."*

"That doesn't mean I can't have a look. Even kludges occasionally have aesthetic appeal."

"Fine, I'll send an image to your ship as soon as I dig one up."

"Just don't mix her up with the Magog." He snapped his fingers, and one of the slaves came in—a human female. "Fetch me a red ensemble suitable for travelling."

"Yes, m'lord," she said without looking up at him. She bent over, picked up the dressing gown, and scurried back out of the room.

"I'll have the message for you by midday," Bolivar said after finishing off the wine. "It should be enough to convince them to stick around. If it doesn't, do whatever's necessary to make them take the job."

"Will do. See you in four days, old friend."

Beka hated being kept waiting.

She, Rev, Harper, Vexpag, and Nabrot had arrived at Schopenhauer in one piece. Nabrot had put them in touch with this Powell person who was willing not only to grant them an appointment, but to give them a place to park the *Maru* free of charge. Since they had quite literally nothing with which to pay for such privileges, the latter was a big relief.

A Chichin slave had met them at the storage lot and taken them in an aircar to a hotel near the spaceport where a small room had been reserved for them. Beka had never liked mudfoot accommodations, viewing them as halfhearted attempts to duplicate the regulated atmosphere of a ship. They didn't bother taking the extra step of installing a proper AG field to keep things steady or tougher walls to keep out the weather. Instead, the rooms just had regulated air and an artificial sealed-in feel.

The slave had said that Powell would be with them "shortly," but gave no indication how long that duration truly was. Harper and Vexpag had actually planned ahead and brought some work with them—they engaged in some small repair projects on *Maru* parts as they sat on each of the two double beds in the room. Rev sat in the corner and meditated.

Beka fidgeted. She sat in a chair and stared at the floor, having long since grown bored with staring at the ugly paintings that stained the walls. *That's the other thing about hotels—they all have the damn ugliest artwork in the Known Worlds.* So concerned was Beka with what would happen next, it didn't occur to her to bring anything along, like her music or a good book—or even a bad book. Hell, she could really sink her teeth into *Heart of the Matador* or *Ride of the Guard* about now. She toyed with the idea of returning to the storage lot to get something, but she had nothing with which to pay for an aircar ride back. The room of course came equipped with a terminal, and she could probably connect to the

Maru's library from here, but she didn't want to make any kind of connection between the Nietzschean systems and her own. And somehow, she didn't imagine that Jaguar Pride's idea of entertainment would match hers. . . .

All in all, this has been a pretty wretched day.

"C-Captain Valentine?"

Beka looked up from her intense visual study of the nonexistent pattern in the monochrome carpet to see Nabrot standing in front of her, in the same arms-in-front-of-him pose he'd adopted when she first met him back on Olivares.

After fixing him with a withering look, she put her head back down, having no interest in looking at the little twerp. "What?"

"I just wanted to say I'm sorry, ma'am. Believe me, if I'd known that it was a hologram, I never would've—"

"It's all right," she said, not meaning it, but not wanting to listen to him whine any longer. "Looks like the Ursans had us all fooled."

"If there's any way I can make it up to you—"

She looked back up at him. "Can you fix the hole in my cargo hold? Can you pay off my father's debts? Can you figure out some way to construct money out of thin air that'll pay off the informants that we still owe money to, and who *will* find us sooner or later if we don't pay by the end of the month? Or the equipment Harper bought on credit so he could jack into the computer?"

"He—he can always sell that back."

Harper sell back a toy he'd gotten his mitts on. Right, that'll happen. "How about the rest of it? Can you do that?"

"N-no. B-but maybe Powell can."

"Right, because Nietzscheans are renowned throughout the galaxies as kind, benevolent, forgiving, charitable figures, right?"

Nabrot looked as if he was trying to make himself smaller.

Beka sighed and plastered a pleasant look onto her face. "I appreciate your apology, and I might even be able to accept it eventually. But right now, I'm just too angry, okay?"

Nodding quickly, Nabrot went off to bother Harper.

"You were a bit hard on him."

Blowing out a breath, Beka turned to see Rev standing behind her, his meditations having apparently been abandoned. "No, I was a *lot* hard on him. But what was I supposed to do? And before you say, 'not tried to steal the sword in the first place,' I didn't hear you coming up with alternative methods of paying for that big hole in the ship."

"True, the Divine did not provide any alternatives for me to suggest. . . ."

"Damn right." Beka leaned back in her chair and sighed. "I'm telling you, Rev, I don't see any way out of this. The only way we're going to be able to keep going is by the charity of Nietzscheans."

"The Divine often provides a Way—sometimes from an unexpected source."

"Well, if it *is* from Archduke Bolivar, it'll be the most unexpected source on record."

Before they could continue, the door opened to reveal a dark-skinned Nietzschean dressed in an impeccably tailored blue suit. The door had been opened by the Chichin slave, who then stood behind his master.

"My apologies for the delay. I am Douglas Powell out of Soon-Li by Francis of Jaguar Pride." He looked at Beka. "You must be Captain Valentine."

"Must I?" Beka said with a sweet smile.

"I would say you have little choice in the matter," Powell said, returning the smile. He held up a hand, which held a data chip. "I have a message from Archduke Bolivar for you, in response to your attempt to secure the Sword of Terpsichore for him."

"Hey," Harper said, "we weren't doing it 'for' anybody but ourselves, pal."

"Shut up, Harper," Beka said, almost by rote.

Powell dropped the smile and gave Harper a look akin to that of an epicure viewing a fast-food lunch. "Keep your place, boy. I speak to Captain Valentine out of respect for what you have accomplished, but do not mistake me for someone who will tolerate your existence for any length of time if you displease me."

The Chichin reentered the room—only then did Beka even realize that the slave had exited after letting Powell in—carrying a tray of drinks and food. It was a standard collection of human, Perseid, and Vedran crudités and bottled water to drink. *Simple and safe—enough to be polite, but no real effort. About what you'd expect from Nietzscheans serving kludges*, Beka thought.

As the Chichin set the tray on the hotel room's table, Powell said, "Help yourselves to the libations and victuals, courtesy of the Jaguar Pride."

Harper walked over to the table and held up a limp red pepper. "I'm whelmed."

"You'll have to excuse my engineer," Beka said, getting up and slapping Harper on the arm. "He has a diarrhea problem relating to his mouth."

"I can see that," Powell said with pursed lips. "In any case, here is Archduke Bolivar's message."

This oughtta be good, Beka thought as Powell placed the chip into the room's reader.

A very attractive face appeared on the screen. Short, wavy

blond hair framed an angular face with magnificent cheekbones and a prominent chin. Beka didn't often think of Nietzscheans as good-looking—adjectives like *intimidating* tended to dominate—but this one definitely had a charisma about him.

I need to be very careful around this one, she thought, slamming down the thoughts that were starting to burble in her head. The roster of men in her life that had complicated it more than necessary was depressingly long, starting with her father and brother and ending with Bobby Jensen. The archduke was just the kind of guy who could add to the list. She took heart in the fact that he probably wouldn't give a kludge a second thought.

"Greetings, Captain Valentine. My name is Charlemagne Bolivar of Jaguar Pride. Nietzsche once said, 'And perhaps a great day will come, when a people distinguished by war and victory, by the highest development of military organization and intelligence, and accustomed to making the gravest sacrifices to these things, will voluntarily exclaim, "We will break the sword into pieces".' Nice words—problem is, our old friend Ogun Bonaparte appears to have taken that rather literally. There were rumors flying about that he shattered the real Sword of Terpsichore to tiny bits about five minutes after he yanked it out of his dear brother's belly.

"You appear to have proven those rumors true. The sword is long gone, and Ursa Pride has been charging outrageous admission fees to look at a hologram. As it happens, this is a piece of information that is of value to me. It's of no value to you, of course, so allow me to make up for that. Jaguar Pride is willing to pay off the expenses you incurred attempting to steal the sword—"

"Good," Beka said.

"—in exchange for taking on a job for me."

"Bad," she said.

"I need you to take care of one of my sisters, Catherine. She carries within her one of our Pride's future leaders—naturally, that makes her a target for our good friends in the Sabra Pride, who've been spending the last seven-and-a-half months trying to kill her.

"What I propose is this: We'll pay off your debts, you protect my sister until her child is born. You'll hide her and her bodyguards on your cargo ship in secret. If you take the deal, we'll be back at Schopenhauer in four days. If you don't take the deal—then you're even stupider than the average kludge and deserve what you get. Ta."

The image faded.

Before Harper could say anything, Beka looked at Powell. "Could you excuse us please? We need to discuss this."

Powell gave her a dubious look. "You're joking."

"Do I look like I'm joking?"

"You only have one choice."

Rev smiled. "The Divine provides many choices. Some are simply easier to see than others."

That got a laugh out of Powell. "Out of the mouths of Magog comes gibberish. Very well." Powell snapped his fingers, then turned and left. The slave, responding to the finger-snap, followed.

Once the door closed, Harper said, "I don't like this guy. He's setting off all my scumbag alarms."

"I'm with the twerp," Vexpag said. It was the first time he'd looked up from his repair job on the bed. Beka hadn't been sure he was even paying attention. "He ain't tellin' us everythin'."

Beka turned to Rev and gave him a questioning look.

"I could point out that it is always dangerous to get involved with Nietzscheans, that such deals never go well for the non-

Nietzschean—but I suspect there will be little point. You have already made up your mind."

Smiling and shaking her head, Beka said, "How do you do that?"

"Years of practice," Rev said with a smile.

"Boss," Harper said, "if you already made up your mind, why'd you tell Jaguar-face to bug out?"

"Because I didn't want him to see you guys arguing with me, and I didn't want you saying anything that would endanger the job."

"Ain't a 'job,' Bek, it's playing baby-sitter for the damn Nietzscheans!" Vexpag said.

"Fine, Fred, tell me exactly how you intend to eat tomorrow."

"Through my mouth, prob'ly."

"Very funny." Beka ran a hand through her hair. "We're out of options. You're right, Rev, there are always other choices, but they all involve taking on *more* debt in order to work to pay off an already-steep one. I'm not prepared to do that, and there's no guarantee we *can* do that. I'm taking Bolivar's offer. That means either you guys take it or you find another ship to serve on. What'll it be?"

Vexpag stared at her for a minute, then sat back down on the bed. "You're the captain."

Damn right, she thought.

Harper did likewise. "What he said. But let me just say that I really don't like it."

"I don't like it either, Harper."

"Nor I," Rev said. "I can only advise that we all watch our backs. This Nietzschean woman is bound to be trouble."

"That's a big ol' duh," Harper said.

Looking over at the Perseid, who sat on one of the beds, study-ing the pattern in the bedspread, Beka prompted, "Nabrot?"

"Me?"

"You're the only Nabrot in the room," Beka said. "Go out and fetch your friend."

"Uh, okay."

Nabrot got up and left the room. He came back less than a minute later trailed by Powell.

"You've come to a decision?"

"Yes. We accept on one condition. The Jaguar Pride also has to pay for the repairs to the *Eureka Maru*."

Powell smiled. "I've seen your ship, Captain. The cost of a proper repair job on it would bankrupt the Pride's treasury."

"Hey!" Harper said, his engineer's ego no doubt bruised, but Rev shushed him.

"At least pay to cover the repair of the hole in the cargo hold. We incurred that damage while escaping from Beros Prime," she lied. "In a sense, it falls under the category of a debt incurred while trying to steal the sword." Powell didn't look convinced, so Beka thought fast. "Besides, if you want us to provide a secret safe haven for the archduke's sister, we'll need to go about our regular business. Our regular business requires that we have a cargo hold that can actually, y'know, *hold* things."

The Nietzschean's round face was all but unreadable. Beka could see why Bolivar used the man as an advisor—he gave no indication what he was thinking. That made him unusual in a race that mostly didn't care if people knew what they thought. *Of course, that's mostly because everyone can guess what they're thinking anyhow: "I'm better than you." It's all Nietzscheans ever think. . . .*

Finally, he said, "I will have to clear it with the archduke, but I believe we can accommodate that request."

Smiling, Beka said, "In that case, Mr. Powell, we have a deal." She put out a hand.

To Beka's surprise, Powell actually accepted the handshake. "A pleasure doing business with you, Captain Valentine."

"No, it isn't, either. Don't lie to me, Mr. Powell. You hate the idea of doing business with me, and you'd much rather I was standing next to your Chichin serving you drinks. But right here, right now, we need each other. So let's just use each other and go our separate ways, okay?"

"She actually said that?"

Bolivar's personal yacht was moving through the Schopenhauer system. Catherine was in her cabin, asleep. Even Nietzschean women tended to nap more when pregnant. As soon they had transited back into normal space from Slipstream, Bolivar had contacted Powell to see if Captain Valentine had accepted the deal. Not that there was any doubt in his mind. The universe was chockfull of stupidity, more so among kludges, but Bolivar thought it unlikely that someone clever and talented enough to pull off the Terpsichore theft was stupid enough to not take this deal.

However, Valentine exceeded his expectations: she not only wasn't stupid, she was impressively clever. She maneuvered Powell into fixing her ship in such a way that made it appear that she was doing them a favor—which, in a sense, she was—and also let Powell know that she knew exactly what was going on and was under no illusion about the reality of the situation.

I like her style.

"Yes, Charlemagne, she actually said that," Powell said.

"You sound bitter."

"She's a kludge, Charlemagne. I don't like it when they get the upper hand."

"Using her was your idea, remember."

"Yes, using her. Not her using us."

Bolivar smiled. "A little using never hurt anyone. I take it the repairs are underway?"

"Uh, no. I didn't want to proceed until I received your authorization, which I couldn't get until you were back in-system."

Sighing, Bolivar said, "Do it. And make it quick. I don't want Catherine on Schopenhauer any longer than necessary. Oh, and *don't* let Valentine tell you where they're going. The less we know, the better."

That seemed to panic Powell. *"If we don't know where she is—"*

"We will. Vanzetti will send regular updates, but I want that information to come from him, not from Valentine. It's better if there's no connection between her and me."

"Understood." Powell nodded. *"How is Catherine doing?"*

Again, Bolivar sighed. "The same."

"My sympathies."

"Yes, well, she'll be someone else's problem for the next couple of months. Frankly, it'd be worth buying Valentine a whole new ship just for her taking her off our hands during the end stages."

An intercom beeped. *"My Lord, we're on final approach to Schopen-hauer."*

"Excellent." Bolivar rose from his chair. "I'll see you soon, Douglas."

The surprise isn't that the Commonwealth fell. The surprise is that such a bloated entity managed to sustain itself for as long as it did. And the Nietzscheans quickly discovered the same thing the Visigoths found out after they sacked Rome: it's a lot easier to topple an empire than build one.

—ANONYMOUS, 57 AFC

Varastaya peered through the scope of her weapon at the hut in the middle of the woods and eagerly looked forward to being able to kill people.

There were other benefits to her job, of course, primary among them being the money. But mostly what she liked was the killing.

She sat in the branch of the large oak tree, waiting for a sign of life that would confirm that she was targeting the right hut.

The door to the hut opened, and out walked a young man wearing the black jumpsuit favored by the forces opposing the Malani Free Army. He drank from a cup of something, seemingly unconcerned, even though he was supposed to be guarding a critical outpost.

Varastaya smiled. Then she pulled the trigger.

She didn't wait to see if her shot actually took the young man's life or not. Her joy for imparting death notwithstanding, that was comparatively irrelevant. The shot was also the signal to attack. So right after she fired, she leapt the ten meters down to the ground. Her cybernetic legs easily absorbed the impact, and she was running practically as soon as she hit the ground.

Twenty members of the MFA were stationed throughout the woods, under Varastaya's command. Tyr had told her that this hut was a supply and communications center for the enemy, and had instructed her to lead a score of troops to take the hut, which was inadequately defended, according to the intelligence the MFA had obtained.

Upon seeing the gunshot from Varastaya, those troops, who were arranged in a circle around the hut, started moving in.

A slight whirring sound accompanied Varastaya as she ran, which annoyed her. It was a sop to skintones, was all—they always got uncomfortable around cyborgs and AIs, and it was easier for them if they knew that the person they were dealing with was part or all artificial. So most manufacturers put in that damn whirring noise to keep themselves from getting sued by skintones who thought that to *not* put in the sounds constituted fraud. As far as Varastaya was concerned, they could all kiss her circuit-laden posterior. The fact that most of her body parts had been replaced by more efficient machine parts was nobody's business but hers and her victims', and it generally wasn't the latter's business for very long.

Three people in black jumpsuits saw her just as she was approaching the hut. Without breaking stride, she lifted her weapon and blasted them each to pieces. They were all dead before any of them even had a chance to aim their weapons.

Among her bionic enhancements was a playback function in her eyes that allowed her to review anything she saw. As she finished her journey toward the hut, she replayed the three bodies exploding from the impact of her weapon in a window inset in her enhanced field of vision. She smiled as she watched the skin burn, the muscles disintegrate, the bones splinter, the blood flow freely. And all by her hand.

That's four down, she thought. *If the reports were right, that's a quarter of the forces right there. And if the reports* weren't *right, I get to kill more people.* She grinned. *A plan with no drawbacks.*

She heard the sounds of multiple gunshots from all around her. At first, she thought that it was her troops making short work of the minimal forces.

Then she realized that what she was hearing was an exchange of gunfire—and the volume of it coming from the hut was far in excess of what they had been led to expect.

As if to accentuate this realization, six troops leapt out at Varastaya.

To a skintone, they were probably moving fast, but to Varastaya's enhanced eyes they were practically crawling. Four of them were dead within a second of her seeing them.

The other two, however, were able to get shots off. She ducked both, but that action took valuable time, which they used to close the gap.

Varastaya grabbed the muzzle of the first one's gun just as he was about to fire it into her face. Flexing her fingers, she crushed it. "Go ahead," she said. "Fire."

Then she punched him in the face hard enough to slam the now-broken fragments of his nose into his brain, killing him instantly. Her eyes were sufficiently acute that she could actually see the nose shattering, observe the fragments as they travelled under the skin. Even as she did so, she kicked to her left, shattering the bones in the other attacker's left leg just as he pulled the trigger on his own weapon, which fired harmlessly into the air.

She then ripped the second attacker's head off.

Blood gushed from the bottom of the head she held as well as the top of the neck that fell to the dirt. Varastaya was pleased with the look of shock and anger and pain that was forever frozen on the skintone's face.

Belatedly, she realized that killing both these men was a tactical error. Obviously, the MFA's intelligence about this place was faulty. Tyr had spoken of a poorly defended hut that could be taken by twenty troops. Varastaya could still hear the exchange of gunfire, and more of it seemed to be coming from the hut itself, not outside it. It was possible that her own people were simply close enough now, but it could also mean that her side was losing.

If she had left one of these people alive, she could have questioned them.

But killing them had been so much *fun*. . . .

She replayed the shattering of the one person's nose again, just for the fun of it.

Enough, she admonished herself, ending the replay before it was finished. *You've got work to do. You can always watch the replays later.*

The snap of a twig caught her attention. Someone was coming.

Her enhanced ears picked out two sets of footfalls heading straight for her from behind the trees.

She peered into the forest and made out two humanoid shapes. Taking aim, she fired at each of them. Their screams were music to her ears.

Running over to inspect the bodies, she was quite proud of the fact that—despite the distance and the number of trees blocking her line of sight—she was able to kill both of them, but mildly distressed to see that they were two of her own troops.

Shrugging off the mistake, she continued forward to the hut. She was now close enough that she could make out heat signatures. Several dozen people—a few she could see normally, and they all wore black jumpsuits—stood around the hut on all sides, firing hand weapons. A few of them dropped, but not nearly enough.

Varastaya peered around the perimeter, and saw that her own people were being massacred. The whole thing would be over soon.

The sensible thing to do would be to retreat and report back to Tyr.

But not right away. After all, she had five of these bastards in her sights. *It'd be such a tragic waste to let them live.*

She shot the fifth one before the first one even hit the ground.

However, that still left some thirty or so troops defending the hut. Even if she had her full complement, she'd be outnumbered. Varastaya had taken on as many as thirty skintones in her time, but they were unarmed. As good as she was, she doubted even she could survive it, even with the support she had. Besides, there was also the matter of reporting this back to Tyr.

So she turned and ran.

As she did so, she replayed each of the deaths. After four of them, she decided she liked the deaths of the two in the trees the best. Sure, technically they were on her side, but not really. They were just local skintones who happened to be working for the same side as the people who'd hired Tyr. If it had been Glasten or Brexos or Tyr or Johnson—or even that scumsucking Nightsider—she might have felt a little bad about it. Maybe.

Her enhancements meant she felt no fatigue, so was free to focus on the replays and think of other things while her arms and legs pumped and carried her away from the hut and back toward Amorin as fast as any aircar. She recalled the childhood accident that had led to several of her organs and limbs being replaced with cybernetic implants and prosthetics. The memory of the pain that accompanied the accident was so vivid that she still, twenty years later, sometimes could feel a phantom version of it, of the blades slicing through her legs, of the fire that burned her arm.

But she liked what the implants did to her. They made her faster and stronger—less weak. Suddenly, she could retaliate when the other children made fun of her instead of flailing about like a weakling.

That led to a recollection of the greatest day of her life, when she was fourteen and snapped the neck of her schoolmate.

Oddly enough, though Varastaya could remember every detail of the look on Irina's face, of the way her eyes seemed to roll backward, of the feel of the bones as they shattered under her touch, of the look of the jagged pieces of neckbone as they sliced through Irina's skin—she could not for the life of her recall *why* she had performed the act. It was some slight or offense on Irina's part, of course, but Varastaya no longer remembered the nature of that offense.

Not that it mattered. What did matter was that Varastaya had finally found a purpose. And, after a stay in a juvenile detention center for the next seven years, she put that purpose to good use. First, she worked as an enforcer for a local gangster, then worked her way up as her reputation—and her abilities—increased. As soon as she could afford another cybernetic enhancement, she got it. By the time she was thirty, she had very little by way of original parts, as it were, left. Most importantly, she instructed the doctors to remove the ability to feel pain. They had been reluctant to do so, but a simple threat of arm removal had solved that problem. True, pain had an important role in a skintone's life, but Varastaya had endured enough pain in her life. She saw no reason to continue to do so when the memories of the past were so vivid.

She had also grown tired of enforcement work by that time. Most of it consisted of intimidation rather than any actual violence, which took all the fun out of it. Besides, she was gaining a reputation—no one would even put up a fight when she came near. Luckily, her boss had a contact on Alamanzar who was able to get her some soldier-for-hire work.

At last, work that allowed her to properly kill people! After all, simply breaking the occasional bone had no joy in it. To Varastaya, if the victim still lived, she hadn't been doing her job properly. Cries of pain and labored breathing just irritated her sensitive ears. When you killed someone, they quieted right down.

One job on Spilimbergo Secondina had put her on opposite sides from a Nietzschean named Tyr Anasazi. Seeing that Tyr was smarter than her employer and likely to remain alive longer, she switched sides. While Tyr's reaction was hardly one of gratitude— he never acknowledged the impact her defection had on the campaign, insisting that it changed nothing of consequence—he did offer her a place on his team.

Varastaya had always admired Nietzscheans. They did with genetic engineering what she herself had done with technology: make herself the best she could be. That was the only way to survive in this universe. *Well*, she thought with a smile, *that and to be a killer. Because if you're not, you'll get killed.*

As for Tyr, he rarely looked happy about anything, but he was noticeably devoid of that emotion when Varastaya reported back to him at the throne room in Amorin. Or, rather, what was once the throne room. The thrones themselves—formerly the seats of power for the now-exiled king and queen—were used as shelves for Minister Saamm and his toadies to store things. Not that Varastaya cared much one way or the other. Politics held no interest for her. As long as Saamm's credits cleared Tyr's bank account, Tyr gave her her share, and she got to kill things, she was content.

They had put a rug down over the royal crest that decorated the center of the floor and put a table on top of that. Tyr and Saamm were seated on opposite sides of that table, with Varastaya standing nearby.

"So you just left them there," Tyr said.

Shrugging, Varastaya said, "I didn't have a choice. We didn't have radios with us."

Saamm made a gurgling noise. "Why didn't you have radios?"

Varastaya looked down at the minister, whose forehead glistened with sweat. "Tyr told me to maintain strict radio silence no matter what. I thought the best way to do that was to not have radios at all."

"A very Alexandrian solution," Tyr said with a small smile. Varastaya had no idea what that meant. "That, however, doesn't answer the most critical question."

"Yes, why did you leave all those troops behind? We can't afford these kinds of losses!"

"Actually," Tyr said, turning to Saamm, "that's not the most critical question. We had been informed that the enemy forces were not strong enough to defend that station. The fact that they were—and were organized enough to rout our people despite the element of surprise—leads me to think that we are not engaging a disorganized, inferior force, as you led me to believe."

Smiling, Varastaya noticed that Saamm's heart rate skyrocketed, and the sweating got worse. "They *were* disorganized and inferior! I can't explain where they got the additional troops."

"It's not simply the troops, but the deployment of them. From what Varastaya described, they were ready for the attack and defended the station with the skill of professionals. That's the fourth such engagement in the last day where we have either lost or had a more difficult time of it than anticipated. Once can be overlooked, twice even can be forgiven. At this point, however, we have to assume that we are engaged with an enemy who will defeat us unless we change our tactics."

"Then change our tactics," Saamm said, as if it were that simple.

"Very well," Tyr said. "First, you should declare martial law. Then you must institute a draft."

Saamm snorted. "You're joking."

"The shift in tactics requires that we make more frontal assaults and engage in actions that will result in heavy casualties. Your precious MFA has suffered tremendous losses thanks to your incompetence prior to my arrival two months ago and more with the onset of this new infusion of talent your enemy seems to have gained in the past week." Tyr leaned forward, his own calm in direct inverse proportion to Saamm's growing nervousness. "You need more people to staff your armies or you will be overwhelmed."

"You don't understand—"

Tyr got up. "No, Minister, *you* don't understand." He started to pace around the room. "You hired me to win this planet for you. If you won't heed my advice, then I have to ask why you bothered to bring me here in the first place."

Saamm also got up, probably not wanting to look small next to the Nietzschean. Varastaya almost laughed. It was completely impossible not to look small next to Tyr. Even Brexos and Glasten, who were the same size, appeared tiny when in proximity to their leader. She wished she could have killed Saamm right then and there—but it was generally bad form to kill one's employers, at least before the job was finished.

"I cannot declare martial law!" Saamm said. "It goes against everything we fought for!"

"You speak in the past tense, Minister, as if your fight has ended. But it only just began when you removed Nwari and Hamsha from this room. Right now, you need soldiers, any way you can get them. You've already bankrupted your treasury bringing me here, so I doubt you have the resources to hire more ground troops. That leaves you with the sole option of a draft."

Saamm started to pace. "The whole point was to give the people say in how they are ruled." He stopped pacing and turned back to Tyr. "If I declare martial law, I become no better than Nwari and Hamsha. I will be forcing my will on the people!"

Tyr sat back down at the table. "If the people want a say in how they are ruled, Minister, then they should be willing to fight and die for that say. If they're not, they don't deserve it."

"What a charmingly Nietzschean sentiment," Saamm muttered.

"No, it's a realistic one. However, if it's a Nietzschean sentiment you want, let me give you this: do not trust *anyone*. It is obvious from what has happened that our intelligence network is compromised."

That's for damn sure, Varastaya thought. One of the things she liked about working with Tyr was that his intel was usually good. The disaster at the hut was out of character for one of his operations.

"You must be sure," Tyr continued, "to treat everyone and anyone as a potential enemy. If you do not, you will surely fail."

"I'll keep that in mind." Saamm's heart rate had not, Varastaya noted, gone down appreciably. "I will put your suggestions in motion, Anasazi. And may the creators have mercy on us."

As Saamm turned to leave the throne room, Tyr said, "One more thing, Minister. You *are* better than Nwari and Hamsha, and do you know why?"

Saamm shook his head.

"Because you're still here."

At that, Saamm snorted, and continued out of the room.

Once he was gone, Tyr added, "For now."

"But not for long," Varastaya added. "Are you sure we're on the right side of this one, Tyr?"

Tyr smiled. "There's only one side that matters, Varastaya. Go get yourself cleaned up, then find Brexos and report to the war room. We're going to need to do some guerrilla attack runs on the shipping lanes while we wait for the minister's draft to take effect."

Only when Tyr used the words "cleaned up" did Varastaya even register that there was blood, dirt, and bits of bone and muscle staining her shirt and pants. Her straight black hair had also come slightly undone.

"Fine," she said, hoping that the shipping lanes were well populated. After all, she had gotten to kill only seventeen people today.

She departed the throne room, replaying the part where she ripped off one soldier's head. That had been *such* fun. . . .

ELEVEN • CANOPY, 302 AFC

> Patience is a virtue, and I have never considered myself
> to be a virtuous person.
>
> —PROFESSOR KARISTOVA MARJ, RETIREMENT SPEECH,
> ALL SYSTEMS UNIVERSITY, CY 9112

"You expect me to eat *this?*"

The Reverend Behemiel Far-Traveller had always thought of himself as being a patient sort. However, Catherine Bolivar of Jaguar Pride was trying that patience rather severely.

"I do not expect anything," he said. "I simply provide the food. What you do with it is your own concern."

"I won't eat this. You probably spit in it."

"Were that the case, madam, it would be steaming and deadly."

"I have no empirical evidence to suggest that it isn't, Magog. Get out of my sight, you disgust me."

Rev bowed. "As you wish."

They were all staying in a hotel suite on Canopy next to the largest spaceport. Catherine had complained about the somewhat minimal accommodations on the *Eureka Maru* pretty much from the millisecond she came on board. The air was stale, she said; the ceilings low, she whined; the floors uncomfortable for her feet, she complained.

To their benefit, Archduke Bolivar had anticipated that his sister would not be enamored of spending all her time on the cargo ship, so in addition to providing Beka with enough money to pay off the debts they'd incurred and to repair the *Maru*, he also gave her sufficient funds to reserve this suite. It needed to be done in Beka's name, since the whole point of the exercise was to keep Catherine's presence with the *Maru* crew a secret from those who would try to kill her.

Before meeting her, Rev had assumed that to refer to members of the Jaguar's chief rival, the Sabra Pride. Now that he had spent time with the tall, sandy-haired, hazel-eyed woman with the porcelain skin and angular features made puffy by pregnancy, Rev had to increase that number to virtually anyone who'd met her. She set new standards for Nietzschean arrogance—which were already appallingly high—and had all the worst difficulties of pregnant mammals. The one benefit of the latter was that she at least slept a lot, though when she awoke she complained about whatever bed she had been in, whether the cot on the *Maru* or the aerogel bed in the hotel suite.

Human reproductive methods are so ridiculously taxing on the females, he thought. Not that he was in a position to judge, given that his own people reproduced by injecting larvae that hatched and fed off the host into living beings. It was a metaphor for how the Magog lived their lives: as near-mindless killing machines that fed off of other life forms. Even when Magog created life, they destroyed.

Rev himself came into the world that way as a Magog named Red Plague—but he was able to see past his own nature, and follow the True Way. Every day, he fought to instead to be Behemiel Far-Traveller—a being far greater than what Red Plague's instincts wanted him to be.

As he left Catherine to pout in her chamber, he found Beka entering the sitting room.

"Ah, Rev, you're here," she said. "I've got news."

"Good news, I hope."

"For a change, yeah," she said with a bright smile. It was that same smile that had drawn Rev to Beka in the first place.

It had been difficult for him, a Magog among "food," to find a place. True, he could have stayed among his fellow Wayists, who accepted him without question, but that, to his mind, defeated the point of his conversion. What better method of reminding the universe what the Divine could do than to have a Magog preaching the Way? He could not do that from the safety of a monastery. True, a Magog founded the faith, but people had a very easy time forgetting that.

However, finding a place to do so in the universe proved a challenge. Few could see past the horns, the teeth, the fur. But Captain Beka Valentine had proven to be one such. She needed someone to help her run her cargo ship—"and," she had said at the time, "to knock my moral compass back into whack."

"Do you truly wish to have a Magog among your crew?" he had asked her then.

"The way I see it," she had said, "if you wanted to eat me, you'd've done it by now. As for what I wish—" There, again, she had smiled, a gesture that seemed to light up the entire flight deck. "We don't usually get what we wish for, we just get what we get. So I may as well take it. Besides, I've done worse."

It was a refreshingly Wayist attitude for a nonbeliever. Wayist orthodoxy stated that everyone was a Wayist, and a monk's job was to simply reveal it. In truth Rev didn't believe that about everyone. He did about Beka, however. Like Rev, Beka became more than what she was. And Rev knew in his soul that she could be something even greater still.

So, despite the fact that her moral compass needed whacking more often than Rev was always comfortable with, he stuck by her. He had yet to have cause to regret the decision.

"What are these felicitous tidings?" he asked Beka now in the hotel suite.

Beka walked over to the table and set down a large bag. "The ship will be fixed up and ready to go by morning—and we have a job. And, you'll be happy to know, it's a legitimate one. There's a Than company that needs some cargo run from here back home to San-Ska-Re over the course of the next couple of weeks. Not the most exciting work in the Known Worlds, but it's a paycheck, and it's low-profile." She smirked as she removed some manner of food from the bag. "That'll keep her royal heinie happy, I'm sure."

Rev tried not to wince as he watched Beka eat. The one concession that Behemiel needed to make to Red Plague was biological necessity—a Magog could only consume live food. He kept a supply of animals for that purpose, but it made the food of other species to be unpalatable at best. "An impossible task, that. While I would never consider taking another life, when around her I can comprehend the instinct to do so."

Beka laughed and took a bite of her lunch. "Either way, we should be able to build the bank account to something tolerable and keep Catherine safe from the ravening hordes of Sabra Pride."

"That would be ideal." Rev hesitated. "I must confess that I still have some trepidation about this arrangement with the Jaguar Pride—but I cannot deny that things are going smoothly so far."

Sighing, Beka said, "That's usually when things go wrong, isn't it?"

"Sometimes. However, other times, the Divine provides us with a respite."

"Believe me, Rev, I could use one of those. Any pull you might have to provide us one? Now's the time."

"I will do what I can," Rev said, returning the smile.

The door to the sitting room opened, and two large Nietzscheans entered—Sacco and Vanzetti, the two bodyguards who had accompanied Catherine. Twin brothers who apparently always worked together, both men had the same icy blue eyes, aquiline nose, near-lipless mouths, and brown goates. However, they could be easily distinguished by their hair: Sacco's was shoulder-length, as brown as his facial hair, and tied back in a ponytail; Vanzetti's was short, spiked, and bleached platinum blond.

"How is she?" Sacco asked without preamble.

Rev smiled. "Irritable."

The smile was not returned by Vanzetti as he asked, "Has she eaten?"

"I provided her with food. What she does with it is out of my meager control, I am afraid."

Sacco smiled, but not in amusement. "Funny, I thought you Magog were expert at forcing people to do your bidding."

"You think incorrectly. But that is hardly surprising."

Vanzetti moved closer to Rev. "Are you insulting me, Magog?"

"If you have to ask—"

"That's enough!" Beka said. "Do you two have actual business here?"

"It's *our* hotel room, kludge," Sacco said disdainfully.

Beka stood up. The Nietzscheans were both much taller than she, but she did not let that keep her from looking right at Sacco. "I reply to only one thing from the likes of you, pal: Captain Valentine. And this is *my* room, not yours."

"Our boss paid for it, kludge. And you'd best mind your manners." Sacco's hand, Rev noticed, went to his sidearm.

"No, you mind yours. You want to stay on my ship—and in my hotel room—you follow my rules."

Vanzetti sneered. "And what if we don't?"

Beka shrugged. "Then you and Archduchess Bitch Queen from Hell can sit out on the street for all I care."

"You wouldn't dare," Sacco said, though he didn't sound convinced of his own words.

When Beka smiled this time, it wasn't the bright one, but rather a much smaller one that was considerably more unpleasant—more like a Magog smile, Rev thought mischieviously. "Only one way to find out, über."

Sacco started to go for his weapon, but Vanzetti put a hand on his partner's arm. "She ain't worth it. Let's just go check on Catherine, all right?"

Though his hand left his weapon, Sacco continued to stare daggers at Beka. For her part, Beka seemed totally unintimidated. "Watch yourself—'Captain' Valentine."

"I'll try to make time in my schedule to be scared later next week, okay?" Beka asked sweetly.

Again, Sacco started to react. Again, Vanzetti held him back. "C'mon," the latter said, and they both retreated to Catherine's room.

As soon as the door closed behind them, Beka let out a long breath and collapsed back into her chair. "Damn."

"Well handled."

"Yeah, right. Well handled. Sure. Now if I can just get my heart restarted."

Rev smiled. "With Nietzscheans, it is better to give a show of strength. If you appear weak to them, they will only exploit your vulnerability."

"Yeah, by shooting you. And if you show strength, they see you as a threat, and they shoot you. Kind of a lose-lose situation, don't you think?"

"Perhaps."

Beka grabbed her lunch, then put it right back down. "Damn. That pretty much killed my appetite." She got up. "I'm gonna go check out the first cargo run—wanna come with me? It's gotta be better than sticking around with Tweedle-dum and Tweedle-dumber."

With a short laugh, Rev said, "Perhaps, but I thought we had agreed that it would be prudent if one of us remained near Catherine at all times."

"Yeah, you're right. Well, you do prudent better than the rest of us. I'll catch you later."

Rev watched her go, then went over to the couch, where he had left his copy of Gershom Scholem's *Kabbalah*. Just as he sat down, a muffled voice from the rear of the suite cried, "Get this swill away from me! I want *proper* food! And my ankles hurt!"

Setting down Professor Scholem's text, Rev closed his eyes and muttered a prayer to the Divine.

Beka approached the diamond-shaped door and entered the codes provided by Sunrise Over Hills, their new employer. This would gain her ingress to the bay that was holding the cargo until the *Maru* got fixed. She had returned to check on it again, partly in order to get out of the hotel room, but mainly because the code-lock system was about thirty years old. A blind Nightsider could crack its code, so she lived in fear of the cargo going missing. *And wouldn't it just be in character for the Thans to blame me for "losing" their stuff when it's their own fault?*

The door obligingly slid open after she'd input the code, a hiss accompanying the air escaping the sealed room. *So far, so good.*

As soon as the door closed behind her, Beka frowned. *I could've sworn I saw something. . . .*

"Do you work here?"

Beka whirled around to see a young woman suddenly standing behind her. She had blond hair and a bright smile. Wearing a fairly simple two-piece outfit, the woman also had pointed ears and, Beka noted after a moment, a tail that curled around her left leg.

All of that, however, was secondary to the woman's skintone, which was purple.

In all the years she had travelled through the galaxies, which was pretty much since birth, Beka had seen many different types of life in assorted shapes, sizes, colors, textures, and attitudes. This was, however, the first time she'd come across a biped with purple skin and a tail. *Come to think of it, I've never seen either one, much less the two in combination. Either she's a human with way more genetic modifications than the usual, or she's a species I've managed to miss.* "Who are you?"

The woman took this as a cue to set her motormouth on full. In a rapid-fire barrage of words spoken in a very high, syrupy voice, she said, "I'm sorry I'm lost I'm trying to find this plant store that someone told me had some really nice orchids and I got turned around and then I wound up in here and the door closed and I couldn't get out and please don't hurt me okay?"

"I won't hurt you." In truth the jury was still out on that one, but Beka thought it better to be reassuring. "And you haven't answered my question."

"Oh. I'm Trance. Sorry. Can you get me out of here?"

Beka wanted desperately to be angry with this strange woman who had broken into her cargo hold, but found her to be so— well, innocent sounding that she couldn't maintain her anger.

That, in turn, made her more cautious. "Why are you here?"

"I told you, I got lost. I don't even know what's in those boxes. I want to get out of here, please?"

Now she was pouting. *I don't believe this.* Beka raised her arms and made as if to force this Trance person to stay immobile. "All right, look. Just stand here, okay? Don't move. Let me check my cargo and I'll figure out what to do with you."

"Okay."

Nodding, Beka turned around and moved toward the largest of the boxes. This one had the marberries.

"Uh, one thing, though?"

She stopped and, without turning around, said, "Yes?"

"I'd be careful of that really big box over there?" Trance sounded hesitant. "I think there's something kinda wrong with it."

"Thank you." Beka tried to sound vaguely sincere, and wasn't sure how well she succeeded. Nor, frankly, did she much care. Instead, she walked over to the box. She had been about to enter the code when she decided to inspect the codepad more closely.

Then she noticed the wire.

Quickly, she put her hands behind her back and leaned in more closely so she could examine the codepad visually but not allow herself to even come close to touching it.

Two years ago, she never would have realized that the stray copper wire was part of a sloppily placed impact explosive, but having Fred Vexpag in her crew had proven educational in many ways.

The explosive hadn't been there when Sunrise had taken her to check the cargo this morning. She turned to the only thing about the cargo hold besides that that was different now. "How'd you know what was there, Trance?"

"Why, what is it?"

"Will you please just answer my question?"

Trance started squirming a little. "I don't know, I just—knew something was wrong. Does that make sense?"

No, not at all. "Well, thanks—I guess. Maybe. How did you get in here again?"

"I told you, I was trying to find the plant store, and I got lost, but then I found this room, and the guy who told me about the plant store said it had a diamond door, so I walked in—"

"How did you walk in? The door was locked."

Trance squirmed some more, but, Beka noticed, her feet didn't budge. Her tail, however, started to curl upward. "Uhm—no, it wasn't. The door was wide open, honest, I swear. Really." Her eyes seemed to grow wider even as the rest of her face contracted. "Please don't hurt me."

It's like talking to a puppy. "I'm not going to hurt you." *At least not yet.* "But I need you to tell me exactly what happened."

"Like I said, I walked up to the door, 'cause I thought it was the plant store but when I came in the door closed behind me and I realized it *wasn't* the plant store and are you sure you're not gonna hurt me?"

"Positive."

"Well, I didn't know what to do after the door closed, 'cause I couldn't get it back open again. So I started looking at the boxes. That one," she pointed at the marberry box, "didn't really look right."

Beka sighed. She couldn't put her finger on why, but she instinctively believed this Trance person. If nothing else, if someone wanted to sabotage the marberry shipment, they wouldn't then draw attention to it. Now they had reason to be cautious.

She checked the other boxes, and saw that some of them also had the looks of tampering. Turning to the purple woman, she said, "I'm going to contact the owner of this cargo, and I want you to tell him everything you told me, all right?"

"Uh, okay. Just one thing?"

"What?"

"Any chance someone can tell me where the plant store is?"

Unable to suppress a smile, Beka said, "We'll see."

Fred Vexpag tried not to growl. He *hated* shopping.

"None of these will do." Catherine Bolivar had expressed that sentiment early and often on this little expedition, presently being applied to about a dozen pairs of shoes. Her ankles having swollen with pregnancy, Catherine had decided that she needed new footwear, in addition to the half-a-dozen other items she insisted on searching for.

It had all started for Fred when he returned to the hotel room, having sent off a gift to Stella. Rev informed him that Catherine wished to go shopping in the drift, but refused to be accompanied by "a smelly Magog." Compared to the average Magog, Rev smelled like a field of orchids, but it wasn't like Catherine was going to be dissuaded. They had all agreed that some member of the *Maru* crew be near the Nietzschean hellspawn at all times, as nobody trusted the bodyguards, and since Beka was checking on the cargo and the twerp was off somewhere, probably getting them all in trouble again, that left Fred—who had been looking forward to a nice nap.

"I want something *nice*," Catherine informed the Umbrite shoe merchant. "There is no dictionary on any planet that would put an image of a single one of these appalling monstrosities next to a definintion of that word. Kindly remove them from my sight and replace them with something that has at least a modicum of aesthetic value."

Fred looked over at Sacco—Vanzetti had remained in the hotel room, under orders to make sure that a full three-course meal would greet Catherine's return—whose face was twisted in a long-suffering grimace. He decided to break his habit of never talking to a Nietzschean—a habit that had begun after a Nietzschean cheated him out of a million thrones back on Enkindu—and ask the bodyguard, "She always like this?"

"No." Sacco grinned. "She's usually worse. But the pregnancy has slowed her down a bit."

"Sorry to hear that."

Sacco folded his arms. "She's from good stock. Her sons will be strong, her daughters will be powerful."

The Nietzschean answer to everything, Fred thought. "So how'd you get stuck with watchin' her back?"

Whatever friendliness might have crept into Sacco's demeanor fell away. "What do you care, kludge?"

Fred shrugged. "Talkin' to you helps drown her out."

At that, Sacco laughed. "Nothing drowns her out, I'm afraid. It's been tried."

"Yeah, I guess." The plastic of the toothpick Fred had in his mouth started getting uncomfortably soft. Fred spit it out and pulled another one out of his pocket.

As he did so, something caught his eye at the doorway to the shoe merchant's. Something seemed odd about the doorjamb. The seams of the individual parts that made up the frame didn't match up. They shouldn't have been so uneven.

He walked over to the door to get a better look.

"What is it?" Sacco asked, following.

"Not sure. Prob'ly nothing." Even as Fred said it, he didn't believe it. He knew *something* was wrong here, he just needed to figure out what. He peered more closely at the doorjamb, moving the toothpick from side to side in his mouth.

"Hey Vexpag!"

Fred looked up to see Beka walking toward the store, alongside a woman who looked like she'd been dipped in a vat of grapes. "Hi, Bek. Who's your friend?"

"Fred Vexpag, Trance Gemini. Trance here stumbled onto a little bit of sabotage of our cargo."

"Aw, hell, what happened this time?" The last thing they needed was another job going south. Fred was seriously starting to question the efficacy of remaining on the *Maru*, given how everything they did seemed to go wrong.

Then again, other opportunities hadn't exactly been lining up to take him on, either—at least not ones with as talented a crew as Beka had put together. The *Maru* ran more tightly than most, and, with Fred's demolition skills, Rev's negotiating talents, Beka's amazing Slip piloting, and—much as he hated to admit it—the twerp's mechanical acumen, the likelihood of living a long, happy life and eventually retiring to Fuchal with Stella was greatly increased.

Still, it'd be nice if something went right just once.

"In the end, nothing," Beka said, prompting relief in Fred. "Someone had busted in and started wiring the boxes to blow up on opening. Trance stumbled into the cargo bay by mistake—the saboteur had left the door open—and scared him off."

"I didn't even *see* him!" The purple woman had a high squeaky voice that set Fred's teeth on edge. "But he left and the door closed, and I was stuck until Captain Valentine saved me."

Beka smiled. "She saved us too."

"Any idea who planted it?" Fred asked.

Shrugging, Beka said, "Sunrise figured it was his chief competitor. Point is, it didn't work, and I never would've noticed it if it hadn't been for Trance here. So I thought I'd take her shopping. What brings you here?"

Fred turned around and pointed to the inside of the merchant's. At Beka's approach, Sacco had gone back inside to keep an eye on Catherine, whose complaints had increased in volume, making Fred grateful he'd put more distance between himself and the woman.

Just as he was about to explain Catherine's sudden desire for a shopping trip coinciding with Fred's return to the hotel room, he caught a whiff of *gleves* oil—the primary component of a particularly popular Nietzschean detonator.

The smell was coming from the very doorjamb he had come over to inspect. The detonation process involved the oil burning, and Nietzscheans also liked to use shaped plastic for their explosives that could be disguised as ordinary objects—*like*, he thought, *part of a doorjamb*.

Leaping right at Beka and the purple woman, Fred cried, "Get *down!*"

The explosion followed half a second later.

Immediately, Fred realized that the explosion was only the beginning. The yield was far too low to be good for anything but a distraction. He struggled to untangle himself from his captain and her new friend and unholster the pistol from his boot.

He saw a small crescent-shaped hole in the wall of the entryway to the shoe merchant, smoke issuing forth from it. Through the smoke, he spied two Nietzscheans running toward Catherine. One of them shot Sacco, the other shot the shoe merchant; both went down immediately. Fred took aim at one and fired.

To Fred's initial surprise, the Nietzschean actually reacted to the shot and was able to dodge it in part—meaning that it only took the man's ear off instead of his entire head. *This one obviously got bred for damn fast reflexes*, Fred thought with annoyance.

Putting a hand up in what was to Fred a vain attempt to stanch the bleeding from the hole where his right ear used to be, the Nietzschean turned and fired back, but Fred had taken up refuge behind a kiosk. Said kiosk proceeded to get shot at.

Fred spared a glance behind him to see that Beka and her friend had taken cover. Beka must not have been armed, otherwise Fred assumed she'd be in the thick of things. *She said she came from the cargo bay—Canopy security doesn't let weapons in there.* At least, that was the theory. The presence of explosives in their cargo pointed to a hole or six in that security. . . .

Putting it in the back of his mind, Fred took a few more shots in the general direction of the Nietzscheans, but without breaking cover.

"Get your hands *off* of me!" whined a familiar voice. Fred saw the other Nietzschean dragging Catherine Bolivar toward the exit. Earless's covering fire prevented Fred from interfering—not that he had any interest in engaging a Nietzschean hand-to-hand. Fred's idea of a fair fight positioned him very far away from the action, holding a detonator or a rifle. Shooting was out of the question, as the Nietzschean had wisely put Catherine between him and Fred, and Catherine's pregnant self was far too big a target for Fred to avoid.

Earless's shots continued to pound on the kiosk, which wasn't going to be long for the world. But then Fred noticed that the angle of the shots started to change—Earless was moving toward the entrance, following his partner, no doubt. That meant he was going to be in Fred's sights in a second—assuming the kiosk didn't shatter first . . .

"Ooof!"

That came from behind Fred, followed by something that sure sounded like the impact of a person onto the floor. Fred refused to visually confirm this, focused as he was on being ready to do a proper job of taking Earless's head off as soon as he came into sight.

"I'm sorry! Are you okay?" That was the purple woman.

The shooting stopped.

Not wanting to look a gift horse in the mouth, Fred stood up, took a microsecond to take aim, and fired at Earless, who now stood only a meter in front of Fred.

Another second later, Earless became Headless.

As the Nietzschean's decapitated corpse fell to the floor, Fred turned to see the purple woman and Beka standing over the other Nietzschean. Catherine was off to the side, holding herself up against the doorjamb—the one opposite the side that had been blown off by the explosive.

Beka, Fred noted, had the Nietzschean's own gun trained on him.

"I'm so sorry, Mr. Nietzschean!" the purple woman was saying. "That was a complete accident, I didn't mean to trip you like that."

"Yeah?" Fred said. "How *did* you mean to trip 'im, then?" Fred wasn't sure what he found more ridiculous, that the woman had managed to use that tail of hers to trip up the Nietzschean or that she was actually apologizing for it.

"My lady, are you all right?"

That was Sacco, who struggled to get to his feet, using his left hand to cover a bloody patch on his left shoulder. *Well, he's damn lucky*, Fred thought. It looked like the shot only missed the body-guard's heart by a few centimeters. The gesture looked awkward, but the Nietzschean was obviously right-handed, as that hand held his pistol.

"No, I'm not all right, you incredible buffoon! This is absolutely outrageous! The whole purpose of this idiotic exercise was to keep me *safe*! Now I'm having kidnapping attempts made on me in *public*!"

Sacco walked forward. "The Sabra Pride must have received word that you were here, m'lady."

"Not necessarily," Beka said. "Please to note the logo on the holster of the gun I'm aiming at Dumbo's head here."

"What are you blathering about, kludge?" Catherine asked snippily.

Fred, however, peered at the holster. "That ain't the Sabra crest."

"No, it belongs to Mandau Pride," Sacco said. He pointed his own weapon at the fallen Nietzschean. "What brings you here, Mandau?"

The would-be kidnapper—who had, up until this point, been staring daggers at the purple woman—turned to Sacco and smiled. "Do you honestly think I'll tell *you*?"

"No." Sacco then shot him twice in the chest.

"What the hell did you do *that* for?" Beka cried. "We could've questioned him."

Sacco shrugged. "I suppose we could have, but such an action would not have produced answers. He would be impervious to torture, and every minute he remained alive would be another minute in which he would attempt to escape and inform his superiors of how he failed. That's a security risk that we cannot take."

Typical Nietzschean, Fred thought.

"Take me back to my room *now*," Catherine said just as Beka was about to reply.

"We still need to—" Beka started.

Catherine turned eyes of fire on Beka. "We need to do what I *say* we need to do, kludge, and don't you *dare* to forget that! Sacco, take me back to my room *now*!"

Under other circumstances, Fred would have pointed out that Sacco needed medical attention, but if the bodyguard wasn't going to be concerned for his own welfare, why the hell should Fred give a damn?

"Great." Beka lowered the gun as Sacco and Catherine walked toward the car service port. "Let's get out of here. Security'll be here any minute, and I'd just as soon *not* explain the three corpses."

Fred removed his toothpick, which had long since gone soft, but did not leave it behind, instead shoving it into a pocket. "Fine by me." *No sense in leaving evidence lying around.*

"I'm *really* sorry, Captain Valentine," the purple woman said.

Shaking her head, Beka said, "It's all right, Trance. You probably saved the day."

Trance blinked. Then her eyes went wide. "Really? Wow! I don't think I've ever done that before."

"First time for everythin'," Fred muttered.

"Wow."

They started to walk in the opposite direction as Catherine and Sacco—while Catherine, of course, could hire an aircar to take her back to the hotel, Beka and Fred's more limited means required taking the monorail, which was on the northern end of the shopping center.

Then Trance spoke up again. "Hey, is there time for me to go to the plant store?"

TWELVE • MALANI'S HAVEN, 303 AFC

> Those who do not learn from history are doomed to
> repeat it. Those who do learn from history are
> doomed to make new mistakes. And those who only
> learn selected lessons from history are doomed to do
> both.
>
> —PROFESSOR SAAMM, ROYAL UNIVERSITY,
> MALANI'S HAVEN, 288 AFC

The city of Amorin burned.

Saamm, former leader of the Liberators, current minister of Malani's Haven, stared out the window of the throne room watching everything he'd worked for literally go up in flames, and he wondered where, precisely, it had all gone wrong.

It had all seemed so sensible at first. A teacher of history at the Royal University, he knew that the hereditary monarchy was corrupt at its heart. You couldn't put absolute power in the hands of two people and expect their offspring to be automatically qualified for the job. Sooner or later, the law of averages would catch up—as it did with Nwari and Hamsha. Bisime, at least, made up for his shortcomings by being popular with the people, allowing him to put his repressive policies into practice without complaint. His son and daughter-in-law, however, had none of his charm, with the added detriment of worse policies.

The time was ripe for revolution.

In the distance, he saw the structures of the university among those currently aflame. That probably saddened him most of all, for it had all begun there. He had spoken to his students, telling them of the mistakes of the past, from the fall of the Roman Empire on Old Earth five millennia ago to the fall of the Systems Commonwealth three centuries ago, and how relevant the events were to their lives on Malani's Haven now. They had listened, learned, even responded. Not all of them, of course, but enough of them.

Unfortunately, others responded as well. Saamm soon lost his post at the university—his punishment for daring to speak out against the rightful monarchs. If anything, it strengthened his resolve. With the help of his former students, he organized the Liberators. He gathered followers, led rallies, made speeches. It had been slow going at first, but the death of the popular King Bisime and the subsequent disaster that life under King Nwari and Queen Hamsha quickly became made an excellent recruitment incentive.

Best of all, Saamm had been able to get a good chunk of the military on his side—aided by the military's own tactical blunder in cutting the salaries of the rank-and-file. Taking revenge against those who had removed food from your mouth proved a powerful lure. Saamm had spent his life teaching the history of dozens of worlds, and he knew that oppressive regimes like that on Malani's Haven relied primarily on the military. The Roman army's support allowed Claudius to rise to the position of emperor after Caligula's assassination, preventing the Senate from finally making Rome the republic it should have been with the madman's death. The Nietzscheans had undermined the High Guard from within when they took up arms against the Commonwealth at Hephaistos, and without the High Guard, the Commonwealth was not long for the universe. Saamm had been determined not to make the same mistake as either the Roman Senate or the High Guard.

Now he wondered how long the Senate would truly have been able to govern Rome, even if they had the military on their side. And he wondered if the Long Night would have happened if the Vedrans had remained instead of disappearing so completely—in much the same way Nwari and Hamsha had done.

Have I brought a new Long Night to Malani's Haven?

He thought about martial law, about a mandatory draft, about imposing a curfew in the cities, and that gave him his answer.

The draft had seemed like a workable idea, but many refused to be taken—others wound up fighting for the other side, supporting the aristocrats and the generals. The very people who had been helping the monarchs keep the people down were now being aided in their attempt to restore the old regime by the very people it had oppressed.

Tyr had told Saamm to put down the rallies and speeches that had started springing up, but the minister found that he could not. How could he justify disallowing the very type of rebellion that put him into power?

Ingrates, he thought with a sudden burst of anger, his hands clenching into fists. *I did all this for them, and this is how they repay me?*

Then he relaxed, his hands opening back up. *No. I can hardly blame them for my own shortcomings. I started this, and I will accept full responsibility.*

Now the armies lay siege to the palace. He simply did not have the troops to defend the city, even with Tyr's help. Saamm wondered how much worse it all would have been without the organizational skills of the Nietzschean and his mercenaries. They had taken charge of the MFA, giving them crash courses in tactics, taking them on campaigns. Sadly, they were only able to delay the inevitable. When the enemy suffered losses, those numbers were replaced. When Saamm's people died, there didn't seem to be any replacements available. It wasn't fair.

As he stood watching the city of his birth going up in flames, he wondered if Nwari and Hamsha had the same feeling of despair in the pit of their stomachs months ago when Saamm himself led his people to the palace.

Saamm, however, would not run. Honorius abandoned Rome to the Visigoths. The Vedrans abandoned the Commonwealth to the Nietzscheans and the Magog. Nwari and Hamsha abandoned Malani's Haven to Saamm's own Liberators. Saamm would not do the same.

Instead, he turned to Tyr Anasazi, who had just entered. "You said you would be able to defend the city."

"I would have been able to defend the city against the rabble or against the enemy army. However, the army has enlisted the rabble and has rather outnumbered us. Someone has brought them together."

"I *know* that!" Saamm sighed. "It wasn't supposed to be like this."

Tyr's pitiless brown eyes stared down at him. "And what precisely did you think it was going to 'be like,' Minister? Adulation from the masses? Gratitude? They're sheep who had been given a barely adequate shepherd who fed them dead grass. You promised them something better only to give them the same barren fields they grazed before."

Saamm threw up his hands. "What was I supposed to do? I gave them the freedom they said they wanted!"

Shaking his head, Tyr said, "You pitiful fool. The rule of men is not a right that is granted, it is a privilege that must be earned and vigilantly maintained. If you don't have the stomach for it, you should never have fought for it in the first place."

The minister opened his mouth to argue, but the words burned to ashes in his mouth. *What is the point?*

Several of Saamm's troops burst in, alongside two of Tyr's mercenaries—the Nightsider named Gerenmar and the augmented human woman Varastaya.

"We can't hold them back any further," Gerenmar said.

Varastaya added, "I took down about twenty of 'em, but they've got three garrisons coming in—we just don't have the damn numbers."

"I'm sorry, Tyr," Gerenmar said, "we tried to hold the line. . . ."

"Don't concern yourself." Tyr sounded remarkably calm.

"We can take that tunnel you guys used before." Varastaya started moving toward the rear of the throne room. "They probably don't know about it. We can regroup."

Both Tyr and Saamm said "No" simultaneously. Saamm then turned to look at Tyr in surprise—a look shared by the two mercenaries.

"What do you mean, no?" the Nightsider said. "We're not gonna surrender, are we?"

"We will stand our ground," said Tyr.

Before Saamm could respond, the door to the throne room opened once again. A tall man with a smooth head, a thick beard, and dressed in the black field uniform of the Royal Army of Malani's Haven entered. Saamm placed the face after a moment as General Isembi. Behind him were a dozen troops, all with weapons drawn.

Holding up a hand, Saamm said, "There is no need for further violence! General, I am willing to discuss terms with you."

Isembi smiled a most unpleasant smile. His teeth were crooked and only served to make the general look demonic. "Are these terms of your surrender, Minister?"

"They are terms that will bring an end to this conflict. I have always wanted what is best for the people of Malani's Haven. It has become painfully obvious that the Liberators have not provided that."

Tyr snorted. "And that, Minister, is why you lost. What is good for the people is very rarely what is good for the government."

"Such a system *can* work, sir. The Commonwealth is perhaps the best example of that."

"Yes, but it too fell."

Isembi continued to smile. "Your mistake was in assuming that all are equal. It is true that all are created equal, but that status quo does not remain for long. You mistook the students whose minds you corrupted at that university of yours as being representative of the people of Malani's Haven. What they were, truly, were the elite. All your rebellion did was pit one group of elite against another."

"As I told you," Tyr added, "the rabble are sheep. They will go to whatever pasture is greener."

Saamm lowered his head. "So we go from monarchy to democracy to military dictatorship, is that it, General? I wonder how the people will find that pasture."

"That," Tyr said, "is where you are mistaken, Minister." Reaching into a pouch on his belt, Tyr removed a communications device of some sort and spoke into it. "The throne room is secure."

Confused, Saamm asked, "Who are you talking to?"

"Yeah," Varastaya said. "Tyr, what the hell's going on? I thought—"

"You're not paid to think," Tyr snapped at the woman. Turning to Saamm, he added, "And you're in no position to ask me anything."

Two more troops came in and reported to Isembi that the entire castle was secure and that the ship carrying something called "A1" had landed on the roof.

The Nightsider walked up to Tyr. "I just want to know one thing, Anasazi—is this sudden folding of ours going to have any impact on whether or not I get paid?"

Tyr didn't even look at Gerenmar. "Have I ever given you reason to doubt that I would pay you in full at the conclusion of a job, Gerenmar?"

Gerenmar seemed reluctant to answer. "No."

"Then don't assume I'll start now."

Saamm found himself more confused than ever. He had hoped to end this without violence, and in that, at least, he had been successful. He would not take the route of his predecessors—he would not kill himself as Orkani had, nor run away like Nwari and

Hamsha. If there was to be a trial, he would face it; if he was to be summarily executed, he would face that. The worst failures of history were those who did not accept responsibility for their actions. Saamm had always admired Albert Speer. He was a high-ranking member of an oppressive regime on Old Earth that had been responsible for the extermination of twelve million humans. When that regime was overthrown and its surviving proponents put on trial, Speer was the only one of the dozen or so defendants who accepted blame and responsibility for the atrocities committed. *If history had more people like Speer who took responsibility for their actions, the galaxies would be a better place. . . .*

"Welcome to Malani's Haven, Field Marshal Augustus," Tyr said.

At that, Saamm looked up—and his jaw fell open. Striding purposefully into the room was a Nietzschean dressed in white armor—

—followed by King Nwari and Queen Hamsha!

Tyr continued. "The palace has been retaken, as promised."

Saamm's mind was a whirlwind of confusion and anguish. "How—what is—I don't—" He couldn't make his mouth finish a sentence.

Nwari walked forward into the room, looking more confident than Saamm could ever remember seeing him. He stepped with a swagger he'd never had before. "You have done well, Tyr Anasazi," he said in a deep, rich voice. He turned to Saamm. "Your time as a usurper is over. You will be remanded to the Royal Dungeon until such time as our Nietzschean masters decide what to do with you."

All this was too much for Saamm to process. "What has happened here?!" he screamed.

The Nietzschean field marshal stepped forward and smiled. "The close of an era. For centuries, Malani's Haven has resisted the Ursa Pride's attempts to subjugate it. Today, that resistance has come to a close."

Saamm reeled. He looked at Tyr, standing there, looking so very placid and unconcerned. *Of course he does, he's just doing what he was supposed to do.* "You betrayed us."

He shrugged—shrugged! "Your interpretation. Keep in mind, Minister, that I did warn you."

"How's that, exactly?"

"I told you not to trust *anyone*. You chose not to heed that advice by continuing to trust me."

"I—" Saamm cut off his objection when he realized, to his devastation, that Tyr was correct. The minister had followed every bit of advice the Nietzschean had proffered without once questioning it or not trusting it. Going over the events of the past few months in his head, he realized that Tyr's instructions had all been designed to make Saamm's own position—especially vis-à-vis the people of Malani's Haven—worse.

Tyr had one final blow. "When I said you were superior to the king and queen—I was obviously mistaken. They, at least, knew enough to retreat and solidify their position. You, on the other hand, trudged headlong into the abyss."

Looking around the room, Saamm saw the faces of his foes— the king and queen, the troops, the general, the two Nietzscheans, the mercenaries—yet none of them truly deserved blame—or credit, depending on how one looked at it, since history was, as he well knew, written by the winners—for what had happened this day. It was Saamm's alone. His arrogance that led him to think that he could make Malani's Haven a better place. His stupidity that prevented him from seeing Tyr Anasazi's treachery.

He looked at King Nwari. "I assume the responsibility and

thus the guilt for everything that was perpetrated since your over-throw, Your Highness. Not the individual mistakes, grave as they may be, but my having acted in the leadership. I will accept whatever punishment you deem fit."

"That is not for me to decide," Nwari said.

Saamm looked over at the field marshal in his white armor. "Indeed. Then it seems we have both been reduced to being dupes of the Nietzscheans, haven't we?"

Nwari looked surprisingly sober as he whispered, "So it would seem."

For his part, the field marshal looked at Tyr. "If you will have one of your people escort the minister to the dungeon the king mentioned, we can get on with the business of preparing this planet for its entry into the Ursan Empire."

"Of course." Tyr shot a look at Varastaya.

"We'll have to start," the field marshal said as the cyborg woman grabbed Saamm by the arm, "by getting those fires under control. I don't fancy the idea of the capital city being razed."

Varastaya almost yanked Saamm's arm out of its socket as she led him out. "C'mon," she said. "And don't give me an excuse."

Unsure as to what she didn't want an excuse for, Saamm simply went along with her. He had been numbed in any case.

He wondered if death would hurt as much as he feared it would.

The Aronberg Company accepts no liability for suits not checked prior to usage.

— TAG ON ALL EXTRAVEHICULAR SUITS
MANUFACTURED BY THE ARONBERG COMPANY

I'm going to kill her, Beka thought for the four-hundredth time in the past week as she transited back into normal space.

The *Eureka Maru* had completed two cargo runs, both of which had gone smoothly and without incident. No one else attempted to blow up the cargo—Sunrise Over Hills had hinted that proper retribution had been taken and Beka needn't concern herself with it—and they had delivered the cargo to San-Ska-Re on time and intact. Indeed, the fact that it arrived in that state of affairs had impressed the Than no end. Rev had told Beka that he overheard one of them saying that they factored in losses due to damage and/or theft as a matter of course. This third trip would put them halfway through the two-week, six-run contract.

However, back on Canopy, things had gotten tense. Beka, Sacco, and Vanzetti agreed that Catherine should stay in the hotel suite—a rare case of a united front between kludge and über, which proved handy when Catherine balked at the idea. However, even she had to admit that she was less of a target if she stayed in an easily defended hotel suite than out in public. To play it safe, however, they switched suites, and gave the hotel manager enough of a kickback to keep that switch quiet.

Unfortunately, while Beka had taken her second run, leaving Vexpag behind to help the two Nietzscheans keep an eye on Catherine, another attempt had been made. This time, the culprits were the expected Sabra Pride. As with the attack in the shoe merchant's, the perpetrators were killed, though, according to Vexpag, this time it was in the line of fire in both cases.

For this third run, Beka had decided that the safest place was the *Maru*. Whoever was after Catherine—a number that appeared to include half the Prides in the Known Worlds—knew they were on Canopy, so the sensible thing was to get her off-planet, and fast. However, Beka wasn't about to give up a lucrative contract, either.

"What kind of Slipstream engines do you *have* in this thing? I've been on *boats* that have smoother rides than this rattletrap."

Here we go again. The run from Canopy to San-Ska-Re took three Slips, taking them through Glastonbury's Retreat and to Herakles Sector. Catherine had spent the entire time in Glastonbury complaining about the state of the *Maru*'s engines, and now that they'd arrived in Herakles, she picked up where she left off. "If you don't like it, lady, walk. I've saved your ass twice already, so—"

"My *bodyguards* have saved my life, kludge. Not surprising, as that's their *job*. You, on the other hand—"

"*Uh, Boss?*"

Never more grateful for an interruption from Harper, Beka tapped the intercom. "What is it, Harper?"

"*I'm pickin' up a signal.*"

"Where?"

"*I'm tryin' to track it now, but—I think it's comin' from the flight deck.*"

Engaging the autopilot and slipping her chair into standby mode, Beka got up and regarded the rest of the flight deck. Rev and Vexpag were at their stations, with Catherine and Vanzetti standing between them. Sacco was back in his quarters, still recuperating from his wounds.

Harper then came up from the engine room holding some kind of hand-scanner of his own design. "It's definitely in here somewhere, Boss. In faaaaaaaact—" he peered at the reading, moved the scanner around the deck, and then pointed it right at Catherine "—it's on her."

Catherine, whose pregnancy left her stooped slightly most of the time, drew herself up to her full height. "I *beg* your pardon!"

Without another word, Harper reached out and grabbed at Catherine's ornate gold brooch, positioned over her heart. The brooch, shaped like a jaguar, held a white scarf that was draped around Catherine's shoulders. Before Harper could get a grip on it, though, Catherine held up her left arm to defend the brooch—with the three spikes fully extended.

"Hey!" Harper cried, pulling his hand back.

"How *dare* you try to molest my person!"

"Trust me, lady, on my list of persons to molest, you're *way* down near the bottom. But—" He started to hold up his scanner.

Vanzetti unholstered his weapon and placed the muzzle at Harper's head. "Move away from her, kludge—*now!*"

"You wanna shoot me, über, fine, but that ain't gonna change the fact that Archduchess Fussbudget over there is carrying a transmitter on her chest—which is a very nice chest as chests go, I might add." Harper held up the scanner so the bodyguard could see the readout. "See?"

Beka took out her own weapon, and she nodded at Vexpag, who did likewise, both aiming at the Nietzschean's head. "Vanzetti, holster that thing *now*, or she's down to one bodyguard. Rev, get the brooch."

The Magog walked up to Catherine, and held out one clawed hand. "If you would be so kind, madam, to allow me to inspect the brooch?"

Vanzetti slowly lowered his pistol, at which point Beka did the same. She signaled Vexpag not to follow suit, but to keep his sights trained on the bodyguard's head. She would, dammit, keep the upper hand here.

"I will do no such thing!" Catherine put a protective hand over the brooch. "This was a gift from Charlemagne, and I will not—"

However, Vanzetti, of all people, interrupted. "My lady, I believe you should acquiesce." He was now looking at Harper's scanner reading. "It would seem the kludge has indeed found something."

"Very well." Catherine looked at Beka. "I will give *her* the brooch." She unclasped the jaguar-shaped pin with one hand, holding the scarf in place with the other, and then handed it to Beka.

For the four hundred and first time, Beka thought, *I'm going to kill her*. Putting on the sweetest smile she could muster up, she said, "Thank you," and then handed the item to Harper.

"Careful!" Catherine cried as Harper pulled a tool out of his belt and used it to prise open the jewelry. "That brooch is worth twice your miserable kludge life!"

"More like your life, lady." Harper looked at Beka. "I got bad news and bad news. This sucker's attached to a homing beacon, and it's been going since we came outta Slip. I'm guessing it's a signal to someone already in-system, giving 'em a nice precise location to home in on and fry our bacon."

"And the bad news?"

"This is just the relay—the actual beacon is coming from the crew quarters."

Before Harper even finished his sentence, Vanzetti was moving, a look of fury on his face. Beka ran after him, as did Vexpag. "Rev, Harper, stay here with Catherine."

"No problem. I don't wanna get between two pissed-off Nietzscheans." Harper's voice receded as Beka got further from the deck.

Ahead of her, Vanzetti approached the door to the captain's cabin—which Beka had, very reluctantly and only because Rev said it was a good idea, allowed Catherine and her bodyguards to take over for the duration of the trip to San-Ska-Re—and shouted, "Sacco!"

Oh, good idea, she thought angrily, *let the saboteur know you're coming.*

"Sacco, we need you up front!" Vanzetti said. "Get out here, now!"

Ah, okay. Beka amended her anger, especially once she noted that the door was locked. *Of course, he could've just asked me to crack the lock since it's, y'know, my ship and all, but perish forbid an über ask a kludge for help. . . .* Never a fan of Nietzschean chauvinism, the last couple of weeks had worn down her tolerance for it to its final nerve ending.

Beka heard the door unlock, then slide open to reveal Sacco, who looked like he'd just woken up. "What is it?"

Vanzetti placed the muzzle of his pistol over Sacco's heart. "I should've realized. I wondered how that Mandau Pride marksman back at the shoe merchant could possibly miss a heart-shot at that range—he was working with you, wounding you to make it look good, but not actually killing you. Pity for you that it failed. Who've you betrayed us to this time? Sabra? Drago-Kazov?"

To his credit, Sacco made no attempt to deny his treachery. "You'll find out soon enough—if you live that long."

"I intend to live a long, happy life, brother mine. Pity you won't be able to say the same. If you're lucky, I might give your final regards to Indira before I take her on as my new co-wife."

Typically, *that* got a rise out of Sacco. But before Sacco could articulate his rage at Vanzetti's designs on his spouse, the latter blew a hole in his chest.

Vexpag stepped over the corpse and went to one of the three beds. "Got us an EVA suit ready to go—and a transmitter, prob'ly tied into that brooch. I'm guessin' he was plannin' on buggin' out in the next twenty minutes or so."

"Which he only would've done if he expected someone to pick him up. Kill that transmitter's signal." Beka started running back toward the flight deck. "*Maru*, go to combat readiness."

"*Combat readiness.*"

As soon as she set foot on the flight deck, she barked orders. "Rev, keep every sensor drone we have out."

"Looking for what?"

"Nietzscheans." She moved toward the pilot's seat.

Vanzetti and Vexpag were right behind her. The former said to

Catherine, "My lady, we have been betrayed. My brother sold us out. He has paid for this transgression with his life."

"What!?"

As Beka climbed into the pilot seat, she asked, "Harper, is that thing still broadcasting?"

"Nope. I gutted it. And don't worry—" he added with what Beka assumed to be a conciliatory look at Catherine "—I'll make sure your pretty brooch is back to normal. It was hollow to start out, so Sack-Face probably just stuck the circuitry inside and closed it back up."

"Any damage will come out of your hide, kludge."

Nice to see threats to her life haven't changed Catherine's sunny disposition. "Get back aft, Harper. I want everything you can give me to get us to the Slip point."

"Uh, okay, Boss, but we've got a full load, and we're goin' at max now."

"Then get us to more than max. I'm hoping that Sacco's friends won't find us before we can go to Slipstream."

Vanzetti snorted as Harper made a quick dash for his domain. "You're running."

"I love the *Maru* dearly, but she's still a cargo ship, complete with a full, heavy load belonging to Thans who are paying me a lot of money to get it to them. Somewhere out there is a Nietzschean ship or twelve that want to fire on your archduchess, and were smart enough to co-opt her bodyguard and set up an ambush in unclaimed space when I've got a load that'll slow me down and make me less maneuverable. You're damned right I'm running."

"It is the prudent course of action," Rev added. "And prudence begets survival. Isn't that what you Nietzscheans value above all?"

"Besides," Beka said, "if we can get to Slipstream, we'll come out in Than space. As in demand as you are, Catherine, I don't think even you're worth going to war with the Than over."

"I still think—" Vanzetti started, but Catherine interrupted.

"I don't give a *damn* about your tactical arguments! Captain, do what you must to keep me alive."

Beka bit back a snide retort.

"Missiles are primed'n ready, Bek, and mines're armed." She heard Vexpag spit out a toothpick as he spoke. "Just need somethin' to aim 'em at."

The flight deck quieted down after that. Beka could hear the sounds of all five of them breathing. Perhaps it was having Harper around for so long, but Beka never liked total quiet. "Rev, time to Slip point?"

"At current speed, nine minutes."

Beka ground her teeth. They were still at thirty-three percent of the speed of light, so they were still three light-minutes from the Slip Point. She hit the intercom. "Harper?"

"Gimme a sec—the dome wasn't built in a day."

She heard Rev snort. "I believe that was Rome."

"There was a dome in Rome? I thought it was a colosseum."

"Harper . . ."

"Okay, okay—hang on—all right, you can go to forty-two PSL."

"Detecting something," Rev said, just as Beka started to accelerate. "Two ships at one-and-a-half light-minutes and closing at fifty PSL."

Fifty? "Shit," she muttered. "Vexpag?"

"Ready when you are, Bek."

"Hit 'em with everything you can, on my mark."

"You got it."

"We're receiving a message," Rev added.

Catherine cried, "Don't answer!"

"Like hell. Answer 'em, Rev," Beka said. "Anything to stall 'em until we can get to the Slip point."

"They're moving into position to block us from reaching the point, Beka."

She made a face. "Of *course*. Why make my life *easy* or anything? Punch 'em up, Rev, and make sure they can only see me. And all of you hang onto something secure."

"Why should we do that?" Catherine asked.

If you have to ask, Archduchess . . . "Fine, don't hang onto something secure, see if I care. Rev?"

"There's still a transmission lag of several seconds," Rev said as he opened the communication.

A strikingly handsome man with small eyes and short black hair appeared on the screen. *"This is Major Hirohito T'ang of the Drago-Kazov requesting your immediate surrender."*

She put on her gee-it's-so-good-to-see-you face and said, "Captain Beka Valentine of the *Eureka Maru*. I'm late delivering supplies to the Than, Major, would you mind not blocking my Slipstream access? I don't think the Than government will appreciate you making me late." Of course, it was likely that the Than Hegemony wouldn't give a Nightsider's ass about a cargo ship working for a private company, but it was worth the bluff—the Than had one of the largest fleets in the Known Worlds, so she had nothing to lose by at least pretending to have their potential backing.

Several tense comm-lag seconds passed. Then T'ang scowled. *"Don't play games with me, kludge. We both know why I'm here. Now you have two choices. Surrender the Jaguar to us, and we'll let you go unharmed, or the Than get their cargo in pieces."*

The two ships were decelerating now, close enough that the image of them Beka had out the viewport was almost real-time—as was their communication. The Dragans' positions cut off two of the best routes to the Slip point, as they required the least maneuvering—and, given their load, that was a major factor. That still left her with one option, though it would strain the *Maru's* hull, especially the cargo struts.

"Well, in that case, Major, there's only one choice, isn't there?"

"I'm glad you understa—"

"That would be, none of the above." As she spoke, she shoved the grips downward, rotating the *Maru* forty-five degrees and between the two ships. "Vexpag, *now!*"

As Vexpag fired the *Maru's* missiles, Beka prepared to engage one of her favorite maneuvers. The trick had actually been pioneered by her father, but Ignatius Valentine had never had the skill to pull it off—Beka, however, mastered it by the time she was twelve. It had gotten her dad, her brother, and Beka herself out of more scrapes than she could count.

"Oof!"

That sounded like Catherine. I told her *to hang onto something.* The *Maru's* creaky old AG field didn't always compensate for course changes with the same speed that Catherine was no doubt accustomed to on her Jaguar Pride yacht.

After two seconds, Beka activated the Slip engines—then veered off, not actually entering the 'stream. It took pinpoint control and lightning-fast reflexes to stop from actually going into the 'stream. For most pilots, it was counterintuitive: activating the Slip engines and following the resultant opening into the 'stream was of a piece. Beka, however, had trained herself to compartmentalize her instincts.

With any luck, the Nietzscheans haven't done likewise. Best case, they'd go into Slipstream and find themselves following nothing; by the time they doubled back to Herakles, the *Maru* would be long gone. Worst case, they'd be sensor-blind for several precious seconds.

Of course, the *Maru* was equally blind, but Beka knew where she was going as she turned the ship around as fast as it would go—which was irritatingly slow—and brought it back toward the proper Slip point. That had been the biggest risk: she had activated the Slip engines while they were still behind the safety line, as it were. Slipstream was only safe a certain distance from a gravity source, and the spot where she had pulled her trick was a hair short of that. *But playing it safe won't get us out of here.*

"Twenty seconds to Slip point," Rev said, though Beka knew that. She had already visualized the course and now simply followed it.

Then the ship jerked nastily as one of the struts that connected the main part of the ship to the larger cargo hold broke under the pressure of Beka's maneuverings.

"We lost a strut!" Harper informed them from aft.

Beka snarled as she struggled to maintain velocity despite the sudden change in the structure. *Thanks, Harper, but I already knew that. Now where in the hell is Major Pain-in-the-Ass?*

"Ten seconds," Rev said. "I'm not seeing the Nietzscheans. Perhaps they went into Slipstream."

"Let's hope," Beka muttered.

Vanzetti barked a laugh. "Hope is for fools and small children."

Beka had a smart-ass reply in readiness, but it was interrupted by an explosion.

"Dammit!" Vexpag yelled. "We got hit by a stray!"

"We're at the Slip point," Rev said.

"About damn time." Beka engaged the Slip engines.

Nothing happened.

A choking sense of helplessness clutched Beka's heart. *No, dammit, don't do this to me.*

"Why aren't we going to Slipstream?" Catherine's voice had lost none of its haughty demeanor.

Luckily, Beka had lost none of her ability to ignore it. "Harper!"

"Two seconds, Boss!"

"Detecting one of the Nietzschean ships," Rev said. "Half a light-second away."

Beka hated many things in this universe, but being helpless topped the list. Now they were sitting ducks. "We don't have two seconds, Harper!"

However, even as she said it, she realized that the words were not entirely true. Major T'ang—or his sister ship, she wasn't sure which it was—had the *Maru* right in its sights. They could take them out easily. *So why aren't they firing?*

"Yeah, we do." Vexpag fired three more missiles as he spoke.

The Nietzschean vessel was consumed by a ball of flame a second later.

"Slip's back on, Boss."

Catherine barked, "Then get us *out* of here, Captain!"

"Why didn't I think of that?" Beka muttered as she slammed the *Maru* into Slipstream.

They transited into normal space, but not in the system that held San-Ska-Re.

"Why not?" Catherine asked belligerently when Beka informed her passenger of this.

"Two reasons. One, I wasn't going to be able to stay in Slipstream any longer with the kind of damage we've taken. Two, one of Major T'ang's ships was unaccounted for, and he knew we were headed to San-Ska-Re, so I thought a detour was probably a good idea. Before we do anything else, I want Harper to give the Slip engines a once-over and we need to fix that strut."

Placing a fresh toothpick in his mouth, Vexpag said, "I take it the twerp's got the engine and I'm on weldin' duty?"

Beka nodded. "Good guess."

"I will assist," Vanzetti said.

That got Beka's attention. "Excuse me?"

"Consider it my way of thanking you, Captain Valentine. You have done—a great service, both to the Nietzschean people in general and to Jaguar Pride in particular today. I believe aiding you in repairing your vessel is an appropriate way to express gratitude." He smiled. "I can even use the EVA suit that my brother intended to depart the ship with."

Grinning, Beka said, "I like a man with a sense of irony. Fine, both of you suit up. And make it quick—we're still on the clock for the Than, and I don't want to be late with the delivery. And Vexpag? *Check* your suit this time?"

"Yeah, yeah."

After the pair of them departed the flight deck, Beka looked at Catherine, who said, "Well, that was more excitement than I ever expected to have. I will retire to my cabin now." She started to move aft.

"Not so fast," Beka said, putting a hand on her shoulder. Catherine gave the hand a disdainful look, but Beka didn't budge it. "I want to know precisely what's going on here. Major T'ang had about four opportunities to take us out. He didn't need to talk to us, and he could've blown us to tiny bits while we were waiting for Harper to put the Slip engines back together. That's the third time they've come after you, and each time, they've tried to *take* you, not kill you. Oh, and then there's the little matter of each attempt coming from a different Pride, only one of whom was on the most-wanted list your brother gave us. I know you and Sabra have been playing I'll-stab-you-in-the-back-if-you-stab-me for centuries, but why the hell are losers like Mandau and heavy hitters like the Drago-Kazov coming after you?"

A look of fury came over Catherine's face, and Beka feared that she would have to suffer through another petulant outburst. However, this look was different—it wasn't the usual arrogant anger that framed her every word. "They're not coming after me, they're coming after *this*." She pointed at her swollen belly. "I have had six children, Captain, but this is the first time I have cursed it and wished that it would go away."

Rev folded his hands together. "That is not a very Nietzschean sentiment."

"No, it isn't, Magog. But it is a true one. How familiar are either of you with the legends of my people? Not the idiotic stories you kludges tell about us, but *our* stories."

"Bits and pieces," Beka said.

"I have heard many tales," Rev added.

"Do you know about the progenitor?"

Beka rolled her eyes. "What, the messiah nonsense? That some Nietzschean will be an exact duplicate of Drago Museveni and unite the Prides?"

Catherine fixed Beka with a glare indicating that her eye-roll was premature. "That 'nonsense,' as you so idiotically put it, is one of the most sacred stories of the Nietzschean race, Captain.

Preliminary in vitro scans indicate a very good chance that this child in my belly may be the messiah."

"Oh." Beka found herself unable to say anything beyond that.

"The matriarch had been hoping that they could keep it under wraps, but since the Drago-Kazov hold the remains of Museveni, and since the verification can't be conclusive until after the baby is born, they needed to do something with me." She snorted. "You should've seen the look on the matriarch's face when Charlemagne suggested trundling me off with you fools."

And here I was just starting to almost feel sorry for her. "This 'fool' is the only reason you're alive. And people who live in betraying-bodyguard houses shouldn't throw stones."

"Indeed. We'll probably have to double-check the genetic worth of Sacco's children. We also need to return directly to the homeworld. Even with Sacco's deserved death, your rattletrap of a ship is no longer a safe haven."

Beka snapped, "Only place we're going directly from here to is San-Ska-Re. I've still got to at least deliver this cargo." Unfortunately, Catherine was right in that they needed to get her back home. *Which means we lose the second week of the job, which means only half the paycheck. Less, if Sunrise decides to get cranky about breaking the contract. Just wonderful.*

The life seemed to drain out of Catherine, then. All of a sudden she deflated, looking less like the archduchess of Jaguar Pride and much more like a tired, pregnant woman. "If you insist, Captain Valentine, that will, of course, be fine."

Beka almost fell over from the shock. *That was the nicest thing she's said since we've met.*

"Now then, I'm really *very* tired. . . ."

"Fine." Beka's questions had been answered in any case. Once Catherine had made her way back to the captain's quarters, Beka said, "And thank you *so* much for sharing that little tidbit from the beginning. . . ."

"You cannot be surprised that Archduke Bolivar was not completely forthcoming," Rev said.

Beka walked over to the small refrigerator in a corner of the flight deck. "Not forthcoming is one thing, but this is kind of a biggie. I can appreciate discretion, but at least a *hint* that we were keeping an eye on the Nietzschean messiah might've been nice." She pushed aside half a dozen of Harper's wretched Sparky Cola cans before finally tracking down a bottle of water.

"Would it have changed anything?"

Taking a sip of the water, Beka considered Rev's question. "Probably not, but I would've liked to have made that choice myself, you know?" She turned on Rev and pointed a finger at him. "And don't you go telling me that the Divine doesn't always give us the choices we expect."

Rev smiled. "What makes you think I would say something like that?"

"Ha ha ha."

"Hey, Bek?"

Opening the intercom, Beka said, "What is is, Vexpag?"

"This thing's in worse shape'n we thought. We can weld it together enough to hold for about three-four more Slips, but that's it."

"Great. Another repair bill."

"And even with that, this thing'll have more jagged edges'n Vanzetti's forearms—or the twerp's hair."

"*Oh very funny, toothpick man.*" That was Harper, listening in from the engine room.

"Now now, Seamus, don't you know it's rude to eavesdrop?" Beka said with an indulgent smile.

"*Yeah, what's your point? Anyhow, the Slip engines are fine. Just a little Harper massage therapy, and they're as good as new—or, rather, good as twenty years old, which is as good as this baby's likely to get.*"

"Don't rub it in. Vexpag, how much longer will you need?"

"*No time at all—we're 'bout done. We just—aaaahhhh! Dammit!*"

"Vexpag?"

"*Activate your seal!*" That was Vanzetti.

"*Yeah, yeah, I'm doin' it, just—*"

Then a strangled cough.

"*Seal it, fool!*"

Silence.

"Vexpag, talk to me!"

"*He cannot hear you, Captain,*" Vanzetti said a second later. "*He's quite dead.*"

"Dead?" Beka didn't believe it. She couldn't believe it. "What happened?"

"*One of those jagged edges he mentioned tore through his suit and the seal malfunctioned. I had assumed he didn't check his suit before depart-ing out of confidence, not stupidity.*"

Rev bowed his head. "Eternal light grant unto him, and may perpetual light shine upon him."

Trying to focus, Beka asked, "Is—is the strut fixed?"

"*As fixed as it can be, yes.*"

"Then—then bring his body back in so we can get the hell out of here." She looked over at Rev. "How could this happen?"

"He was never exactly—assiduous about checking his suit."

"I told him." She shook her head. "Dammit, I *ordered* him to check the suit! Why wouldn't he *listen*? Just for once in his life, why couldn't he *listen* to me?"

Checking his console, Rev said, "Vanzetti and—Vanzetti is back on board. The airlock is sealed."

Throwing her water bottle against the bulkhead, Beka let out a very loud, very low-pitched scream. *They keep leaving me*, she thought angrily. *First Rafe, then Sid, then Dad, then Bobby. Now Vexpag. What's next? Rev walking out on me to follow some crusade or other? Harper buggering off with a pretty face he stumbles across at a drift?*

How can he be dead? I was just talking to him and now he's just gone.

The thing that irritated her the most was that she didn't even *like* Fred Vexpag all that much. But for three years he had been a constant, steady presence, always there watching her back—half the time blowing up whatever she happened to be standing in front of, but still . . .

"Beka?"

It took Beka several seconds to bring herself to look at Rev.

"I'm detecting a Slip portal opening. It could be unrelated—but on the off chance that it is Major T'ang's other ship, it might be wise if we were elsewhere."

Beka nodded and moved silently to the pilot's chair. Oddly, she found herself missing the squeak as she moved it into the ready position.

Dammit.

"Transiting to Slipstream now."

FOURTEEN • HAUKON TAU, 302 AFC

> The biggest mistake we Nietzscheans made was betraying the Commonwealth. Not because it brought on the Long Night, though that's hardly something to celebrate. No, what it did was shift our arrogance in the wrong direction. As long as we were part of the Commonwealth, we could concentrate on how much better we all were than everyone else. Once the war and the Magog invasion wiped out all remnants of civilization, all we had left was to focus on how much better individual Nietzscheans were than other Nietzscheans. It's no wonder we turned on each other. . . .
>
> —ARTURRO BOLIVAR,
> "DIVIDED WE STAND, UNITED WE FALL," 235 AFC

Tyr stood upright and faced Alaric Augustus directly. The Ursa had insulted his Pride, and by extension himself, and Tyr Anasazi did not suffer insults lightly or easily. "There is nothing 'inferior' about the Kodiak, Field Marshal. We were betrayed by the Drago-Kazov, and—"

"Is that supposed to mitigate your failure? If you were so incompetent as to allow yourselves to be betrayed so completely, you deserved your fate."

That brought Tyr up short.

"You are the last remnant of a failed Pride. If you truly wished to improve the bloodlines of the Nietzschean race, you would take that knife in your boot and plunge it into your own heart. I would shoot you myself, but I have no desire to waste ammunition on one such as you. The Kodiak's play *has* ended, Tyr Anasazi, you were simply never informed of its close. My recommendation would be for you to take your curtain call and remove yourself from the stage."

With that, Augustus turned his back on Tyr and moved toward the exit of Ferahr al-Akbar's office.

Ferahr swallowed audibly and said, "Well, that didn't go *too* badly. . . ."

Tyr snarled. "Shut up, Ferahr. Field Marshal, wait!"

"Our meeting is ended, Kodiak," Augustus said without turning around.

"What if I can give you something you want?"

"You cannot possibly have anything I desire." Belying those words, Augustus stopped, turned around, and regarded Tyr, as if challenging the Kodiak to prove him wrong.

"Tell me, sir, for how long has your Pride attempted to add Malani's Haven to your empire?"

Augustus's eyebrows shot upward. "We have, in fact, long since abandoned Malani's Haven as being more trouble than it was worth to conquer. Why?"

"I can give you Malani's Haven on a platter, Field Marshal. Think of the prestige attached to accomplishing that, where so many others of your Pride have failed." Tyr saw Augustus hesitate, so he pressed his advantage. "Think about what I am offering you, sir: I am a survivor, who lived through the destruction of my Pride. My mother was Victoria, and my father was Barbarossa, son of Temujin—my genes are *strong*, and I will happily provide you with a genetic sample to bring to your matriarch. And I can give you Malani's Haven. Are these the actions of a man whose play has ended, as you so eloquently put it? Or are they, perhaps, signs of a resource that your Pride should exploit?"

Tyr found that he could not read anything from the expression on Augustus's face. *Is he considering the offer, or changing his mind as to whether or not he should "waste" the ammunition to shoot me?* Tyr did not know, but he was not afraid. Augustus was a sensible man from all accounts, and he would not dismiss so beneficial an offer out of hand. He had nothing to lose and far too much to gain.

"Very well," the field marshal finally said. "If you can deliver on this—rather outlandish promise, then I will see to it that you receive your reward."

Tyr smiled. Augustus, of course, did not know just how familiar Tyr was with the situation on Malani's Haven, nor the current dire straits of the planetary government, which Tyr was in a unique position to exploit.

"Oh," the field marshal added as he turned around, "and feel free to provide that genetic sample, if you wish. My ship will be docked in the drift for another day; the sample can be messengered there."

"Thank you, Field Marshal."

Augustus shrugged. "I have done nothing." With that, he left Ferahr's office.

Excellent. It hadn't gone the way he'd hoped, but at least it was a start. Of all the Prides out there, Ursa was hardly ideal. True, there were worse—Ursa, at least, had a homeworld and a thriving, if small, empire—but there were also much better. Still, Ursa could give Tyr the platform he needed. They would provide wives, enable him to sire progeny, start a line of his own. *And I will reclaim my birthright. The remains of the progenitor will be wrested from the Drago-Kazov's hands and put back with the Kodiak where they belong!*

"You mind tellin' me what that was all about?" Ferahr asked.

"Yes, I do mind. I will need you to send a message to Terra Verde for me to Nwari and Hamsha. I'll send the text to you within the hour."

Typically, Ferahr made grousing noises, but Tyr had long since learned to ignore them. Ferahr's bleatings didn't matter—in the end, he had always come through for Tyr.

Soon, he thought. From the day he was sold into slavery on Zocatl, he had been working toward the day when he would restore the Kodiak—and raise himself to the rightful glory that he deserved. Now, at last, those first steps were being taken. . . .

MALANI'S HAVEN, 303 AFC

Months later, in the throne room of Amorin on Malani's Haven, Tyr approached Field Marshal Augustus. Order had been restored in the capital city and Augustus had set up a provisional military government to rule until such time as Ursa Pride sent a proper governor.

Augustus had, Tyr noted with amusement, not changed the throne room much from how Saamm had redecorated. He also worked from a table in the center of the room, situated on a rug that covered the royal crest of Malani's Haven. The only difference was the rug, which now had the image of a large bear, representing Ursa Pride, stitched into it. The thrones formerly occupied by Nwari and Hamsha—who were still monarchs of the planet in name, at least, if not function, in order to ease the transition—still served as ornately designed shelf space.

Under other circumstances, Tyr might have appreciated the irony. But the fortunes of Malani's Haven had been nothing more than a means to an end for him, and that end was in sight. After today, he could live a long and productive life without ever hearing of or setting foot on Malani's Haven again.

"Field Marshal."

Augustus looked up from a flexi he was reading over. Turning off its display, he said, "Ah, yes, Anasazi. We do have some unfinished business, don't we?"

"Yes, sir, we do."

The field marshal started rummaging through the flexis on his desk. "I do have it here, somewhere . . ."

Tyr assumed that Augustus searched for the results of the scan Ursa Pride's matriarch performed on Tyr's genetic sample that showed him to be of good stock.

It therefore came as something of a shock when Augustus pulled out a credit chit.

Staring down at the display on the chit, Augustus said, "This is for twice your usual fee for such a thing—I believe it is a million thrones for the first month, three hundred thousand thrones a week following that. The fee here covers the fifteen weeks you were on Malani's Haven, for a total of eight million, six hundred thousand thrones." He looked up and smiled a most insincere smile at Tyr as he held out the chit. "It should clear the account you maintain on Haukon Tau within the week."

"I beg your pardon?" Tyr asked with barely contained fury. He did not take the chit.

"That, added to what Saamm paid you to betray him should

keep you and your merry band of kludges well for some time. Perhaps you can use your portion to buy an even larger weapon—I understand that, for some, it serves as a compensatory tool."

Curling his hands into fists so tight he thought his fingernails might draw blood, Tyr said, "Sir, we had an arrangement—"

"Yes we did." Augustus dropped the smile and fixed Tyr with his round, soulless eyes. Never raising his voice above the pleasant, smooth tone he seemed to maintain perpetually, he continued: "I told you that, if you would fulfill your promise to deliver Malani's Haven to Ursa Pride, you would receive your reward. Here it is. You are a mercenary, Tyr Anasazi, out of a dead woman by a dead man of a dead Pride. Monetary compensation is all the reward you should expect—or that you deserve. If your line is to continue, it will not be with Ursa Pride."

When Tyr still did not take the chit, Augustus shrugged and put it down on the table. It was simply a receipt in any case—the money would be in Tyr's account ere long.

Whether he wanted it or not.

Tyr had no conscious recollection of leaving the throne room and telling his team that their apparent betrayal of their employer had reaped impressive dividends, but the next thing he knew, he was listening to their cheers. Gerenmar, Varastaya, and Glasten were especially enthused by their increased rewards. Tyr knew that the Nightsider had gambling debts back on Haukon Tau and that Varastaya had more enhancements and upgrades she'd been eager to incorporate into her cyborg body. As for Glasten, he was simply greedy. Brexos and Johnson, for their part, just smiled.

Tyr retreated to the *Abraxas* after that. It was good that this whole pathetic business had come to a close. The actual owner of the vessel would be by Haukon Tau to claim it in another month, and probably would not be happy to know that it had spent its time allegedly in long-term storage being used as a ferry ship for a band of mercenaries.

Though now I have sufficient funds to pay off the owner and just buy the damn ship.

He tried to do his exercises, but the forms would not coalesce. He was awkward, sloppy; the movements unfocused. They relied on soundness of mind *and* body, and while the latter was up to the task, the former was awash in turmoil.

I forgot my own first lesson, and fell victim to the same trap I lured Saamm into. I trusted. Thinking back over his original conversation with Augustus, he saw the flaw in his assumptions. In hindsight, of course, the avenues for the field marshal's treachery were obvious, but so eager was Tyr to establish himself with Ursa Pride that he willfully blinded himself—much as Saamm had.

Saamm, of course, paid for his treachery with the loss of everything—probably including his life, pending the outcome of his trial, though Tyr couldn't imagine any other ending.

However, Tyr still lived. And Tyr learned. Rarely did Tyr make a mistake; never did he make the same one twice. Throwing himself in with another Pride was not a course he would take a second time—at least, not without much better preparation.

Augustus had made one critical error. He thought humiliation to be his best weapon, mistakenly believing that Tyr could so easily be broken.

It was the critical difference between a wound and a deathblow. Wounds eventually could heal, after all.

I must teach him the error of his ways as he taught me the error of mine.

A plan now formulating in his head, Tyr continued with the exercises. They flowed freely and crisply.

———

Alaric Augustus slept soundly in his bed, dreaming of Hildegarde.

Shortly before he departed for Malani's Haven, the matriarch had given her approval to be his third wife. Much as he admired Lucrezia and Elizabeth—and they had provided him with fine children—his love for Hildegarde had burned within him since he was a boy. It had taken a great deal of effort to secure her. He could not be sure which was more difficult, setting up the ambush that killed Hildegarde's husband and making it look like an accident, or persuading the matriarch to let him stake a claim to her.

Hildegarde herself wanted it, of course—they had desired each other since they were teenagers—but political reality interfered. As a descendant of Ogun, Zeus Bonaparte had first claim on Hildegarde. Never mind that he was a muscle-bound idiot.

Luckily, that made him very easy to fool into walking into that cave. . . .

On top of all that, he had been handed a prime opportunity by the last of the Kodiak.

Even if he had not been able to win Hildegarde before, he was sure that the taking of Malani's Haven would have cemented his claim on her. After all, it was one thing to play kludges against each other for one's own ends, but to manipulate a fellow Nietzschean—and, for all that Augustus dismissed Tyr Anasazi to his face, he was a most worthy foe—made victory all the sweeter.

And so much more impressive for his credentials as a father to Nietzschean children.

We shall have many children, he thought. *Strong sons, fertile daughters.* Augustus had not been born to one of the primary families of Ursa Pride, so he had had to make his own glory. The campaigns he'd waged had earned him much of that, and made it easier for his children to strive for even greater heights.

And I have Anasazi to thank for improving my legacy. As he dozed, Augustus wondered if he should have taken the Kodiak up on his offer to join the Pride instead of allowing him to depart Malani's Haven with his troop of kludge mercenaries a week ago. Anasazi's lineage *was* good, and he had indeed proven a worthy foe.

But no. His eagerness to prove himself is a weakness. I was able to exploit it, and it would be a liability to the Pride as well. If he wishes to restore the Kodiak, let him do it himself, not on our backs. The course Augustus took was the proper one. Certainly, they could afford the eight-point-six-million-throne fee, even with the short-term economic burden of absorbing Malani's Haven. Acquisition of the planet would pay huge dividends for centuries, once the initial infrastructure problems were ironed out—a problem for whatever planetary governor the Bonapartes decided to send along. *I wonder who it will be—probably Claudius, he's been eager for a planet to rule since he was a boy.* . . .

He drifted off to sleep, an image of Hildegarde, naked and desirable, dancing for him, just as she did when they were teenagers having illicit meetings. He missed those days so. . . .

That image was shattered by a noise from outside his chamber.

The room was far more elaborate than anything he could have had on his ship—indeed, the room was twice the size of the flight deck and engine room combined on his flagship. The bed sat under a decadently soft aerogel mattress. It was the most comfortable Augustus had been in over a decade, and he didn't appreciate his sleep being interrupted.

Immediately, Augustus was wide awake and holding his sidearm, which he kept under his pillow. He glanced around the room and saw nothing.

Then he closed his eyes and listened.

He heard nothing.

Still, he was not convinced. He had heard a noise. So he got up, padded to the door, and opened it, weapon at the ready.

The two guards stationed at his door for the night lay dead on the floor, their throats cut.

Several possibilities flew through Augustus's head, even as he sent out an alarm on his wrist-comm, which he never took off. Perhaps Saamm's people were attempting to avenge him—the trial had been that morning, with the execution scheduled for the following week. Perhaps Nwari and Hamsha were getting delusions of grandeur.

He turned around to see a third possibility he hadn't even counted upon: Tyr Anasazi. Before Augustus had the chance to react, Anasazi knocked the gun from his hand. It clattered to the smooth, marble floor and skittered across to Augustus's oh-so-comfortable bed.

What is he doing back here?

The Kodiak held a large knife, stained red with the blood of Augustus's two bodyguards. He seemed the picture of calm, yet the eyes with which he stared at Augustus burned with fury.

"Your play has ended, Field Marshal Alaric Augustus. I am hereby informing you of its close. I suggest you to take your curtain call, for I am about to remove *you* from the stage."

Keep talking, fool. My troops will be here any minute, and then you will pay. "Very droll, mercenary. But my performance will go on for some time. I have dozens of children on Beros Prime, with more on the way once I return to my new wife."

"I'm afraid I have bad news. You see, I have not been idle this past week. Both your wives, your children, and even your precious Hildegarde are all dead."

Augustus felt his heart leap into his throat. "No."

"She will never provide you with children, Field Marshal. And your lineage dies with you today."

He refused to accept it. "You couldn't have. It's only been a week. You couldn't have found all of them and made it back here in time."

"Can't I have?" Anasazi sounded so matter-of-fact that Augustus suddenly found himself furiously calculating in his head how quickly one could Slip from here to Beros Prime, how long it might take someone of the Kodiak's skill and determination to track down Lucrezia, Elizabeth, all his children, *and* Hildegarde.

However, even addled as he was by the Kodiak's mind games, Augustus's battle instincts saved him. Anasazi thrust at him with his knife, and Augustus raised an arm to defend himself against it. Parrying Anasazi's strike with ease, Augustus extended his forearm spikes and slashed at the Kodiak's throat.

He too parried, their spikes interlocking. Anasazi thrust his arm downward. Augustus saw the move coming, but found himself unable to fight against it—the Kodiak was simply too strong.

The move sent Augustus stumbling to the floor. He tried to scramble to his feet, but Anasazi leapt down onto his back, using his bent knees to hold Augustus in place by the rib cage. Augustus tried to move, but Anasazi's knees pressed into each side of his chest. He found it difficult to breathe. The field marshal attempted to slash at his opponent with his forearm spikes, but both angle and leverage were completely wrong, and he succeeded only in flailing about like a beached Castalian.

Then Anasazi laughed mirthlessly. "Perhaps I didn't kill your entire family, Field Marshal. But you will die without ever knowing for sure."

As the blade sliced through the flesh of his throat, blood pouring out of the wound, Field Marshal Alaric Augustus thought of his children, and prayed to a god he had thought long deceased that Anasazi had lied and that his boys and girls were alive and well.

FIFTEEN • THE *EUREKA MARU*, CANOPY, 302 AFC

Don't ever get into bed with a Nietzschean. Their expectations for performance are always way in excess of what's realistic.

—KANT KORBLAN, STAND-UP ROUTINE, 300 AFC

Beka sat in the bunkroom, watching Fred Vexpag bend to put the welding torch back in the case attached to the belt of his EVA suit. The motion brought the back of his suit in contact with one of the jagged edges of the cargo hold strut, tearing a massive hole. Air came out, in the form of what looked like steam, through the tear. Vexpag hit the switch on the suit's belt buckle, to no avail. His face twisted as he desperately tried to breathe air that the suit could no longer provide, even as the Nietzschean next to him screamed exhortations at him to activate a seal that didn't work.

It was Beka's fourteenth viewing of the external camera feed of the *Maru*. It told her the same thing as the first thirteen viewings—not to mention her own aural recollection of the event itself.

Now Vexpag's body lay in the cargo hold alongside Sacco's corpse, mute testimony to the rigors of space travel.

"Beka?"

Turning her attention away from Vexpag's dying paroxysms, Beka looked up to see the concerned face of Rev Bem.

"We've arrived at Canopy. I would recommend we not tarry—there may well be other Nietzscheans who wish to make off with Catherine and claim the messiah for themselves."

"Fine, whatever." Beka turned back to the recording.

"Does that help you?"

"What?"

Rev pointed at the image of Fred's horrific struggle for air. "Repeated viewings of Vexpag's death."

Blowing out a breath, Beka got up from her cot. "I don't know. I just feel like I should do *something*. Try to explain it."

Rev folded his arms. "The universe does not always provide easy answers for us—but in this case, I believe the explanation is quite simple. While the Divine may forgive, space does not. It is the most inhospitable environment in the universe. We may attempt to tame it, to build drifts and ships and stations and atmospheric domes, but ultimately, space will destroy us if we are not careful. Vexpag was *not* careful, and he paid the ultimate price. For that, we should mourn him. But what we should not do is misapportion blame."

"I *told* him to check the damn seal." Beka shook her head. "You know what the worst part is? I have no clue what to do with the body. I don't know who his family is, or that 'lady' he's always sending gifts to. Harper tried to find out once, and almost got himself shot."

"What about his personal effects?"

Snorting a laugh, Beka said, "Lots of journals on guns and explosives. Fiction about people who use lots of guns and explosives. Enough toothpicks to build a life-sized plastic replica of the *Maru*. And a computer chip that's in a code that Harper's been trying and failing to hack since we transited back into normal space."

"The Divine will provide answers eventually, Beka, of that I am sure." Rev put a comforting hand on the captain's shoulder. "For now, however, we must clean out our hotel suite and proceed to the Jaguar homeworld."

Nodding, Beka said, "Yeah, you're right. The sooner we get rid of Catherine, the happier I'll be." She managed to dredge up a smile. "If nothing else, I want my room back."

The pair of them proceeded to the flight deck, where Beka negotiated the final approach to the storage lot near the hotel.

"Oh, we received a message from the planet from your friend Trance."

Beka couldn't help but smile at that. "What's the strange purple gal want from me now?"

"Only that she's looking forward to seeing you again and wants to show you the plants she bought."

"Of course she does." Beka shook her head as she maneuvered the *Maru* into Canopy's atmosphere. "Unfortunately, I'm not gonna get the chance to check out her horticulture. We need to be in and out."

The heavy tread of Harper's workboots signalled the engineer's arrival. "Break out the champagne, Seamus Zelazny Harper has done it once again! The crowd cheers!"

"Why is the crowd cheering, Harper?" Beka asked. "Did you crack Vexpag's code?"

"'Fraid that miracle's still on standby, but I have in the meantime solved the third greatest mystery of all time. The first, of course, is how to get to Tarn-Vedra, followed closely by who put the bop in the bop-shoo-bop-shoo-bop, but very close behind both of them is, drumroll please—who is Fred Vexpag's lady?"

Rev asked, "And you have ascertained this piece of information?"

"Naturally. After all, as we know, secrets are only secrets until I get my hands on 'em. The lady in question is named Stella DiAmico, and she lives on Tekka Shiro."

Beka had been hoping for more information than that. "Is that it?"

"Hey, c'mon, this took some major detective work on my part. What else did you want?"

Shrugging, Beka said, "An occupation, maybe?"

"Well, her address on Tekka is right in the heart of the capital city."

An address is something, at least. "All right, fine. Rev, could you put together some kind of message to her? Let her know what—what happened, and if she can give us any clue about silly things like next of kin and where to ship the body?"

"Of course," Rev said.

As she maneuvered the *Maru* into the storage lot, she added, "We can have the hotel courier it when we check out."

Once they landed, Vanzetti and Catherine appeared from aft. "Why have we landed?"

Beka closed her eyes and counted to five. "Vanzetti—"

"I tried to explain to her, but she insists on asking you, Captain." Vanzetti spoke through clenched teeth.

"Fine." Beka got up from the pilot's seat. "We need to close out the account with the hotel. There are some personal items in there—"

"I have nothing there that can't be replaced."

As usual, Catherine couldn't see past her own nose. "I still need to close out the account. The room's in my name, and I really can't afford to incur any more debt, since I'm willing to bet that your brother isn't going to float a hotel suite on Canopy indefinitely."

Catherine sighed. "Very well. But hurry up about it!"

Gee, I was going to take my time. Like I want to stay here with a target painted on my hull any longer than necessary. But she stopped herself from voicing the thought—it obviously would do no good save to aggravate Beka even further.

She headed for the airlock. "We'll be back in a bit. Try not to touch anything, okay?"

The look Catherine fixed her with was all the satisfaction Beka could ask. *Sometimes Nietzscheans are too easy. . . .*

She opened the airlock door and was shot in the shoulder.

Searing pain sliced through her entire left arm as she fell to the deck. It was a glancing shot, not fatal, but it still hurt like hell.

Grinding her teeth and trying not to scream, she looked up and saw a Nietzschean holding two pistols start to shoot the interior of her ship. Rev and Vanzetti both ducked for cover. Catherine, of course, couldn't move with the same speed as the others, and didn't even try, instead standing with her mouth hanging open.

The Nietzschean ran past Beka and grabbed Catherine by the arm. Beka tried to focus past the pain that spread to her entire chest and rendered her left arm useless and grab her own sidearm. It took focusing all her willpower just to get her right arm to move to the holster. By the time she was able to get a grip on it, the Nietzschean had already led Catherine—who was bellowing "Let go of me!" at the top of her lungs, to no effect—back out through the airlock.

Why do people do that? Do they really think that someone who's taking them away at gunpoint is going to let go of you just because you ask? I mean, how stupid is that?

Wincing at the pain—which had now spread to her entire thoracic region—Beka unholstered her pistol and fired. The shot went about ten meters over the Nietzschean's head.

However, it did get his attention. He stopped and turned around. "Quit while you're behind, kludge."

He raised his pistol and aimed it right at Beka's face.

Her pistol was aimed right at his, also. Under other circumstances, Beka would be willing to pit her aim even against an über, especially at this close range, but the pain from her wound barely enabled her to keep her eyes open, much less hold her gun steady.

"Beka, you there?" said a high, syrupy voice from the storage lot just beyond the airlock. "It's me, Trance!"

The Nietzschean looked away at the voice for only a second, but it was as long as Beka needed. She squeezed the trigger on the pistol four times.

Then she fell unconscious.

Images swam in her head . . .

. . . Vexpag promised that he'd check his suit before going EVA . . .

(*So why is his body decaying as he speaks?*)

. . . Daddy promised he'd bring her back the best birthday

present, but she should stay with Rafe on the drift while he and Uncle Sid went to "take care of some business" . . .

(*"Sorry, Rocket, I forgot, but next time, I promise!"*)

. . . Harper promised to fix the A/P valve with his teeth . . .

(*So why will it cost me eight million thrones?*)

. . . Trance promised to keep saving her life . . .

(*"You're my good-luck charm."*)

. . . Rafe promised he'd be back in a few minutes . . .

(*So why didn't he ever return?*)

. . . Uncle Sid promised Daddy would be only a few days late . . .

(*"Something came up, Rebeka, you know how it is. He asked me to give you this, though."*)

. . . Bobby promised he would never lie to Beka no matter what, which turned out to be the biggest lie of all . . .

(*"In that case, I pick mine—you're lookin' at her."*)

. . . Rev told her that she was going to be fine . . .

(*"Thank the Divine you're all right."*)

It took Beka a moment to realize that Rev was real, and standing over her. "R-Rev?"

"Yes, Beka, I'm here."

She blinked a few times, then took in her surroundings. *I'm in the bunkroom, which means Catherine's still on board and using my cabin.* She closed her eyes again, and felt the vibrations of the ship—they were in space, moving, but not in Slipstream. She also couldn't feel her left arm or shoulder, but that was the pleasant numbness of anaesthetic. Putting her right hand to that shoulder, she felt the bandages, no doubt applied by Rev.

"What happened?"

"Is she okay?" said a high voice before Rev could answer.

Looking past Rev, Beka saw the purple face of Trance coming into the room. "Trance? What're you doing here?"

"You asked her to come on board," Rev said. "I believe the exact words you used were 'good-luck charm.'"

Beka blinked. *I thought that was part of the dream.* "Will someone *please* tell me what happened?"

"Boss, you're awake!"

Great. Harper too. "Who's flying my ship?"

"We're on autopilot. We're about an hour out of the Jaguar homeworld."

Opening her mouth, then closing it, Beka finally got out the words, "Who flew us into Slipstream?"

"Only the most good-looking person on the ship."

Beka smiled. "Oh, so Rev was piloting?"

"Check her wound, Rev, I think she's delirious. Anyhow, to answer your question, when the purple chick here—"

"My name's Trance."

"Uh, right, Trance—sorry. Anyhow, when the purple chick here distracted the Nietzschean, you shot him so full of holes he'd make a good Swiss cheese. Vanzetti said he'd dispose of the body and take care of everything. You said the purple chick—"

"It's *Trance!*"

"—was a good luck charm, and how'd she like to join the crew, then you fell unconscious."

"What happened to Catherine?" Beka asked.

Rev smiled. "She complained, of course."

Snorting, Harper said, "Yeah, she had a problem with how you saved her, like usual. You know, if she wasn't a Nietzschean who could kick my ass so hard it'd go through my head, I'd probably tell her a thing or two."

"Yeah, well, I, for one, have had enough of this." Beka started to climb out of bed as best she could with the use of only one arm.

Sounding almost panicked, Rev asked, "What are you doing?"

"Getting out of bed."

"You should rest, Beka."

Sitting up—and hesitating for about two seconds while her head swam—Beka said, "I'll rest later. Right now, I want some answers."

As she staggered toward the exit to the bunkroom—having to push her way past her three crewmembers—Trance asked, "Hey what happened to that other guy, the one with the ponytail? He seemed nice."

Beka winced, this time in mental rather than physical anguish. The last thing she wanted was another reminder of how, precisely, everything had gone to hell.

Harper, bless him, came to her rescue. "He . . . ah . . . he bought the farm."

"Oh." Trance sounded confused, but didn't ask any further questions on the subject, instead following Beka out of the bunkroom. "So did you mean what you said before? I'm only asking because you seemed kinda loopy when you said it, so I'm not sure if you really meant it, 'cause people don't always say what they mean when they're loopy."

It took Beka a moment to extract the actual question out of Trance's verbal barrage. "What did I say before?"

"You said I could join the crew. I don't know a lot about ships, but I learn really really fast, I promise. And I don't have anywhere else to go."

Beka didn't want to think about this right now. But Trance had thrice been in the right place at the right time, and Beka was pretty sure that, were it not for the purple woman, she'd be dead right now. *Maybe she really is a good-luck charm. I know I could certainly use some of that right now.*

"Tell you what—we'll take you in and show you the ropes. If you work out . . ." She smiled. "Yeah, you can stay."

Trance jumped up and down, her tail flailing about behind her, and clapped.

"Yay! Thank you *so* much, Captain Valentine!"

Unable to avoid laughing—Trance's childlike enthusiasm was infectious—Beka said, "Don't thank me yet, kiddo. You've got a lot of work ahead of you. And it's 'Beka.' Harper, why don't you take our new mate on a tour of the ship and show her the basic systems? I'm going to have a word with our Nietzschean nutcase."

"No problem, Boss. If you will be so kind as to come with me, my purple pixie." Harper indicated the way to the flight deck.

"Okay, but—what's a pixie?"

As the two of them headed for the flight deck, Rev followed Beka back to the captain's cabin. "I think you have made a wise choice, Beka. I sense a good soul in that one."

"Yeah, well, right now she's mainly a pair of hands that we need. This ship has always run best with a crew of four." She thought back to her days growing up with Daddy, Rafe, Uncle Sid, and her running the ship. Not always consistently, of course, but still, the *Maru* was tightest with four hands on deck. And something about Trance just gave her a good feeling, though she couldn't quite figure out what it was. . . .

Beka sighed, and opened the door to the captain's cabin. She noted that Catherine—or Vanzetti—had changed the code again, but Beka's override worked no matter what the code.

Several dozen questions died a-borning on Beka's lips as soon as the door opened and she saw Catherine Bolivar lying on the bunk, screaming. Sweat glistened on her aristocratic face, which twisted into an expression that Beka had previously only seen on rabid animals. Her hair was plastered to her head, also by sweat. She gripped her belly as if trying to keep it from falling off.

Vanzetti stood over her, looking more helpless than Beka had ever seen any Nietzschean.

"What's happening?" Beka asked.

The bodyguard started to answer, but Catherine screamed over him, "What does it look like, you gibbering imbecile? *I'm going into labor!*"

"And just when I thought this day couldn't get any worse," Beka muttered. She turned to Rev. "I don't suppose—"

"I don't want that *thing* anywhere near me!" Catherine bellowed.

Rev held up his arms. "Even were the patient willing, I would have to decline—human birthing is a bit beyond even my experience."

Beka hit the intercom just as Catherine started moaning very loudly.

"Geez, Boss, what're you doing to her?"

"I'm not doing anything, Harper, but our possible Nietzschean messiah has decided to put in his appearance." She looked over at Vanzetti, who still looked baffled. "I thought she wasn't due for another month or so?"

Smiling wryly, Vanzetti said, "The average gestation for a pregnancy is nine months. But that *is* only an average. I suspect that the stress of the past—"

"Will you shut up and get this baby *out* of me!?"

Oh, this is gonna be fun, Beka thought irritably. "How far are we from the Jaguar homeworld?"

"*About fifty minutes. I can slam us up to forty PSL or so, but that'll only shave about ten minutes at most.*"

While Catherine started casting verbal aspersions on his lineage, Vanzetti said, "I can send a signal to Archduke Bolivar—perhaps there's a nearby ship that can be diverted."

"What good'll that do? By the time they get here and dock with us, we can have made it to the homeworld."

Catherine screamed, "Damn you all!"

"I take it that none of your crew has experience in these matters?" Vanzetti asked.

Shaking her head, Beka said, "That would be a big no, unless there's something you haven't told me, Harper?"

"*No chance, Boss—I don't know nothin' 'bout birthin' no babies.*"

"*I might be able to help.*"

That was Trance. "If you think you can help, Trance, get your purple posterior down here."

Vanzetti walked past her, heading toward the flight deck. "I'd still feel better trying to contact one of ours."

"And again I ask, what good'll that do?" Beka asked.

"I can guarantee that any Nietzschean ship will have at least one person, and more likely several dozen, who are greatly experienced in the birthing process."

Figures. "Fine, send out an SOS." Catherine screamed again, prompting Beka to add, "It certainly couldn't hurt."

Trance came back to the cabin then. "Hi," she said with a small smile.

"Do you know what you're doing, Trance?"

"I think I can help."

Catherine's screams grew louder, as she outlined how and where she wanted this baby eliminated. Beka had heard torture victims that weren't this loud. "Well, you certainly couldn't make it any worse. Do what you can—but be careful. I'm willing to bet that she bites."

Trance smiled. "Then I'll bite back."

Chuckling, Beka said, "Good girl. Keep me posted."

As she headed to the flight deck, Beka heard Trance speak in a soothing voice. "You need to regulate your breathing—that's it— very good."

"She is quite a strange creature, this Trance Gemini," Rev said.

Beka didn't have an adequate response to that, so instead she flexed her left arm, which actually responded to her attempt at movement.

"Be careful, Beka," Rev said. "You should be able to control your arm enough to pilot the ship, but do not attempt too much lateral or upward movement of your left arm, or you risk further damage."

"Whatever you say, Doc," Beka said with a smile. "And thanks for patching me up."

Rev simply bowed in reply.

As they entered the flight deck, Harper said, "Uh, Boss, we got a problem."

Now what? "What is it this time, Harper?"

"The Drago-Kazov," Vanzetti said with a snarl. "*Here!* In our home system, they *dare* to invade us!"

"And they're headin' right for us," Harper added.

Beka leapt into the pilot's seat. "Vexpag, arm the missiles, and—" She winced. *Dammit, dammit, dammit.*

Vanzetti said, "I have already armed your meager weaponry, Captain, but it will not be enough against—"

"We are being hailed by the Drago-Kazov," Rev interrupted. "Correction: we are being hailed by Archduke Bolivar."

"What!?" Vanzetti couldn't have sounded more surprised if the Magog had said that Drago Museveni himself was hailing them. "How is that possible?"

"All things are possible," Rev said with a smile, "though I grant you that this is very improbable."

Beka blinked. "Well, since we're in no position to argue, let's answer him, just for shits and grins."

"Very well."

Bolivar's attractive face filled half the screen over Beka's main viewport, with another Nietzschean, an older woman, next to him. *"Greetings, Captain Valentine. If those missiles you've armed are meant for me, that's very generous, but I've already got plenty of my own, thanks."*

"What the hell is going on, Bolivar?"

The archduke indicated the woman to his left. *"This is the matriarch of the Drago-Kazov. She was in the neighborhood anyhow. My sister—another one, Beatrizia—is marrying one of their admirals."*

"We are hopeful," the woman said in a deep, commanding voice, *"that this marriage will bring unity to the Prides."* She held up one arm and indicated Bolivar with it.

"Since we had this whole temporary truce thing," Bolivar said, *"we thought this might be an ideal opportunity to see once and for all if we really can unite the Prides. If you'll dock with us, we'll take my darling sister off your hands, and let you be on your way."*

"Not that simple, Chuckles," Beka said. "See, we've been play-ing target practice with half the Prides in the Known Worlds for the last few weeks, due mainly to one of the bodyguards you sent being a treacherous bastard even by Nietzschean standards, one of my crew got himself killed keeping your 'darling sister' safe, and to top it all off, she's gone into labor."

"*What!?*"

Beka smiled. "Which part didn't you get?"

The matriarch looked like she would explode. "*You will dock with us* immediately*! We cannot have our future entrusted to the hands of such as you.*"

A squeal from aft startled Beka, but also brought a smile to her face. "I think you might be too late to worry about that."

Beka turned around and saw Trance entering the flight deck, a little baby swathed in what looked like Catherine's scarf in her arms. The purple woman wore as wide a smile as Beka had ever seen. "Isn't he adorable? The only thing nicer than a newborn baby is a sunflower."

Not wanting to pursue that analogy, Beka instead just said, "That was fast."

"Actually," Vanzetti said, "it was, if anything, slow. Nietzschean women rarely spend more than fifteen minutes in labor."

"Handy, that." Beka turned back to Trance. "How's Catherine doing?"

"She's fine." Trance's smile somehow managed to grow even wider. "Once she started breathing properly, everything went just *great*."

"*You know,*" Bolivar said, "*it's going to be pretty damn ironic if this child turns out to be the progenitor reincarnated, and he was midwifed by a—what are you, anyhow?*"

"I'm Trance."

The matriarch turned on Bolivar, her arms spread and her fists clenched. *"Do not even joke about such a thing."* She turned back to the viewer and pointed at Beka. *"You will bring the baby onto our ship immediately, or I will have you all killed in the most heinous manner imaginable."*

"What," Harper muttered, "she's gonna scold us to death?"

"We'll dock in a few minutes," Beka said quickly. *"Eureka Maru* out."

Rev cut the connection. Vanzetti regarded Harper. "Do not joke about such things, kludge. The matriarchs are figures to be reckoned with. If it was a choice between facing the entire Drago-Kazov fleet led by Field Marshal Cuchulain himself or the Drago-Kazov matriarch, I'd take my chances against Cuchulain."

Harper shrugged, and walked over to Trance, who still held the baby. "Doesn't look much like a messiah," he said as he peered in close, pulling the scarf off the baby's face. "Looks more like a prune."

Trance pulled the baby away from the engineer. "Harper! Be nice!"

"Frankly," Beka said as she maneuvered the *Maru* toward the Nietzschean ship, "I'll be just as happy to hand the baby—and his mother—back to the Nietzscheans and end this whole mess."

The matriarch waited for them in the airlock, and practically yanked the child out of Trance's hands, then left.

"Don't mind her," Bolivar said with a smile. "The Drago-Kazov tend to breed for attitude."

"Tell me about it," Harper muttered.

"Jaguar Pride, however, is made of kinder stuff. So let me say, Captain Valentine, that, on behalf of my entire Pride, I thank you for caring for my sister, and also offer our sincerest condolences on the death of your crewmate."

Beka was having none of it. "I'd give you points for sincerity if you faked it a little better. Why didn't you tell me Catherine was carrying the Nietzschean messiah?"

"Why didn't you tell me that the hole in your cargo pod that you coerced me into paying to fix came from Resters on Tychen?" Bolviar asked with a smirk. "You said it yourself, Captain Valentine, we were using each other. We shouldn't quibble over how we each accomplished that. Let's just move on, shall we? I fulfilled my end of the bargain, and then some, by repairing your—" he looked around the airlock and coughed "—ship. You fulfilled your end by keeping my sister safe until she gave birth."

"Which she did in my cabin. That wasn't part of the deal. Neither was my getting shot, or having a job get screwed up, or losing a crewmember."

Bolivar nodded in utterly false sympathy. "We *do* live in an imperfect universe, it's true. I'd speak to the designer, if I were you."

"Some of us do," Rev said, "but answers to such questions are rarely forthcoming."

"Ah yes, you must be the Magog Wayist. Some day I'd love to hear the story of how that happened." He looked Rev up and down. "On second thought, perhaps not. In any case, Captain," he said, turning back to Beka, "I'll just collect my sister and then you can be on your way."

Beka started to object, then realized she didn't have a worthwhile reason. At least, not one that Bolivar couldn't refute with the greatest of ease. He had, indeed, fulfilled his end of the contract, and Beka hers. *Of course it didn't turn out like I wanted, but considering who we were getting into bed with, we were lucky to get out alive.*

Vexpag didn't even manage that much.

Still, for a deal with the devil, they didn't do nearly as badly as they could have. *Hell, if it wasn't for Trance, it probably would've gone a lot worse.*

Vanzetti came out a moment later, guiding Catherine by the arm. "Where's the baby?" she asked in a dreamy voice—she sounded exhausted. *Given the way she was screaming*, Beka thought with a small smile, *it's no wonder.*

Bolivar walked up to his sister, and took the other arm. "He's with the matriarch, love, doing the test."

"Good. I want to end this whole mess."

"This 'mess' is quite ended," came an imperious voice from the airlock.

Beka turned to see that the matriarch had returned, sans baby. "That was fast," she repeated.

"Genetic tests *are* fairly quick with the proper equipment," Rev said. "And when it comes to this particular test, I am sure the Nietzscheans have the best equipment possible."

Snorting, Beka said, "That's their credo, isn't it?"

"Where's my baby?" Catherine asked.

Waving a hand dismissively, the matriarch said, "With one of your servants, I assume. It is of no consequence. I have compared his DNA with that of the the genetic sample from the progenitor that I brought with me. It is not a match."

"Damn," Bolivar muttered.

"Good," Catherine said more emphatically.

"I suppose marrying Bea off to Cuatemoc will have to suffice," Bolivar said to the matriarch with a smile.

"My approval for that union does stand, Archduke," the matriarch said with a nod, "but I cannot guarantee the continuance of the truce between our Prides now that the identity of your sister's baby has been verified."

Before Bolivar could respond, the matriarch turned on her heel and departed.

"Lovely woman," Bolivar said. "Probably became matriarch by dint of always getting the last word anyhow." He turned to Beka. "Again, Captain, thank you for your service to our Pride. If you ever find yourself on Schopenhauer, look me up."

He departed, along with Catherine. Vanzetti, however, lagged behind.

Beka stared at him. "Anything I can help you with?" she asked a bit snidely.

"You're not bad for a kludge, Valentine. Hope I don't have to kill you someday."

With a smile, he turned and followed the others out.

Trance frowned. "That sounded like a compliment. But it wasn't. Was it?"

"By his standards," Rev said, "I believe it was."

"Whatever," Beka said. "C'mon, let's get out of here."

Harper practically ran back into the *Maru*. "Suits me fine. You ask me, I'm glad that kid wasn't the messiah. The last thing in the world we need is the Nietzscheans *united*. I like it better when they kill each other. It distracts 'em from tryin' to kill the rest of us."

"Amen to that," Rev said.

Beka closed the airlock behind them, then turned to head toward the pilot seat.

She stopped when her foot came down on a piece of plastic. She bent down to pick it up.

One of Vexpag's toothpicks.

The Than had only paid them thirty percent of the fee for the week of work they did, and most of that was probably going to wind up going to do a proper repair job on the cargo strut whose jagged edge had killed Vexpag. Not to mention whatever it was going to cost to dispose of the body.

Oh, dammit, what about Sacco's body? Shaking her head, she decided not to worry about it. At their next stop, she'd just dump it. If the Jaguar had wanted it, they'd have asked. And if they didn't think to ask, it was their problem. Beka certainly wasn't feeling especially charitable toward them right now.

Putting the toothpick in her pocket, she sat in the pilot's chair, slid it forward, and piloted the *Maru* out of the Nietzschean hold.

Maybe that DiAmico woman will pay to have Vexpag's body taken care of, Beka thought, then decided that things couldn't possibly go that well.

SIXTEEN • OLIVARES TRUST, 302 AFC

> As hatchlings, they literally eat their own siblings to survive. As a result, their society is ruthlessly competitive, with little or no check on even the most despicable behavior.
>
> —ENTRY FOR NIGHTSIDERS,
> ALL SYSTEMS UNIVERSITY DATABASE, CA.
> CY 9780

"Is good as new," Vasily told Beka as they both stood in his repair bay.

"A likely story," Beka said, holding up Vasily's bill. "If it was as good as new, this would be much higher."

Chuckling, Vasily said, "True, true. But still, I fix the strut up good. Now you ready to fly without worrying about cargo going into next star system without you."

"Yup. All I need is somewhere to fly to."

Vasily patted her on the shoulder. "You will find somewhere, I am sure." He turned to walk off, then whirled back around. "Oh, and Beka?"

"Yeah?"

"Am sorry about Vexpag. He was a little crazy, but good kid."

She smiled. "Thanks."

So good, his body's still in the cargo pod. Beka had just picked up a message from Tekka Shiro which she hoped would put at least one mystery to rest.

Entering her ship, she put the message in a reader. The face of a woman appeared on the screen—presumably the infamous "lady" herself, Stella DiAmico. On the surface, she was beautiful, with gorgeous, sculpted features, flame-red hair, and the kind of rich lips that guys like Harper seemed to think were attractive. At first, Beka intended to dismiss her as another pretty little thing who had lived a happy life of privilege, but then she got a good look at the woman's eyes. Those eyes betrayed a hard, difficult life.

"This is in response to the message from Captain Beka Valentine of the Eureka Maru. *I assume you're related to the Captain Ignatius Valentine of the* Eureka Maru *I met fifteen years ago. If so, you have my sympathy."*

Beka shook her head. *Figures. Daddy never could resist a sexy redhead.*

"As for Fred Vexpag, if he was in your crew, once again, you have my sympathies. We met seven years ago and went on a few dates. He bored me silly, so I broke it off. He didn't believe me. I have to admit, I'm kind of glad he's dead—it means he won't be sending me any more crap every time he stops in at a port. He had some dumbass pipe dream that he and I would retire to Fuchal once he made his fortune. I don't even like Fuchal, but Fred was never one to let reality intrude on his mental image of the universe. In any event, I doubt he had any family—and even if he

did, would you admit to being part of it? Thanks for the information, and the next time you see Ignatius, tell him to stay away from me. Good-bye."

"Somehow, that just figures." Harper walked in from aft. "I mean, we could even put that on his tombstone. 'Fred Vexpag, two-sixty whatever to three-oh-two AFC: he never let reality intrude on his mental image of the universe.' Has a nice ring, don't it?"

"Well, he's not gonna get a tombstone. We'll dump the body when we head out next."

"Which is when?"

Beka blew out a breath. "That is a very good question. Our track record lately isn't exactly shining—our last three jobs either got yanked out from under us or we yanked it out ourselves. And Quantum just bought out a whole bunch of smaller companies, so we're probably going to have fewer jobs we can afford to take on while they go around undercutting people."

Harper held up a can of Sparky Cola in mock toast. "Here's to the little guy trying to make a fast buck."

"Incoming message."

"Joy of joys," Beka muttered. "Who from?"

"Sender is listed as Gerentex."

Frowning, Beka looked at Harper, who shrugged. "Don't look at me, I don't know him."

"Put it through."

A Nightsider face appeared on the screen. *"Is this Captain Beka Valentine of the* Eureka Maru?"

"Is this Gerentex?"

"Yes, it is. I understand you're a salvage operator looking for work."

Beka folded her arms. "The *Eureka Maru* does run cargo and perform salvage runs, yes, but we have many possible—"

"Captain Valentine, don't play games with me. I need someone with tal-

ent and time on her hands. In exchange, I can promise you the biggest score of your career. I happen to know that you're between jobs at the moment, and with Quantum's latest shenanigans, I'm willing to bet you won't find much in this galaxy anytime soon, unless you sign up with them."

"Not bloody likely," she muttered.

"Exactly. What I'm proposing is extremely lucrative."

"So you said. Tell you what—come on board the *Maru* in an hour and I'll take a look."

"Excellent! I'll see you soon."

An hour later, the Nightsider appeared at the airlock. He was dressed in a metallic jacket that almost blinded Beka when it caught the light, and wore several medallions around his neck. Beka also noticed that the jacket, flamboyant as it was, attempted to cover up a sidearm.

Rev, Trance, and Harper were also present. Gerentex held up a flexi. "Tell me, Captain Valentine, how well do you know history?"

"I know I don't like it told to me like I'm a child by a Nightsider who's wasting my time."

Gerentex smiled. "Straight to the point. I like that."

This guy's worse than Bolivar, Beka thought. *At least he had style.* "Could we get on with this?"

"Three hundred years ago, the Systems Commonwealth and the Nietzscheans fought a very long and brutal war that ended with the Commonwealth's defeat. Most of the High Guard ships were, of course, destroyed. But not all of them."

Beka rolled her eyes. "I've heard those fairy tales about derelicts too. I even chased one once. But that's all they are."

"I don't think so. I've found leads on over thirty High Guard vessels that may still be intact and salvageable."

"Thirty?" Harper was almost salivating. "Are you serious?"

"*Over* thirty," Gerentex said, leaning forward and handing Beka the flexi. "I freely admit that many of them probably are false leads, but that still leaves us with many possibilities. I have paid good money for this information, Captain Valentine, but I am lacking in one essential component."

Beka looked over the list. Some of them matched rumors she'd heard about, including the ghost ship at Herodotus (which had become a legend among salvagers for being a place no one returned from), the Slip fighters in the asteroid belt in Mitalbo (which Beka knew was a dead end), the fleet of ships in Tartarus (which had the drawback of nobody knowing where Tartarus was, since no star chart anyone had found had such a place listed), and the *Andromeda Ascendant* in a black hole (the one in the Hephaistos system, according to the list).

She looked up at Gerentex. "You need someone to perform the salvage."

"Once we find a ship, yes. Think how valuable a High Guard ship of the line would be. You would receive five percent of the profits and—"

"Fifteen percent."

"Seven."

"Get off my ship."

"All right, ten!"

Smiling, Beka said, "Deal. When do we leave?"

Returning the smile—which immediately made Beka feel dirty somehow—Gerentex stood. "Immediately. I have a planet-hopper here at the drift that should fit in your cargo hold."

Gerentex left a moment later—Beka could not bring herself to actually shake hands on the deal, but they did nod—and as soon as he cleared the airlock, Rev spoke. "Are you sure this is wise, Beka?"

"This from the man who was on my side of the should-we-team-up-with-Nietzscheans argument?"

Rev bowed. "A wise man knows when to admit his mistakes, and it was a mistake to work with Jaguar Pride."

"Yeah, and Rat-Face here doesn't exactly inspire confidence," Harper said. "I mean, did you see what he was wearing?"

Trance frowned. "I thought he looked kinda nice."

"And that proves my point."

"What's that supposed to mean?"

Beka blew out a long breath. "Children!" She regarded her crew. "Look, Gerentex gives me the heebie-jeebies too, but if we can find even *one* of these High Guard ships, it'll be the biggest of the big scores. Nobody's built anything like this stuff in three centuries. Even ten percent of what this would go for on the open market will be enough for us to retire."

"She's got a point," Harper said, sipping thoughtfully from his soda can.

"The decision is, of course, yours, Beka," Rev said with a respectful bow of his head.

"I'm with you no matter what, Beka." Trance smiled. She had been coming along very well. She didn't quite pick up on every system, but she did well enough to get by, and she hadn't actually broken anything.

"All right, then, let's chase us down some ghosts."

HAUKON TAU, 303 AFC

"Have I ever told you about my cousin?" Gerenmar asked Tyr as they walked from the storage lot.

They had just finished purchasing some new arms, which Fer-ahr was going to have shipped to Tyr's apartment when they were ready. Gerenmar had needed special weapons that would account for his inferior vision, a criterion Tyr was ill-equipped to judge. Though Tyr had no problem leading these mercenaries into bat-tle as needs be, he had no interest in socializing with them, and Gerenmar's sudden interest in doing so annoyed him.

"My interest in your family life is minimal at best, Gerenmar. Indeed, I thought Nightsiders had no family loyalty." It was one of many Nightsider customs that Tyr had found repellent.

Gerenmar snorted. "I don't. But Gerentex got in touch with me because he found out I was working for you. He's always been the ambitious one of the family, you see."

"A Nightsider with ambition is never a good thing." They were almost at Tyr's apartment. When they got there he could end this tedious conversation.

"It could be for us. He's been investigating old High Guard relics, and he thinks he's found one."

"High Guard?" That got Tyr's interest. As far as he knew, the only High Guard ships still intact were the ones the Drago-Kazov had captured and sent to one of their systems code-named Tar-tarus. The actual location of Tartarus was a well-kept secret—less well-kept was the fact that the Pride had been unable to depro-gram the ships' AIs, rendering them useless to the Dragans.

"Gerentex has been trying to dig up High Guard ships for years. He's been tracking down leads, and four months ago, he hired some clapped-out old cargo ship to do the salvage. Looks like they found one to pick out."

"This is all very fascinating," Tyr lied, "but why are you sharing this idiotic story with me?"

Gerenmar grinned, as unsavory a sight as Tyr had ever seen. "Because he wants to hire us."

"For salvage?"

"Not exactly. The ship they've found is the *Andromeda Ascendant*—it's a warship that was trapped in the event horizon of a black hole back at the beginning of the war. Because of that, there may still be some High Guard officers on board."

Nodding, Tyr said, "And he will need us to secure the ship?"

"Yes. And he'll pay seven hundred thousand."

For work as easy as that sounded, seven hundred thousand was overpaying. "Good work," Tyr said. "How soon does this cousin of yours want us?"

INFINITY ATOLL, 303 AFC

Harper scratched the itch on his neck. The rash hadn't extended to the side of his neck that contained the dataport, thankfully—itching there would've been a major nightmare—but it still was driving him nuts.

Beka still hadn't come back from whatever weird meeting she suddenly ran away to. They'd been spending the last four months digging around looking for High Guard ships, most of which were dead ends. And speaking of dead ends, they also had to share living space with Gerentex. Harper had heard lots of stories about Nightsider hygeine that turned out to be false—the reality was much worse. Rat-Face had awful taste in clothes, worse taste in food, and a stink that made Rev Bem smell like one of Trance's houseplants.

At least they'd traded up in one regard. Harper wasn't happy that Vexpag was dead, of course, but he wasn't sorry to see him gone, exactly. Trance was a big improvement. She was sweet, she didn't abuse Harper, she shared his predilection for grand larceny, and she was easy to talk into adventures.

Of course, the last adventure I talked her into was last night, and I came out of it with this damn rash.

What worried him more was the "mysterious message" Beka had gotten two days after Gerentex had gotten into his planet-hopper and gone off to "run errands." That had left the rest of them at liberty, and Harper—after sixteen weeks of High Guard hunting—was grateful for the rest.

He was less grateful for the rash, or for the look on Beka's face. The last time she looked like that was the last time Bobby showed up. Harper had feared Beka would rekindle their disastrous romance then, and when they didn't, it took a week of Rev consoling Beka before she climbed back out of her funk. What Beka saw in that steroid case, Harper would *never* get.

However, Beka soon returned with Rat-Eyes. "We've got confirmation," Beka said with that light-minute-wide smile of hers. "Tomorrow, we're heading for Hephaistos."

Harper blinked. "Not the *Andromeda*?"

"No, we're just going to fly into the singularity for the hell of it," Rat-Mouth said. "Of course the *Andromeda*, you idiot!"

Scratching his rash, Harper said, "Look, Rat-Nose, this isn't your usual dig out of a moon crater or an asteroid crevice. We're talking the event horizon of a black hole."

"Actually," the Nightsider said, handing Harper a flexi, "it's the accretion disk."

Taking the flexi, Harper looked the diagram over. "C'mon, the only way to get that thing out would be to use extra-strength bucky cables, and you'd have to align them perfectly so that they don't cross into the event horizon. In order to do it right, we'd need active sensors *way* better than what we've got on the *Maru* just to *find* the stupid thing—the disk'll have more gas, dust, and radiation than the bathroom after you've used it. Then we'd have to get all the right sweet spots on the ship."

"None of that will be a problem," Rat-Cheeks said. "I have already ordered the active sensors to be installed, and if you need other equipment, let me know."

That brought Harper up short. "Really? Uh, okay. You have the specs for the *Andromeda* handy?"

The Nightsider smiled. "Naturally."

Harper had finished his Sparky Cola an hour earlier, but he took a dry sip from the empty can anyhow. Setting it aside, he started thinking through the ways they would need to retrofit the *Maru* in order to make this work.

He heard Beka chuckle, though he didn't look up to see it. "While the genius gets to work over there, Rev, Trance, and I will see to your cargo."

"Good," Rat-Brain said. "Be *very* careful with it. It's—valuable. Family merchandise."

"Family?"

"Relates to my cousin. It's a long story."

Harper remembered something. "Hey, Boss? What about Bobby?"

"Bobby?" Beka frowned. "As far as I know, he's on Cascada, why?"

"So he's not why you went off all crazy?"

"No, that was to pick up Gerentex at customs."

Through clenched, pointed teeth, the Nightsider said, "They objected to my cargo."

"I talked 'em into letting him come on board. And hey, Harper?"

"Yeah, Boss?" he asked, scratching his neck.

"You probably shouldn't scratch that."

Harper smiled insincerely. "Thanks, Doc. I'll just take two aspirin and call you in the morning."

EPILOGUE ·

The universe has changed, and we must change with it. The High Guard must become leaner and meaner, taking advantage of technology to fill in the gaps left by our diminished numbers. We must embrace new, nontraditional missions that are ideally suited to our superior organization and resources. We must apply our knowledge, our capabilities, our traditions of service and sacrifice to operations other than war. And while we must maintain our readiness to fight when the need arises, we should pour equal energy into offering a hand to those in need and those who seek to push the frontiers of science and technology for the betterment of sentient species everywhere. We must become more than what we are—not just soldiers, but diplomats. Not just engineers, but scientists. We must do more than patrol the wastes between the stars; we must explore them and share what we learn so that we may grow wiser and more humble in the face of Creation.

—ADMIRAL COSTANZA Q. STARK,

"WATCHERS ON THE WALLS OF PARADISE," CY 9764

The Reverend Behemiel Far-Traveller stood on the observation deck of the *Andromeda Ascendant.* After so many years on the

Eureka Maru, it humbled him to stand in so much wide-open space yet still be on a starship. Even on a drift, one could never see the stars with this much clarity yet still be able to do so in such spacious solitude.

The salvage mission with Gerentex had not gone according to plan, but the end result wound up being more amazing than Rev could possibly have imagined. It began well; Harper's engineering acumen remained as keen as ever, and they managed to retrieve the High Guard ship from the black hole's accretion disk without incident.

After that, however, the salvage mission took several unexpected turns. The ship's AI was still functional, and its captain, Dylan Hunt, was still on board, alive and well after three hundred years frozen in time. Then Gerentex revealed the mercenary team he had secretly hired, led by a Nietzschean named Tyr Anasazi, to aid in the salvage. Hunt's presence had already made the salvage's legality questionable, and when Trance raised that very question, Gerentex killed her—or so they all believed.

Then they learned Gerentex's true reason for wanting a High Guard ship: the vessel was armed with forty nova bombs, the worst weapons of mass-destruction ever conceived. The idea of weapons that could wipe out an entire star system coming into the Nightsider's possession filled Rev with dread.

In the end, Hunt, Anasazi, and the *Maru* crew—including an alive-and-well Trance Gemini—had worked together to keep Gerentex from getting his hands on the bombs or the *Andromeda*. Then Hunt made them all an offer to help him rebuild the Commonwealth.

Captain Hunt's dream was, in truth, an insane one. But the universe insisted on being equally insane, so why not a mad quest?

Besides, the journey mattered far more than the destination. Trying to rebuild the Commonwealth was the right thing to do, and even if the effort turned out to be a catastrophic failure, Rev knew in his soul that he had to be a part of it. True, they had much to lose, but no more than they did on the *Maru*. Unlike the mere monetary gain they had achieved in the past—and those gains were often mere indeed—the benefits should they succeed would be beyond anybody's wildest dreams.

Besides, he thought with a smile, *it will give Beka, Harper, and Trance a chance to become something greater than themselves. They deserve to be more than salvagers, cargo runners, and thieves. The Divine has given them a means to a much better end than they might have otherwise reached.*

He stared out at the stars as viewed from the Hephaistos system. *A better end than poor Vexpag.*

Rev issued up a prayer to the Divine for Vexpag's soul, and for hope for the future of Dylan Hunt's mad dream.

"This place is the *coolest*!"

"I'm glad you approve."

Harper turned to see that the babe-o-licious hologrammatic avatar of the *Andromeda Ascendant's* AI had appeared in the machine shop. As much as he loved the innards of this ship, the avatar was by far the part that lit his indicator light the brightest. *The High Guard knew how to motivate their engineers*, he thought with a grin. After all, how much more would you want to do repair work when the repairs were requested by someone with those lips? It certainly put the spring in his step a lot more than that clunky male voice on the *Maru*. "Oh, believe me, I approve. Lock me in here with all this stuff and a few cases of Sparky Cola, and I'll build you an entire drift that'll make Olivares Trust look like Takilov."

"I'd settle for you dismantling the security overrides you put on me when you boarded."

"Not a problem, uh—hey, what do I call you? Andromeda? Babe? Hot Mama? Hey You?"

The hologram looked thoughtful. *Damn*, Harper thought, *whoever programmed her did an amazing job.*

Finally, she said, "Dylan nicknamed me 'Rommie' when he took command. I think that will suffice."

"Okay, Rommie—I will gladly take out those overrides." He took a gulp of his cola.

"Harper, were you the one who did the upgrades on the *Eureka Maru?*"

"Yeah, most of 'em. We made a few when Gerentex hired us, but I installed 'em all. Why?"

"It's impressive work, given the limitations you were working under."

And she knows genius when she sees it. God, I'm in love! "Well, thank you, Rommie. I hope I can do the same for you."

"I doubt it." Now Rommie spoke in a haughty tone. "This *is* a High Guard ship of the line, and we have—had the finest engineering crew."

"Ship of the line, shmip of the line, it's all machinery, and trust me, machinery is putty in the hands of the master. Give me a few weeks, and you'll be seeing that engineering crew for the amateurs—*talented* amateurs," he added quickly, not wanting to insult Rommie, "they truly were."

"You're very sure of yourself aren't you?"

He grinned. "Somebody has to be. Anyhow, trust me, Rommie, with my brains and your parts, we're gonna make this puppy into the most kickass ship in the Known Worlds."

Dryly, Rommie said, "I can hardly wait."

Tyr Anasazi sat in crew quarters that were twice the size of any place he had lived in the two decades since the fall of the Kodiak Pride. His entire apartment on Haukon Tau could fit in the bathroom of this cabin.

"I have worked for a great many fools in the past few years—perhaps it's time for something new," he had told Hunt in the observation deck, and the words were not truly lies. Of course, they were not the whole truth, either.

Tyr couldn't give less of a damn for Hunt's idiotic quest to restore the Commonwealth, which had a chance of success roughly equivalent to that of Enga's Redoubt being consumed by a giant space-faring goat. He had loftier goals in mind.

The past months had taught him many lessons, the primary one being that he needed resources and needed to rely solely on himself. His mercenary team had all been killed or sent off in a lifepod with the Nightsider to drift for months, but Tyr hadn't spared them more than a thought. They were always merely a means to an end, and Tyr's means had improved greatly with Hunt's oh-so-generous offer.

By signing onto Hunt's crew, Tyr availed himself of the *Andromeda Ascendant*. Someday, the ship would belong to Tyr. Hunt would not lose the ship by force—Tyr had already tried that tactic and failed. That left a more treacherous route: familiarize himself with the territory and with his opponent, and eventually usurp him.

That was long term. In the short term, this High Guard relic would also make a most useful platform for Tyr's long-sought-after goal of restoring the progenitor's remains to their rightful place with Kodiak Pride.

Hunt had foolishly proclaimed himself to be one who let his enemies live. Tyr knew better than to make such a mistake, as Field Marshal Augustus learned in the end. He looked forward to teaching Captain Dylan Hunt a similar lesson some time in the future. . . .

Beka sat on the flight deck of the *Maru*, looking at the interior of the *Andromeda Ascendant*'s bulkheads. In one day, she'd gone from the brink of the biggest score of her career to almost dying in a black hole to signing up for a cause.

I don't do causes.

Beka Valentine was born on the *Eureka Maru* and she fully expected to die on it as well. And when she did go, it would be on *her* terms, not somebody else's. That was why she had broken it off with Bobby, all those years ago.

Then along comes Captain Dylan Hunt, ancient relic of a long-dead military, sounding for all the world just like Bobby, with his own noble cause to fight and probably die for. When Bobby dangled a cause in front of her, she rejected him.

"No, Beka," Bobby had said then, "everybody does causes. Only question is, will you pick yours or will it pick you?"

Back then, she picked a cause: herself. She wouldn't die like her father—flash-fried, his own son and best friend unable to even bother showing up to pay respects. She wouldn't die like Vexpag, either—the victim of her own stupidity.

So why have I signed up for Hunt's stupid dream?

Part of it was her own crew's enthusiasm. Hell, even the Nietzschean mercenary decided to give it a whirl.

And where has going after the big score gotten me, exactly? Dead bodies, a mountain of debt, a broken heart, a theft of a hologram, and Nietzscheans shooting me.

Perhaps Bobby had been right. A cause had picked her—it just wasn't Bobby's cause. It was something even greater.

"What do you think?"

Dylan asked Rommie the question as he changed out of his uniform and into something more comfortable. The *Eureka Maru* crew and the Nietzschean mercenary had accepted his offer. He had his crew—now he just needed to figure out how to begin his crusade.

"I think it's a start. Not a promising start, but a start nonetheless. Harper is dismantling the security overrides—and yes, I'm keeping an eye on him. The overrides are actually pretty impressive. He's good—I can only imagine what he'd be like with proper training."

Dylan put on a bathrobe. "And the rest of them?"

"The Magog appears to be what he says he is, which is—peculiar to say the least. But I think of all of them, he's probably the one we can trust the most. His spirituality is genuine, but it isn't mindless."

"That's my impression too." Dylan poured himself a glass of water. "What about the purple one—Trance?"

"She's a mystery—I still don't know how she revived herself after Gerentex shot her—but her enthusiasm is also genuine. And she's brought over some fascinating plants from the *Maru* to add to the hydroponics bay."

Smiling, Dylan said, "We can always use someone with a green thumb. Even if it's actually purple."

"The trouble spots are Captain Valentine and the Nietzschean."

"You won't get any argument from me on Tyr Anasazi of the Kodiak Pride," Dylan said with appropriate mock-gravity. "I learned the hard way about the dangers of trusting Nietzscheans with Rhade." Unbidden, the image of Rhade killing Refractions of Dawn and almost doing the same to Dylan came into the captain's mind. *Why did you do it, Rhade?* he asked again, even though he knew the answer.

Casting out the unpleasant memory, he continued: "But why Valentine?"

"She's used to being in charge, running her own ship. Based on the *Maru*'s database, she's run that ship for almost a decade—and she's hardly run it as a model of efficient military discipline."

There's that distaste for civilians again, Dylan thought with a smile. "Efficient military discipline doesn't seem to be the order of the day anymore, Rommie. You've seen the *Maru*—the fact that she's kept that thing intact, much less survived this long, is a testament to her abilities. Let's give her a chance. I'll bet we can learn at least as much from her as she can learn from us."

"Perhaps. But I'm not sure how she'll take to being second in command."

Dylan shrugged. "We're not sure of anything."

"Except that we will restore the Commonwealth."

From the mouths of AIs comes confidence. "Maybe. Honestly, I don't know if we can do it—I'm not even sure where to begin. But I do know that we have to try. Even if we're just tilting at the universe's biggest windmill, it's our duty to make the attempt. We can't afford not to succeed."

Rommie smiled. "Then we will succeed. Captain's orders."

Holding up his glass of water, Dylan said, "As one of our new

crewmembers might say, from your mouth to the Divine's ears."
He gulped down the rest of his water. "I'm going to take a
shower," he then said, putting the glass down on the countertop
of his quarters. "It's been a very, very long day."

Trance Gemini put the last of her plants in the *Andromeda*'s hydroponics bay. This was a much better home for them than the *Eureka
Maru*, which really wasn't ideally suited for life. Even though Beka
called the ship home, it was truly only a means of travel and very little else.

The *Andromeda*, though, was a home. It had been home to four
thousand people, and now to Trance and her new friends.

As she set the last of her plants on one of the hydroponics
tables, situated under the UV lamp, Trance smiled.

Everything was going precisely as expected. . . .

THE BEGINNING

ABOUT THE AUTHOR

Keith R.A. DeCandido has been, at various times in the past thirteen-plus years, an editor, novelist, short-story writer, comic book creator, critic, musician, book packager, and TV personality. He has contributed to the worlds of *Star Trek* four novels, one comic book miniseries, a novella, and half-a-dozen eBooks. He has also written bestselling novels, short stories, and nonfiction books based on *Farscape*, *Buffy the Vampire Slayer*, *Doctor Who*, *Xena*, Spider-Man, the X-Men, and more. His work has received wide acclaim ranging from the magazines *Entertainment Weekly*, *TV Zone*, *Dreamwatch*, and *Publishers Weekly* to various online e-zines and bulletin boards. Future projects include more *Star Trek* work, an original novel entitled *Dragon Precinct*, and editing the original anthology *Imaginings*. DeCandido lives in New York City with his girlfriend and the world's two goofiest cats. Find out more at his official Web site at DeCandido.net, or join his equally official fan club at www.kradfanclub.com.